Author photo © www.mattchristie.com

Vina Jackson is the pseudonym for two established writers working together for the first time. One a successful author, the other a published writer who is also a city professional working in the Square Mile.

Eighty Days Yellow

Vina Jackson

An Orion paperback

First published in Great Britain in 2012
by Orion Books Ltd,
Orion House, 5 Upper St Martin's Lane,
London WC2H 9EA

An Hachette UK company

3 5 7 9 10 8 6 4 2

All the characters in this book are fictitious, and any resemblance to actual persons, living or dead, is purely coincidental.

A CIP catalogue record for this book is available from the British Library.

ISBN (Paperback) 978 1 4091 2774 1
ISBN (Ebook) 978 1 4091 2775 8

Typeset at The Spartan Press Ltd,
Lymington, Hants

Printed in Great Britain by Clays Ltd, St Ives plc

The Orion Publishing Group's policy is to use papers that are natural, renewable and recyclable products and made from wood grown in sustainable forests. The logging and manufacturing processes are expected to conform to the environmental regulations of the country of origin.

www.orionbooks.co.uk

Eighty Days Yellow

I

A Girl and Her Violin

I blame it on Vivaldi.

More specifically, on my CD of Vivaldi's *Four Seasons*, which now sat face down on the bedside cabinet, alongside the body of my softly snoring boyfriend.

We'd had a fight when Darren had arrived home at 3 a.m. following a business trip and found me lying on the wooden floor in his living room, nude, the concerto playing as loudly as his surround-sound system would allow. Loud.

The *presto* movement of 'Summer', the Concerto No. 2 in G minor, was just about to kick into full swing when Darren flung open the door.

I hadn't noticed that he'd returned until I felt the flat of his shoe resting on my right shoulder and shaking me back and forth. I opened my eyes and saw him leaning over me. I then noticed that he'd turned the lights on and the CD had come to a sudden halt.

'What the fuck are you doing?' he said.

'Listening to music,' I replied in my smallest voice.

'I can hear that! I could hear it all the way down the street!' he yelled.

He'd been away in Los Angeles, and looked remarkably fresh for someone who had just got off a long flight. He was still wearing half of his business suit, a crisp white shirt, leather belt and dark-navy trousers with a very thin pinstripe, the matching jacket slung over one arm. He was gripping the handle of his wheelie case tightly. It had evidently been raining outside, though I hadn't heard a thing over the sound of the music. His case was slick with rain, rivulets running down the side and pooling onto the floor alongside my thigh. The bottoms of his trousers were wet where his umbrella had not been able to shield him, and were stuck to his calves.

I turned my head towards his shoe and saw an inch of damp calf. He smelled musky, part sweat, part rain, part shoe polish and leather. A few drips of moisture fell from his shoe and onto my arm.

Vivaldi always had a very particular effect on me, and neither the early morning hour nor the look of irritation on Darren's face did anything to distract me from the feeling of warmth that spread rapidly through my body, lighting the blood in my veins in much the same way that the music had.

I turned so that his shoe was still pressed lightly to my right arm and I ran my left hand up his trouser leg.

He stepped backwards, immediately, as if I'd burned him, and shook his head.

'Jesus Christ, Summer . . .'

He wheeled the case up against the wall next to the CD rack, removed *The Four Seasons* from the player and then walked to his room. I considered getting up and following him, but decided against it. There was no way that I could win an argument with Darren when I didn't have any clothes on. I hoped that if I just continued to lie still, I could defuse his rage by appearing less visible, hopeful that my unclothed body would blend better into his wooden flooring if I was lying horizontally rather than standing upright.

I heard the sound of the wardrobe door open and the familiar rattling of wooden coat hangers as he hung up his jacket. In the six months that we had been dating, I hadn't once seen him throw his coat over a chair or the back of the couch, like a normal person would. He hung his jacket straight into the wardrobe, then sat down to take off his shoes, then removed his cufflinks, then unbuttoned his shirt and put it straight into the washing basket, then took off his belt and hung it over the wardrobe rail alongside half a dozen others in varying sombre shades of navy, black and brown. He wore designer briefs, the style I like best on men, tiny pairs of stretch-cotton shorts with a thick waistband. I loved the way that the briefs hugged him, tantalisingly tight, although to my eternal disappointment he would always cover himself with a robe and never walked through the flat with just his underwear on. Nakedness offended Darren.

We'd met at a recital in the summer. It was a big deal for me; one of the scheduled violinists had called in sick and I had been drafted in at the last minute to play in the orchestra, a piece by Arvo Pärt, which I hated. I found it jerky and monotonous, but for a classical slot on a real stage, albeit a small stage, I would have played Justin Bieber and found a way to look as though I was enjoying myself. Darren had been in the audience and he'd loved it. He had a thing for redheads, and he said later that he couldn't see my face because of the angle of the stage, but he had a great view of the top of my head. He said my hair had shone in the stage light as though I was on fire. He'd bought a bucket of champagne and had used his connections with the concert organisers to find me backstage.

I don't like champagne, but I drank it anyway, because he was tall and attractive and the closest thing I'd ever had to a bona fide groupie.

I asked him what he'd have done if I'd been missing my front teeth or had been, in some other way, not to his taste, and he replied that he'd have tried his luck with the percussionist, who wasn't a redhead but was still fairly attractive.

A few hours later, I was drunk and flat on my back in his room in Ealing, wondering how I ended up in bed with a man who stopped to hang up his jacket and lay his shoes carefully together before he climbed on top of me. However, he had a big cock and a nice apartment, and although it turned out that he hated all the music I loved, we spent most of our weekends over the following months together. Unfortunately, to my mind, not nearly enough of that time was spent in bed, and far too much of it was spent going to see highbrow art affairs that I didn't enjoy and was convinced Darren didn't understand.

Men who saw me play in proper classical music venues instead of pubs and tube stations seemed to make the same mistake that Darren had, believing that I would possess all of the traits they associated with a female classical violinist. I would be well mannered, proper, cultured, educated, ladylike and graceful, in possession of a wardrobe full of simple and stylish gowns for wearing on stage, none of them vulgar or showing too much flesh. I would wear kitten heels and be unaware of the effect that my slim ankles might arouse.

In fact, I had only one long, formal black dress for concerts, which I'd bought for a tenner from a shop in Brick Lane and had altered by a tailor. It was velvet with a high neck and a low back, but had been at the dry cleaner's the night I met Darren, so I had bought a bandage dress from Selfridges on my credit card and tucked the tags into my underwear. Fortunately, Darren was a tidy lover and had left no stains either on me or the dress, so I was able to return it the next day.

I had my own place, where I spent my weeknights, part of a block of flats in Whitechapel. It was a bedsit, more of a room than an apartment, with a moderately large single bed, a standing rail that functioned as a wardrobe and a small sink, fridge and cooker. The bathroom was down the hall, shared with four others, whom I did bump into occasionally, but generally they kept to themselves.

Despite the location and the run-down building, I could never have afforded the rent had I not struck a deal with the leaseholder, whom I met in a bar one night after a late-night visit to the British Museum. He never fully explained why he wanted to rent the room out for less than he was paying for it, but I presumed that beneath the floorboards lay either a body or a cache of white powder and I often lay awake at night expecting to hear the stampeding footsteps of a SWAT team running up the hall.

Darren had never been to my flat, partly because I had a feeling that he couldn't have brought himself to set foot on the premises without having the whole building steam-cleaned, and partly because I liked to have a portion of my life that belonged entirely to me. I suppose deep down I knew that our relationship was unlikely to last, and I didn't want to have to deal with a jilted lover throwing rocks at my window in the night.

He had suggested, more than once, that I move in with him and save the money that I was spending on rent so that I could put it towards a nicer violin, or more lessons, but I refused. I hate living with other people, particularly lovers, and I'd rather make money moonlighting on a street corner than be supported by a boyfriend.

I heard the soft snap of his cufflink box closing, shut my eyes and squeezed my legs together in an attempt to make myself invisible.

He stepped back into the living room and walked straight past me into the kitchen. I heard the rush of the kitchen tap, the soft hiss of the gas lighting and, a few minutes later, the rumble of the kettle. He had one of those modern but old-fashioned-style kettles that needs to be heated on the stove until it whistles. I couldn't understand why he didn't just get an electric one, but he claimed that the water tasted better, and that a proper cup of tea should be made with a proper pot of water. I don't drink tea. Even the smell of it makes me ill. I drink coffee, but Darren refused to make me coffee after 7 p.m. as it kept me awake, and he said that my restless nocturnal fidgeting kept him awake too.

I relaxed into the floor and pretended that I was somewhere else, slowing my breathing in a concentrated effort to stay perfectly still, like a corpse.

'I just can't speak to you when you're like this, Summer.' His voice floated from the kitchen, disembodied. It was one of my favourite things about him, the rich tone of his public-schoolboy accent, at turns soft and warm, and at other times cold and hard. I felt a rush of warmth between my thighs and locked my legs together as tightly as I could, thinking of how Darren had laid a towel down the one and only time we'd had sex on the living-room floor. He hated mess.

'Like what?' I replied, without opening my eyes.

'Like this! Naked and stretched out on the floor like a lunatic! Get up and put some fucking clothes on.'

He drained the last mouthfuls of his tea, and hearing the sound of his gentle gulps, I imagined how it would feel to have him kneel with his mouth between my legs. The thought made me flush.

Darren didn't normally go down on me unless I wasn't more than five minutes out of the shower, and even then his licks were tentative, and his tongue replaced by his finger at the earliest possible polite opportunity. He preferred to use only one finger and had not responded well when I had reached my hand down and tried to guide two more inside me.

'Jesus, Summer,' he'd said, 'you'll be gaping by the time you're thirty if you carry on like that.'

He'd gone into the kitchen and washed his hands with dishwashing liquid before coming back to bed and rolling over, falling asleep with his back to me while I lay awake and stared at the ceiling. From the vigorous sounds of splashing, it seemed that he'd washed all the way up to his elbows, like a veterinary nurse about to birth a calf, or a priest about to make a sacrifice.

I hadn't ever encouraged him to try more than one finger again.

Darren put his cup in the sink and walked past me to the bedroom. I waited a few moments after he had disappeared from sight before getting up, embarrassed at the thought of how obscene I would look to him as I rose nude from the floor, although I'd now fallen thoroughly out of my Vivaldi-induced reverie and my limbs were beginning to ache and chill.

'Come to bed, then, when you're ready,' he called back behind him.

I listened to him undress and get into bed, pulled my underwear on and waited for his breathing to deepen before slipping between the sheets beside him.

I was four years old the first time I heard Vivaldi's *Four Seasons*. My mother and siblings had gone away for the weekend to visit my grandmother. I had refused to leave without my father, who couldn't come because he had to work. I clung to him and bawled as my parents tried to bundle me into the car, until eventually they relented and let me stay behind.

My father let me skip nursery school and took me to work with him instead. I spent three glorious days of almost total freedom racing around his workshop, climbing stacks of tyres and inhaling deep rubber-scented breaths as I watched him jack up other people's cars and slide beneath them so that just his waist and legs were visible. I always stayed close by, as I had a terrible fear that one day the jack would fail and the car would drop and cleave him in two. I don't know if it was arrogance or foolishness, but even at that age I thought I would be able to save him, that given the right amount of adrenaline, I would be able to hold up the body of a car for the few seconds that it would take him to escape.

After he'd finished working, we'd climb into his truck

and take the long way home, stopping for an ice cream in a cone on the way, even though I wasn't usually allowed to eat dessert before dinner. My father always ordered rum and raisin, while I asked for a different flavour every time, or sometimes half a scoop of two different sorts.

Late one night, I'd been unable to sleep and had wandered into the living room and found him lying on his back in the dark, apparently asleep, though not breathing heavily. He'd brought his record player in from the garage and I could hear the soft swish of the needle with each turn of the record.

'Hello, daughter,' he said.

'What are you doing?' I asked.

'Listening to music,' he replied, as if it was the most ordinary thing in the world.

I lay down alongside him so I could feel the warmth of his body near me and the faint smell of new rubber mixed with heavy-duty hand cleaner. I closed my eyes and lay still, until soon the floor disappeared and the only thing that existed in the world was me, suspended in the dark, and the sound of Vivaldi's *Four Seasons* on the hi-fi.

Thereafter, I asked my father to play the record again and again, perhaps because I believed that I had been named after one of the movements, a theory that my parents never confirmed.

My early enthusiasm was such that for my birthday that year my father bought me a violin and arranged for me to have lessons. I had always been a fairly impatient child, and independent, the sort of person who might not seem predisposed to taking extra lessons or to learning music, but I dearly wanted, more than anything in the world, to play something that would make me fly away, like I had that night I'd first heard Vivaldi. So from the instant that I set my tiny hands on the bow and the instrument, I practised every waking moment.

My mother began to worry that I was becoming obsessive, and wanted to take the violin away from me for a time, so that I could pay more attention to the rest of my schoolwork, and perhaps also make some friends, but I had flat refused to relinquish my instrument. With a bow in my hand, I felt as though I might take flight at any moment. Without it, I was nothing, just a body like any other body, welded to the ground like a stone.

I quickly worked through the levels of my music primers, and by the time I was nine years old, I was playing far beyond the capacity my astounded school music teacher could conceive.

My father organised more lessons for me, with an older Dutch gentleman, Hendrik van der Vliet, who lived two streets away from us and rarely left his house. He was a tall, painfully thin man who moved awkwardly, as if he were attached to strings, and as if the substance he moved through was thicker than air, like a grasshopper swimming through honey. When he picked up his violin, his body became liquid. Watching the movements of his arm was like watching waves rise and fall in the sea. Music flowed in and out of him like a tide.

Unlike Mrs Drummond, the school music teacher, who had been shocked and suspicious of my progress, Mr van der Vliet seemed largely unmoved. He rarely spoke and never smiled. Though the population of my town, Te Aroha, was small, few people knew him and, as far as I was aware, he did not have any other students. My father told me that he had once played in the Royal Concertgebouw

Orchestra in Amsterdam under Bernard Haitink and had left his classical career and moved to New Zealand when he met a Kiwi woman at one of his concerts. She had died in a car accident on the day that I was born.

Like Hendrik, my father was a quiet man, but interested in people, and he knew everyone in Te Aroha. At some point or other, even the most reclusive person would fall victim to a flat tyre, whether attached to a car, a motorbike or a lawnmower, and with a reputation for taking on even the smallest repair job, my father's time was often consumed with doing odd jobs for various locals, including Hendrik, who had come into his workshop one day to have a bicycle tyre repaired and had left with a violin student.

I felt an odd sort of loyalty towards Mr van der Vliet, as if I was responsible in some way for his happiness, having come into the world on the same day that his wife left it. I felt bound to please him, and under his tutelage I practised and practised until my arms ached and the tips of my fingers were raw.

At school, I was neither popular nor an outcast. My grades were consistently average, and I was unremarkable in every way, other than in music, where my extra lessons and aptitude put me far ahead of my peers. Mrs Drummond ignored me in lessons, perhaps fearing that my extra expertise would make my classmates feel jealous or inadequate.

Every night I went into our garage and played the violin, or listened to records, usually in the dark, mentally swimming across the classical canon. Sometimes my father would join me. We rarely spoke to each other, but I always felt connected to him through the shared experience of listening, or perhaps by our mutual oddity.

I avoided parties and didn't socialise much. Consequently, sexual experiences with boys my own age were limited. Even before I grew into my teens, however, I felt a quickening inside that signalled the early onset of what would later become a hearty sexual appetite. Playing a violin seemed to heighten my senses. It was as if distractions were drowned in the sound and everything else disappeared into the periphery of my perception other than the sensations of my body. As I entered my teens, I began to associate this feeling with arousal. I wondered why I was so easily turned on, and why music had such a powerful effect on me. I always worried that my sex drive was abnormally high.

Mr van der Vliet treated me as if I were an instrument rather than a person. He moved my arms into position or laid a hand on my back to straighten my spine as if I were made of wood not flesh. He seemed completely unconscious of his touch, as though I were an extension of his own body. He was never anything other than completely chaste, but despite that, and his age and slightly acrid smell and bony face, I began to feel something for him. He was unusually tall, taller than my father, perhaps about six foot six, and he towered over me. Even grown to full height, I was only five five. At thirteen years of age, my head barely reached his chest.

I began to look forward to our lessons together for reasons beyond the pleasure of perfecting my own playing. Occasionally I affected an ill-considered note or an awkward movement of my wrist in the hope that he would touch my hand to correct me.

'Summer,' he said to me softly one day, 'if you continue to do that, I will teach you no longer.'

I never played a bum note again.

Until that night, a few hours before Darren and I fought over *The Four Seasons*.

I'd been at a bar in Camden Town, playing a free set with a minor would-be blues rock group, when suddenly my fingers had frozen and I'd missed a note. None of the band members had noticed, and aside from a few hard-core fans who were there for Chris, the lead singer and guitarist, most of the audience was ignoring us. It was a Wednesday-night gig, and the midweek crowd was even tougher than the Saturday-night drunks, as aside from the die-hard fans, the punters were just at the bar for a quiet beer and a chat, inattentive to the music. Chris had told me not to worry about it.

He played viola as well as guitar, though he had largely given up the first instrument in an attempt to create a more commercial appeal with the second. We were both string musicians at heart and had developed a bit of a bond because of it.

'It happens to all of us, sweetheart,' he'd said.

But it didn't happen to me. I was mortified.

I'd left the band without having a drink with them afterwards and caught the train to Darren's flat in Ealing, letting myself in with the spare key. I had mixed his flight times up, thinking he'd arrive later in the morning having taken the red eye and gone straight to the office without dropping by home first, giving me a chance to sleep in a comfortable bed the whole night and listen to some tunes. Another of my reasons for continuing to date him was the quality of the sound system in his flat, and because he had enough floor space to lie on. He was one of the few people I knew who still had a proper stereo, including a CD player, and there wasn't enough space in my flat to lie on the floor, unless I put my head in the kitchen cupboard.

After a few hours of Vivaldi on repeat, I concluded that this relationship, while mostly pleasant, was strangling my creative drive. Six months of moderate art, moderate music, moderate barbecues with other moderate couples and moderate lovemaking had left me pulling at the chain I'd allowed to grow round my own neck, a noose of my own making.

I had to find a way out of it.

Darren was usually a light sleeper, but he regularly took Nytol to help him avoid jet lag after his flights back from Los Angeles. I could see the packet glinting in his otherwise empty wastepaper basket. Even at 4 a.m. he had dutifully disposed of the rubbish rather than let an empty wrapper rest on his bedside cabinet until morning.

The Vivaldi CD sat face down next to his lamp. For Darren, leaving a CD out of the case was the ultimate expression of protest. Despite the Nytol, I was surprised he'd been able to sleep at all, with it lying beside him, getting scratched.

I slipped out of bed before dawn, having had one or two hours of sleep at best, and left him a note on the kitchen bench. 'Sorry,' I said, 'for the noise. Sleep well. I'll call you, etc.'

I took the Central line tube into the West End with no real idea of which direction I was headed. My flat was permanently messy, and I didn't like to practise there too often as the walls were thin and I worried that the tenants in the rooms next door would eventually tire of the noise, pleasant though I hoped it was. My arms ached to play, if for no other reason than to wear out the emotions that had built up over the previous night.

The tube was packed by the time I'd reached Shepherd's Bush. I'd chosen to stand at the end of the carriage, leaning against one of the cushioned seats by the door as it was easier than sitting with my violin case between my legs. Now I was crushed in a throng of sweaty office workers, more cramming in at each stop, each face more miserable than the last.

I was still wearing my long, black velvet dress from the gig the night before, along with a pair of cherry-red patent leather Dr Martens. I played in heels for classical gigs, but preferred to wear the boots home as I felt they added a threatening swagger to my walk as I made my way through East London late at night. I stood straight, with my chin high, imagining that, dressed as I was, most of the carriage, or at least those who could see me among the crowd, suspected I was on my way home from a one-night stand.

Fuck them. I wished I had been on my way home from a one-night stand. With Darren travelling so much and me playing as many gigs as I could get, we hadn't had sex in nearly a month. When we did, I rarely came, and only as the result of a hurried, embarrassed shuffling, me desperately trying to reach orgasm while worrying that my self-pleasuring after sex would make him feel inadequate. I still did it, even though I suspected that it did make him feel inadequate, because it was that or spend the next twenty-four hours pent up and miserable.

A construction worker got on at Marble Arch. By now

the end of the carriage was completely rammed, and the other passengers scowled as he tried to squeeze into a small gap by the door in front of me. He was tall, with thick, muscled limbs, and he had to crouch a little so that the doors could shut behind him.

'Move down, please,' a passenger called out in a polite, though strained, voice.

Nobody moved.

Ever well mannered, I shifted my violin case to create a space, leaving my body unencumbered and directly facing the muscled man.

The train set off with a start, throwing the passengers off balance. He jolted forward and I straightened my back to keep myself steady. For a moment I felt his torso squeeze against me. He was wearing a long-sleeved cotton shirt, a safety vest and stone-washed denim jeans. He wasn't fat, but he was stocky, like a rugby player in the off-season, and crunched up in the carriage with his arm stretched out to hold the overhead rail, everything he was wearing looked slightly too small for him.

I closed my eyes and imagined what he might look like beneath his jeans. I hadn't had a chance to check below the belt as he'd got on, but the hand holding the rail overhead was large and thick, so I figured that the same was true of the bulge in his denims.

We pulled into Bond Street station and a petite blonde, her face fixed with grim determination, prepared to wedge herself in.

Fleeting thought – would the train jerk again as it left the station?

It did.

Muscle Man stumbled against me, and feeling daring, I

squeezed my thighs together and felt his body stiffen. The blonde began to spread herself out a bit, poking the construction worker in the back with her elbow as she reached into her hefty handbag for a book. He shuffled closer to me to give her more room, or perhaps he was simply enjoying the nearness of our bodies.

I squeezed my thighs harder.

The train jolted again.

He relaxed.

Now his body was pressed firmly against mine, and emboldened by our seemingly coincidental proximity, I leaned back just a fraction, pushing my pelvis off the seat so that the button on his jeans pressed against the inside of my leg.

He moved his hand from the rail overhead to rest on the wall just above my shoulder so that we were nearly embracing. I imagined I heard his breath catch in his throat and his heart quicken, though any noise he might have made was drowned by the sound of the train rushing through the tunnel.

My heart was racing and I felt a sudden twinge of fear, thinking that I had gone too far. What would I do if he spoke to me? Or kissed me? I wondered how his tongue would feel in my mouth, if he was a good kisser, if he was the kind of man who would flick his tongue in and out horribly, like a lizard, or if he was the sort who would pull my hair back and kiss me slowly, like he meant it.

I felt a hot dampness spreading between my legs and realised with a mixture of embarrassment and pleasure that my underwear was wet. I was relieved that I had resisted my defiant urge to go commando that morning and instead found a spare pair of knickers at Darren's to put on.

Muscle Man was turning his face towards me now, trying to catch my gaze, and I kept my eyes lowered and my face straight, as if the press of his body against mine was nothing untoward and this was the way that I always travelled on my daily commute.

Fearing what might happen if I stood trapped between the carriage wall and this man any longer, I ducked under his arm and got off the train at Chancery Lane without looking back. I wondered, briefly, if he might follow me. I was wearing a dress; Chancery Lane was a quiet station; after our exchange on the train, he might suggest all manner of anonymous dirty deeds. But the train was gone and my muscled man with it.

I had meant to turn left out of the station and head to the French restaurant on the corner that made the best eggs Benedict I'd had since I left New Zealand. The first time I ate there, I told the chef that he made the most delicious breakfast in London, and he had replied, 'I know.' I can understand why the British don't like the French – they're a cocky bunch, but I like that about them, and I went back to the same restaurant for eggs Benedict as often as I could.

Now, though, too flustered to remember the way, instead of turning left I turned right. The French place didn't open until nine anyway. I could find a quiet spot in Grey's Inn Gardens, perhaps play a little before heading back to the restaurant.

Halfway down the street, searching for the unsignposted lane that led to the gardens, I realised that I was standing outside a strip club that I had visited only a few weeks after I first arrived in the UK. I had visited the club with a friend, a girl with whom I had worked briefly while travelling through Australia's Northern Territory and bumped into again at a youth hostel nearby on my first night in London. She'd heard that dancing was the easiest way to make money here. You spent a couple of months or so at the sleazier joints and then you could get a job at one of the posh bars in Mayfair where celebrities and footballers would stuff wads of fake money down your G-string as if it were confetti.

Charlotte had taken me along to check the place out and see if she could pick up some work. To my disappointment, the man who had met us at the red-carpeted reception area didn't lead us into a room full of scantily clad ladies getting their groove on, but instead took us into his office, through another door off to the side.

He asked Charlotte to outline her previous experience – of which she had none, unless you counted dancing on tables at nightclubs. Next he looked her up and down in the way that a jockey might assess a horse at auction.

Then he eyed me up from head to toe.

'Do you want a job too, love?'

'No, thanks,' I replied. 'Got one already. I'm just her chaperone.'

'It's no touching. We throw them out straight away if they try anything,' he added hopefully.

I shook my head.

I did briefly consider selling my body for cash, though, aside from the risks involved, I would have preferred prostitution. It seemed more honest to me somehow. I found stripping a little contrived. Why go that far and not commit to the full deal? In any event, I decided I needed my nights free for gigs, and I needed a job that left me with plenty of energy to practise.

Charlotte lasted about a month at the club in Holborn

before she was sacked when one of the other girls reported her for leaving the premises with two customers.

A young couple. Innocent-looking as you like, Charlotte said. They'd come in late on a Friday night, the chap pleased as punch and his girlfriend excited and skittish, as if she'd never seen another woman's body in her life. The boyfriend had offered to pay for a dance, and his girlfriend had surveyed the room and picked Charlotte. Perhaps because she hadn't bought any proper stripper outfits yet, or had fake nails done like the other girls. It was Charlotte's point of difference. She was the only stripper who didn't look like a stripper.

The woman had become obviously aroused within seconds. Her boyfriend was blushing bright red. Charlotte enjoyed subverting the innocent, and she was flattered by their response to the movements of her body.

She leaned forward, filling the small space that was left between them.

'Want to come back to mine?' she'd whispered into both their ears.

After a little more blushing, they'd agreed and they'd all bundled into the back of a black cab and driven to her flat in Vauxhall. Charlotte's suggestion they go to theirs instead had been summarily turned down.

Her flatmate's face was a picture, she said, when he'd opened her bedroom door in the morning, without knocking, to bring her a cup of tea, and found her in bed with not just one stranger but two.

I didn't hear from Charlotte often now. London had a way of swallowing people up, and keeping in touch had never been a strong point of mine. I remembered the club, though.

The strip joint was not, as you might expect, down a darkened alleyway, but rather right off the main street, between a Pret a Manger and a sports retailer. There was an Italian restaurant a few doors further down that I'd been to on a date once, made memorable when I accidentally set the menu on fire by holding it open over the candle in the centre of the table.

The doorway was slightly recessed, and the sign above was not lit up in neon, but nonetheless if you looked at the place directly, from the blacked-out glass and the seedy-sounding name – Sweethearts – there was no mistaking it for anything other than a strip club.

Struck by a sudden burst of curiosity, I tucked my arm tightly over my violin case, stepped forward and pushed the door.

It was locked. Shut. Perhaps unsurprisingly at eight-thirty on a Thursday morning, they weren't open. I pushed against the door again, hoping it would give.

Nothing.

Two men in a white van slowed as they drove by and wound down their window.

'Come back at lunchtime, love,' one of them shouted. The expression on his face was of sympathy rather than attraction. In my black dress, still wearing last night's thick rock-chick make-up, I probably looked like a desperate girl looking for a job. So what if I was?

I was hungry now and my mouth was dry. My arms were beginning to ache. I was hugging my violin case tightly to my side, which I had a habit of doing when I was upset or stressed. I didn't have the heart to go into the French restaurant unshowered and dressed in yesterday's clothes. I didn't want the chef to think me uncouth.

I took the tube back to Whitechapel, walked to my flat, stripped out of the dress and curled up on my bed. My alarm was set for 3 p.m., so I could go back underground and busk for the afternoon commuters.

Even on my worst days, the days when my fingers felt as clumsy as a fist full of sausages and my mind felt like it was full of glue, I still found a way to play somewhere, even if it was in a park with pigeons for an audience. It wasn't so much that I was ambitious, or working towards a career in music, though of course I had dreams of being spotted and signed, of playing at the Lincoln Center or the Royal Festival Hall. I just couldn't help it.

I woke up at three feeling rested and a great deal more positive. I'm an optimist by nature. It takes a degree of madness, a very positive attitude or a bit of both to lead a person round the other side of the world with nothing but a suitcase, an empty bank account and a dream to keep them going. My poor moods never lasted long.

I have a wardrobe full of different outfits for busking, most of them garnered from markets and from eBay, because I don't have a lot of cash. I rarely wear jeans, as, with a waist much smaller, proportionately, than my hips, I find trying on trousers tedious, and I wear skirts and dresses nearly every day. I have a couple of pairs of denim cut-off shorts for cowboy days, when I play country tunes, but today, I felt, was a Vivaldi day, and Vivaldi requires a more classical look. The black velvet dress would have been my first choice, but it was crumpled in a heap on the floor where I had ditched it earlier that morning and needed to go back to the dry cleaner's. Instead, I selected a black, knee-length skirt with a slight fishtail and a cream silk blouse with a delicate lace collar that I had bought from a vintage store, the same place I got the dress. I wore opaque tights and a pair of lace-up ankle boots with a low heel. The full effect, I hoped, was a little demure, gothic Victorian, the sort of look that I loved and Darren hated; he thought that vintage was a style for wannabe hipsters who didn't wash.

By the time I had reached Tottenham Court Road, the station where I had an agreed busking spot, the commuter crowd had just begun to pick up. I settled myself in the area against the wall at the bottom of the first set of escalators. I had read a study in a magazine that said that people were most likely to give money to buskers if they'd had a few minutes to make up their mind to tip. So it was handy that I was situated where commuters could see me as they rolled down the escalator and have a chance to fish out their wallets before they walked by. I wasn't immediately in their way either, which seemed to work for Londoners; they liked to feel as though they'd made a choice to step to one side and drop money in my case.

I knew that I ought to make eye contact and smile my thanks at the people who left coins, but I was so lost in my music I often forgot. When I was playing Vivaldi, there was no chance that I would connect with anyone. If the fire alarm had gone off in the station, I probably wouldn't have noticed. I put the violin to my chin and within minutes the commuters disappeared. Tottenham Court Road disappeared. It was just me and Vivaldi on repeat.

I played until my arms began to ache and my stomach began to gnaw, both sure signs that it was later than I had planned to stay. I was home by ten.

It wasn't until the next morning that I counted up my earnings and discovered a crisp red bill tucked neatly inside a small tear in the velvet lining.

Someone had tipped me fifty pounds.

2

A Man and His Desires

The tides of coincidence move in curious ways. Sometimes he felt as if his whole life had flown by like a river, its zigzagging course all too often dictated by random events or people, and he had never been truly in control, had just drifted from childhood, teenage years and early struggles onwards to the quiet waters of middle age, like a drunken embarkation on foreign seas. But then again, wasn't everyone in the same boat? Maybe he had merely proven to be a better navigator, and the storms hadn't been too fierce along the way.

Today's lecture had overrun: too many questions from his students interrupting the flow. Not that that presented him with a problem. The more they enquired, queried, the better. It meant they were attentive, interested in the subject. Which was not always the case. This academic year's was a good intake. Just the right proportion of foreign students and home-based ones to make for a challenging mix, which in turn kept him alert and on his toes. Unlike so many other professors, he varied his courses a lot, if only to sidestep the traps of boredom and repetition. This semester his comparative literature seminars were exploring the recurrence of suicide and the death element in writers of the 1930s and 1940s, examining the novels of F. Scott Fitzgerald in America, the often erroneously labelled fascist writer Drieu La Rochelle in France and the Italian author Cesare Pavese. Not a particularly cheerful subject, but it seemed to be hitting a nerve of some sort with much of his audience, especially the women. Blame Sylvia Plath, he reckoned. As long as it didn't drive too many of them in the direction of their gas cooker in emulation, he smiled inside.

He didn't need the job. He had come into money some ten years ago, after his father had passed away and left him a tidy sum. He had never expected this to happen. Theirs had seldom been a particularly easy relationship, and he had long assumed his siblings, with whom he had neither regular contact nor much in common, would inherit the lot. It had been a pleasant surprise. Another of those unseen crossroads on the road of life.

Following the lecture, he'd met with a couple of students in his office, arranging future tutorials and answering questions, and had found himself short of time. He had originally planned to see a new movie at the Curzon West End, a late-afternoon performance, but this was no longer possible. Not to worry – he could catch it at the weekend.

His mobile vibrated and beeped, shuffling crablike over the smooth surface of his desk. He picked it up. A message flashed.

'Care to meet? C.'

Dominik sighed. Should he? Shouldn't he?

His affair with Claudia had been going on for a year, and he wasn't certain how he felt about it, about her, any more. Technically speaking, he was in the clear, as it had begun after she had completed her classes with him. By just a few days, mind. So the ethics were OK, but he was no longer sure if he wanted the relationship to continue.

He decided not to respond right now. Time for reflection. He took his black scuffed leather jacket from the wall hook, gathered his books and lecture files into his canvas tote bag and made his way onto the street. Zipped up against the chilly wind racing up from the river, he made his way towards the Tube. It was already getting dark outside, the dull metal-grey shade of London autumn. The crowds felt menacing as the rush hour descended swiftly, streams of commuters hurrying in both directions, brushing against him anonymously in their slipstream. Usually by now, he'd be out of the centre of town. It was a bit like seeing another side of the city, an uncommon dimension in which the robotic world of work was in the ascendant, heavy, leaden, out of place. Dominik casually picked up the free evening paper he was handed and entered the station.

Claudia was German, not a true redhead, and a wonderful fuck. Her body often smelled of cocoa oil because of the fragrant cream she regularly used to condition her skin. After a whole night in bed with her, Dominik normally ended up with a faint headache from the prevalent odour. Not that they often spent whole nights together. They made love, chatted perfunctorily and parted until the next time. It was that sort of affair. No strings, no questions, nothing exclusive about it. Fulfilling mutual needs, almost hygienic in virtues. It was a relationship he had somehow drifted into; no doubt she had provided signs, a green light of some sort in the early days, and he was aware he hadn't consciously taken the first steps. The way things sometimes happen.

The train came to a halt as he daydreamed on. This was where he had to change onto the Northern line, through a further labyrinth of corridors. He hated the tube, but loyalty to his earlier, less affluent years deterred him most days from taking taxis when travelling to the college and back. He'd bring his car, and damn the congestion charge, were it not for the lack of parking facilities at the institution and in the nearby area, together with the regular infuriating traffic bottlenecks down the Finchley Road.

The familiar smells of rush hour – sweat, resignation and depression – casually kept on assaulting his senses as he journeyed towards the escalator, and the faint sound of music reached his ears.

The barista had brought them their coffees outside. Dominik's usual double espresso and some more sophisticated cappuccino variation with pseudo-Italian add-ons for Claudia. She'd lit a cigarette after he'd offered no objection to it, although he didn't smoke.

'So were you satisfied with the course?' he'd asked her.

'Absolutely,' she confirmed.

'So what are you planning to do now? Staying in London, more studies?'

'Probably.' She had green eyes, and her dark-red hair was piled up in a chignon, if that was what it was still called these days. A thin fringe swept across her forehead. 'I'd like to do a doctorate, but I don't think I'm quite ready for it yet. Maybe I'll do some teaching somewhere. German. Quite a few people have asked me.'

'Not literature?' Dominik enquired.

'I don't think so,' Claudia answered.

'A pity.'

'Why?' she queried, flashing him a quizzical smile.

'I think you'd be quite good at it.'

'You think so?'

'I do.'

'It's kind of you to say so.'

Dominik took a sip of his coffee. It was hot, strong and sweet. He'd put four sugar cubes in and stirred them into oblivion, erasing all the original bitterness.

'Not at all.'

'I thought your lectures were great,' she added, lowering her eyes and almost fluttering her lashes, but he wasn't sure if she actually had because of the moist penumbra of the cafe. Maybe he had imagined it.

'You always had great questions to ask, demonstrated you had a good understanding of the subject.'

'You have a strong passion . . . for books,' she pointed out quickly.

'I'd hope so,' Dominik said.

She looked up again and he noticed that her neck was flushed all the way down to her rather spectacular cleavage, where a white push-up bra exposed the smooth, shiny upper orbs of her constrained breasts. She always wore tight white shirts, cinched at the waist, emphasising her opulence.

The signal was unmistakeable. This was why she had suggested they meet for a drink. It had nothing to do with academic pursuits any longer. This was now obvious.

Dominik held his breath for an instant as he considered the situation. Damn, she was attractive, and – a glancing thought – it had been a couple of decades since he had bedded a German woman, at which time he had just been in his teens and Christel had been over ten years older, a generational gap then to his ignorant perception. He had since enjoyed so many female nationalities in an unformed quest into the geography of pleasure. Why not?

He moved a hand slowly across the wooden texture of the tabletop and grazed her extended fingers. Long, sharp nails painted scarlet, two heavy rings, one with a small diamond.

She looked down at her hand, answering his unformulated enquiry.

'Been engaged for a year. He's back home. Visits every few months. I'm no longer sure if it's really serious, though. Just if you were wondering.'

Dominik was enjoying the way her German accent was modulating her words.

'I see.' Her palms were unseasonably warm.

'You wear no rings?' she asked.

'I don't,' Dominik said.

One hour later, they were in her bedroom in Shoreditch, the sound of Hoxton nightclub clients crowding onto the outside pavement in loud conversation percolating through her open window.

'Let me,' he said.

They'd kissed. Her breath a cocktail of cigarette, cappuccino, lust and heat rising from her stomach. Her breath halting as his hands wandered across her waist and his chest pressed against hers, the hard tips of her breasts squeezing into him, betraying her arousal. Her breath exhaling across the drawn skin of his neck as he delicately burrowed his tongue in the hollow of her left ear, in turn nibbling her lobe and then licking her depth to immediate effect as she tensed with pleasure and expectation. Claudia closed her eyes.

He began to undo the buttons of her white shirt as she held her breath in. The thin material was stretched so tight he wondered how she could breathe. Button after button released the softness of her skin, and with each successive loosening the shirt flapped aside with liberated abandon. There was something spectacularly joyful about her breasts. Steep hills he could bury himself in, although in normal sexual circumstances he usually went for less expansive examples of opulence. Claudia was a big girl, from her personality, her natural exuberance, to every single curve of her body.

Her hand lingered across the front of his now strained trousers. He took a step back, in no hurry to be released.

Dominik extended a hand towards Claudia, threaded a couple of fingers through her fire-coloured hair, met the soft resistance of dozens of hairpins holding the delicately shaped construction in place. Sighed. Began to extract each hairpin in slow, deliberate motion, freeing whole strands at a time, watching them detach themselves from the mass and flop down to her shoulders, settling calmly across the taut, thin straps of her bra.

These were the moments he lived for. The quiet before the storm. The ritual of unveiling. Knowing the point of no return had been reached, breached, and the fuck was now inevitable. Dominik wanted to savour every single moment, slow them down to a crawl, imprint every memory on his grey cells, brand-new visions coursing from fingertip and throughout his body, along the hardening shaft of his erection, all the way to his brain, bypassing the visual nerve in the process so that they were encrypted in a most particular manner and rendered unforgettable and immortal. The stuff of memories he could spend his whole life feasting on.

He drew a deep breath, caught the faint, unfamiliar whiff of cocoa oil.

'What's your perfume?' he asked, intrigued by the uncommon fragrance.

'Oh, that,' Claudia said with an enticing smile. 'It's not a perfume, just the cream I massage into my skin every morning. Keeps my body soft. You don't like it?'

'It's unusual, I must admit,' he replied, then reflected, 'It's you.'

He would quickly get used to it. Strange how every woman had a distinctive smell, a signature, a delicate sensory equilibrium of natural scent, artificial perfumes and oils, sweet and sour.

Claudia unhooked her bra and her breasts fell out, surprisingly high and firm. Dominik's hands journeyed down to her hard dark-brown nipples. One day in the future, he would enjoy clamping them with her hairpins and get hard watching the pain and pleasure it caused fly across her watery eyes.

'Often, during your lectures, I would catch you looking straight at me, you know,' she remarked.

'Did I?'

'Oh, yes, you did,' she smiled.

'If you say so,' he added, in a mischievous tone.

How could he have not? She had always worn the shortest of skirts and invariably sat in the first row of the amphitheatre, crossing and uncrossing her stockinged legs in gay and distractful abandon, calmly observing his roving gaze with an enigmatic smile drawn across her full lips.

'Let's see you, then,' Dominik said.

He watched her as she unzipped the Burberry-patterned skirt, allowing it to drop to the floor and stepping out of it, still wearing her knee-high brown leather boots. She had strong thighs, but her tall frame was in unison, and as she stood still, topless, her breasts at full imperious mast, clad only in her straight-waisted black knickers, matching hold-up stockings and well-polished boots, there was a warlike Amazonian demeanour about her. Fierce but pliant. Aggressive but ready to bend. They locked gazes.

'You,' she ordered.

Dominik unbuttoned his shirt, let it drift to the carpeted floor, as she watched attentively.

A complicit smile breezed across Claudia's lips, as Dominik remained impassive, his eyes urging her silently to keep on undressing.

Claudia bent over, unzipped the boots and kicked them both off in rapid succession. She rolled down the thin nylon stockings until they were bunched up round her ankles, then pulled them off. She was about to slip out of her knickers when Dominik raised his hand.

'Wait,' he said. She interrupted her motion.

He walked over to Claudia, moved behind her back and kneeled down as he stuck a finger inside the undergarment's tight elastic, admiring the solidity and round perfection of her arse cheeks from his new perspective, the scattered moles dotted here and there across the panorama of her bare back. He pulled in a downwards motion, revealing the white landscape of her hard buttocks. He nudged her calf and she stepped out of the knickers, which he bunched up in his fist and threw across the room.

He rose from his knees, stood behind her. She was totally naked now.

'Turn round,' Dominik said.

She was fully shaven, unusually plump, her opening cleanly delineated, a straight geometric line of opposing thin ridges of flesh.

He extended a finger towards her crotch. Felt the heat radiating outwards. Insolently slipped a finger inside her. She was very wet.

He looked up into her eyes, seeking the hunger.

'Fuck me,' Claudia said.

'I thought you'd never ask.'

The strains of a familiar melody reached him faintly as he allowed himself to march down the corridor that led to the Northern line platform, escorted by the rush-hour crowds like a prisoner under close guard.

The sounds of a violin piercing the muted evening rumour of all the travellers filtered its way towards him, louder with every step forward, then a moment of recognition when Dominik realised someone in the distance was playing the second section of Vivaldi's *Four Seasons*, albeit just the lead violin part without the bustling business of the whole orchestra counterpointing the concerto. But the tone was so sharp it didn't require the support of an orchestra. He hastened his pace, music flowing by his attentive ears.

At the crossroads of four tunnels, in a larger open space, where a parallel set of elevators both swallowed streams of commuters and disgorged a set of counterparts into the depths of the transport system, stood a young woman playing her instrument with her eyes closed. Her flame hair cascaded across her shoulders, halo-like, electric.

Dominik came to an uncomfortable halt, blocking other travellers until he stepped back into a corner where he wasn't interrupting the rush-hour flow, and took a close look at the musician. No, she wasn't plugged in. The richness of the sound was solely due to the area's acoustics and the vigorous glissando of her bow against the strings.

Damn, she is good, Dominik reflected.

It had been a long time since he'd listened closely to anything classical. When he had been a kid, his mother had arranged for him to enjoy a season ticket for a series of concerts held on successive Saturday mornings at the Théâtre du Châtelet in Paris, where his father had set up business and the family lived for a whole decade. Over six months, usually using the morning concerts as a rehearsal of sorts for the actual performances held in the evening for a proper adult audience, the orchestra and guest soloists afforded a wonderful introduction to the world and repertoire of classical music. Dominik had found it fascinating, and thereafter had spent most of his meagre pocket money on acquiring records – those were still the years of glorious vinyl: Tchaikovsky, Grieg, Mendelssohn, Rachmaninov, Berlioz and Prokofiev leading his personal pantheon – much to the bemusement of his father. It would be more than a decade later before he graduated to rock music when Bob Dylan went electric and Dominik also began to wear his hair a touch longer in response, always having been on the late side to ride musical and sociological trends. Still to this day he would invariably play classical music on the radio in his car when driving. It made for serenity, cleared the mind, banished the all-too-numerous calls of road rage that his impatience often summoned.

The young woman's eyes were closed as she swayed gently from foot to foot, as she melded with the melody. She wore a black, knee-length skirt and a whitish Victorian-collared blouse that shimmered slightly in the artificial subterranean light, the material swimming against the unknowable shape of her body. Dominik was immediately taken by the exquisite pallor of her neck and the fragile angle of her wrist as she moved the bow in white heat and gripped the neck of the violin.

The violin itself seemed old, patched together in two separate places by tape, on its last legs, but the colour of its wood accorded perfectly with the colour of the young musician's fiery mane.

Dominik stood there for five whole minutes, time suspended, ignoring the continuous stream of commuters as they rushed by on their way to anonymous lives and activities, watching the violin player with rapt attention as she ran through the intricate Vivaldi melodies with gusto and a total lack of interest in her surroundings and involuntary audience or the frayed velvet lining of her violin case, on the ground by her feet, where coins were slowly accumulating, although no passer-by made any further contribution while Dominik was present and all ears and fascination.

Not once did she open her eyes, lost in a trance, her mind engulfed in the world of the music, flying on the wings of song.

In turn, Dominik closed his eyes too, unconsciously seeking to join her in this other world of her making, where the melody erased all forms of reality. But again and again he would open them, hungry to see the way her body moved in imperceptible inch-like movements, every sinew in her unseen muscles reaching for the ecstasy of otherness. Fuck, he'd die to know what the young woman was feeling right now, mentally, physically.

She was fast reaching the end of the 'Winter' *allegro*. Dominik pulled his wallet out of the left inside pocket of his leather jacket and hunted for a note. He'd been to a cash machine earlier in the day on his way to the university. He briefly hesitated between a twenty and a fifty, looked up at the young red-haired woman and followed the nascent wave of movement coursing through her whole body as her wrist launched the bow at an odd angle towards the instrument's strings once again. The silk of her blouse was stretched to breaking point for an instant and pulled tight against the black bra that she wore visibly underneath it.

Dominik felt a tightening in his groin and he couldn't blame it on the music. He took the fifty-pound note and quickly deposited it in the violin case, rapidly shuffling it under a layer of coins so as not to attract the attention of venal passers-by, all this unnoticed by the young woman who was now living within the music.

He walked away just as the music came to a halt with a flourish and the normal sounds of the tube took over again and the hurried commuters kept streaming on by in all directions.

Later, back home, he lay on the couch, listening to a recording he'd found somewhere on his shelves of the Vivaldi concertos, a CD he hadn't taken out of its case for years. He couldn't even recall buying it; maybe it had come free with a magazine.

He recalled the young woman's closed eyes (what colour could they have been?) as she lost herself in the music, the turn of her booted ankle, wondered what she might smell of. His mind raced on, evoking Claudia's cunt, its depth, his fingers exploring her, his cock pounding against her, the time she had asked him to fist her and how he had fitted so snugly and wetly inside her, and the sound of her moans, the scream on the tip of her tongue, and the way her nails had embedded themselves in one savage thrust into the sensitive skin of his back. Catching his breath, he decided that the next time he fucked Claudia, he would play that music. Indeed. But in his mind it wasn't Claudia he was fucking.

He wasn't lecturing the following day; his timetable had been arranged so that all his courses were compacted into two days of the week only. Nevertheless, he impulsively walked out of the house when the rush hour came and travelled to Tottenham Court Road station. He wanted to see the young musician again. Maybe find out what colour her eyes were. Discover what other pieces of music she had in her repertoire. Whether she would dress differently, depending on day or choice of music.

However, she wasn't there. Just a guy with long, greasy hair standing in her spot, swaggering with attitude, playing 'Wonderwall' badly and then inflicting an even more sloppy version of the Police's 'Roxanne' on the impervious commuters.

Dominik swore under his breath.

For the following five evenings he returned to the station. In hope.

Only to come across a succession of buskers playing Dylan and the Eagles with varying shades of success, or singing operatic tunes to pre-taped orchestral accompaniments. No violin player. He knew buskers had appointed locations and hours, but he had no way of finding out what her schedule was. For all he knew, she could have been a totally unregulated performer and unlikely to make a further appearance there.

Finally, he called Claudia over.

It felt like a revenge fuck, as if he had to punish her for not being another, imperiously positioning her on all fours and taking her more roughly than he was in the habit of doing. She said nothing, but he knew it was not to her taste. Holding her arms across her back, brutally gripping her wrists and forcing himself inside her as far as he could reach, ignoring the dryness, basking in the burning fire of her innards as he kept on pumping with metronomic precision, perversely watching her arse yielding under the intense pressure he was applying below, a pornographic vision he shamelessly wallowed in. Had he been gifted with a third hand, he would have cruelly pulled her hair back at the same time. Why did he get so angry at times? Claudia had done nothing wrong.

Maybe he was getting tired of her and it was time to move on. To whom?

'Do you enjoy hurting me?' she later asked him as they sipped drinks in bed, exhausted, sweaty, troubled.

'Sometimes I do,' Dominik answered.

'You know that I don't mind, don't you?' Claudia said.

He sighed. 'I know. Maybe that's why I do it. But does that mean you like it?' he asked.

'I'm not sure.'

The customary post-coital silence that often divided them returned and they drifted into sleep. She left fairly early in the morning, leaving an apologetic note about an interview of some sort, just a strand of her red hair on the pillow to remind Dominik she had spent the night.

A month went by, during which Dominik no longer played any classical CDs when he was home alone. It just didn't feel right. The end of term was soon approaching and he felt the urge to go travelling again. Amsterdam? Venice? Another continent altogether? Seattle? New Orleans? Somehow all these destinations he had once freely indulged in no longer held the same attraction. It was a most unsettling feeling and one he had seldom experienced before.

Claudia was back in Hanover spending a few weeks with her family and he just hadn't the energy to seek someone else out for fun and pleasure, and there was no one from his past he felt any inclination to spend time with again. Neither was this a time for friends or relatives. There were days when he even came to the conclusion that his powers of seduction might have abandoned him for parts unknown.

On the way to a film screening at the National Film Theatre on the South Bank, he picked up a free newspaper from a vendor lurking outside the station entrance at Waterloo and casually stuffed the folded freesheet into his tote bag and then forgot all about it until mid-afternoon the following day.

Halfway through the paper, Dominik came across a brief item of local news that hadn't made that morning's *Guardian*, in a section called 'News From the Underground', which more usually related tales of weird lost and found objects or silly stories of pets and commuter rage.

A violin-playing busker had been inadvertently caught in an affray the previous day while performing at Tottenham Court Road station, it appeared. A group of regional drunken soccer fans passing through on their way to a match at Wembley had become involved in a large fight in which London transport officers had been obliged to forcibly intervene, and although not directly involved, she had been severely jostled in the process and dropped her instrument, on which one of the guys had then heavily fallen and it seemed her violin was now a total write-off.

Dominik hurriedly read through the short piece twice, rushing to the end. The woman's name was Summer.

Summer Zahova. Despite the Eastern European surname, she appeared to be from New Zealand.

It must be her.

Tottenham Court Road, violin . . . who else could it be?

She was unlikely to go busking if she was presently without an instrument in working order, so the chances of meeting her again, let alone listening to her play, had now evaporated into thin air.

Dominik sat back, unwittingly crumpling the newspaper in his fist and throwing it to the ground in anger.

He did have a name though: Summer.

He collected his thoughts, remembered how, some years before, he had gently stalked an ex-lover across the Internet, if only to find out what had become of her and how her life after him was proceeding. Unilateral stalking as it turned out to be, as she remained quite unaware of his discreet surveillance.

Moving to his study, he booted up his computer and Googled the young musician's name. There were very few hits, but it did indicate she was on Facebook.

The photo on her Facebook page was artless and at least a few years old, but he recognised her in an instant. Maybe it had been taken in New Zealand, which led him to speculate how long she might have been in London, in England.

At rest and not pursed in the throes of playing her violin, her mouth stood lipsticked brilliant red, and Dominik couldn't help speculate how it would feel having his erection enveloped by the fiery lusciousness of those lips.

Summer Zahova's page was in part privacy-protected and he was unable to take a peek at her wall or even a list of her friends, and the personal details were somewhat sparse beyond her name, town of origin and London as place of residence, plus a declared interest in both men and women, as well as a list of classical composers and some pop among her likes. No mention of books or movies; clearly she was not someone who spent much time on Facebook.

But he had an 'in'.

Later that evening, having weighed up a multitude of pros and cons, Dominik returned to the deafening silence of his laptop screen, logged on to Facebook and created a new account under a pretend name, albeit with a minimum of personal details that made Summer's page chatty in comparison. He hesitated over his choice of photo, considered downloading an image of someone wearing an elaborate Venice Carnival mask, but eventually left his picture blank. It would have been a tad melodramatic. The text alone was sufficiently intriguing and enigmatic, he felt.

Now, as his new persona, he typed out a message for Summer:

> Dear Summer Zahova,
>
> I was most sorry to hear of your ordeal. I am a great admirer of your musicianship, and to ensure you are able to continue your practice, I am willing to gift you with a new violin.
>
> Are you willing to accept my challenge and my terms?

He left the message deliberately unsigned and clicked on 'send'.

3
A Girl and Her Arse

I stared at the broken remains of my violin with a strange sense of detachment.

Without the instrument in my hands, I felt as though I wasn't really present, as if I had watched the whole scene unfold from above. Disassociation, my high-school guidance counsellor had named it, when I tried to explain the way that I felt when I wasn't holding a violin. I preferred to think of my peculiar mental flights both into and out of music as a type of magic, though I imagined that my talent for disappearing into melody was really just a heightened awareness in onc part of my brain, resulting from a very focused sort of desire.

I might have wept if I'd been the weeping sort. It wasn't that I didn't get upset about things, just that I have a different way of dealing with emotion, my feelings seeping through my body and usually leaking out through either my bow or some other physical expression, such as angry, emotional sex or swimming furious lengths up and down one of London's outdoor swimming pools.

'Sorry, love,' slurred one of the drunks, stumbling close to me, his alcohol-soaked breath hot on my face.

There was a football match somewhere in town today, and two groups of fans in their regulation team kit, each supporting opposing teams, had clashed in the station on their way to the match. The ruckus had broken out a few feet from where I was playing. As usual, I was so wrapped up in my music I didn't hear whatever remark one side had made to the other in order to light the fuse. I didn't even notice the fighting until I felt a beefy body knock into me, slamming my violin against the wall and overturning my case, coins flying all over like marbles in a school playground.

Tottenham Court Road station is always busy and well staffed. A pair of portly London transport officers pulled the brawling fans apart and threatened to call the police. The fire soon went out of the men, who disappeared like rats into the bowels of the station, racing up escalators and Tube tunnels, perhaps realising they'd be late for their match, or possibly arrested, if they lingered any longer.

I sank down against the wall where I'd earlier been playing 'Bittersweet Symphony' and held the two broken pieces of my violin to my chest as if I was nursing a child. It wasn't an expensive violin, but it had a beautiful tone and I would miss it. My father had picked it out from a second-hand store in Te Aroha and given it to me for Christmas five years ago. I prefer second-hand violins, and my father always had an ear for them, an ability to survey a pile of junk and pick out the instrument that still had some use in it. He made a habit of buying my instruments, in the way that my mother and my sister bought clothes and books they thought I might like, and each one was perfect. I liked to imagine who had played it before me, the way that they had held it, the number of warm hands it had passed through, each owner leaving a little bit of their own story, some love and some loss and some madness, in the body of the instrument, emotions that I could coax out through the strings.

This violin had travelled across New Zealand, and then across the world with me. It was on its last legs, granted; I'd had to patch it up with tape in two places where it had been knocked about on the long journey to London the previous year, but the sound was still true, and it felt just right in my arms. Finding a replacement would be a nightmare. Though Darren had nagged, I'd never got round to having it insured. I couldn't afford a new instrument of any quality, or even an old instrument of any quality. Scouring the markets for a bargain could take weeks, and I couldn't bring myself to buy a violin on eBay without feeling it in my hands and hearing the tone.

I felt like a tramp walking around the station, picking up the coins that had scattered all over, my mangled violin in hand. One of the London transport officers asked for my details, to make a report, and he was obviously annoyed that I could provide him with so little information about the actual event.

'No great talent for observation, eh?' he sneered.

'No,' I replied, staring at his plump hands as he flicked through his notepad. Each of his fingers was pale and squat, like something that you might be disappointed to find on a plate at a party, attached to a cocktail stick. He had the hands of a person who didn't play a musical instrument, or interrupt fights very often.

In truth, I hate soccer, though I wouldn't admit as much to anyone English. Football players, as a general rule, are too pretty for my liking. At least during rugby games, I could forget the sport and concentrate on the thick, muscled thighs of the forwards, their tiny shorts riding up and threatening to expose beautifully firm buttocks. I don't play any organised sport myself, preferring the more singular pursuits of swimming and running, and weight training alone at the gym, to keep my arms in shape for long stretches of instrument-holding.

Finally I managed to collect all of my takings, bundle the broken pieces of the violin into the case and escape the watchful glare of the London transport officers.

I hadn't gathered more than ten pounds in coins from the passing commuters before the louts had broken my violin. It had been a month since the mysterious passer-by had dropped the fifty into my case. I still had the note, tucked safely inside my underwear drawer, although God knows how desperately I needed to spend it. I had increased my hours at the restaurant I worked at part-time, but hadn't had a paid gig for a few weeks, and despite subsisting on cafe food and Pot Noodles, I'd had to dip into my savings to cover last month's rent.

I had seen Darren only once since we fought over the Vivaldi record, and I'd explained to him, badly probably, that things weren't working out for me and I needed a break from our relationship to concentrate on my music.

'You're breaking up with me to be with a violin?'

Darren had looked incredulous. He was well-off, good-looking and of baby-making age; no one had ever broken up with him.

'Just taking a break.'

I'd stared at the gleaming leg of one of his stainless-steel designer bar stools. I couldn't look him in the eye.

'No one just takes a break, Summer. Are you seeing someone else? Chris? From the band?'

He'd taken one of my hands in his. 'God, your palms are cold,' he'd said.

I'd looked down at my fingers. My hands have always been my favourite part of me. My fingers are pale, long and very slender, piano-playing hands, as my mother says.

I'd felt a sudden rush of affection for Darren and turned to him, running my hand through his thick hair, tugging a little on his locks.

'Ow,' he'd said, 'don't do that.'

He'd leaned forward and kissed me. His lips were dry, his touch tentative. He made no move to pull me towards him. His mouth tasted like tea. I'd immediately felt ill.

I'd pushed him away and stood up, preparing to pick up my violin case and my bag with some spare underwear, a toothbrush, the few things that I kept in a drawer at his flat.

'What, you're turning down sex?' Darren had sneered.

'I don't feel well,' I'd said.

'So, for the first time in her life, Miss Summer Zahova has a headache.'

He was standing now and placing his hands on his hips, like a mother berating a petulant child.

I'd picked up my bag and my case, turned on my heel and left. I was wearing his least favourite ensemble: red Converse ankle boots, denim shorts over opaque stockings and a skull T-shirt, and as I'd pushed open his front door, I'd felt more like myself than I had in months, as if a weight had lifted from my shoulders.

'Summer . . .' He'd run after me and grabbed my arm as I stepped through the door, spinning me round to face him. 'I'll call you, OK?' he'd said.

'Fine.' I'd walked away without turning, imagining that he was watching my back disappear down the stairs. I heard the door click on the lock just as I turned the corner to the next flight of steps, out of his sight.

He'd called me regularly since then, at first every night and then dying away to twice or thrice weekly as I ignored all of his messages. Twice he'd called me at 3 a.m., drunk, and left slurred messages on my voicemail.

'I miss you, babe.'

He had never called me 'babe' – in fact, he professed to hate the word – and I began to wonder whether I had ever really known him at all.

For certain, I wouldn't be calling Darren now, though I knew that he would jump at the chance to buy me a new violin. He had hated my old one, thought it looked shoddy and was not suitable for a classical violinist. He also hated my busking, considered it beneath me, though I knew that for the most part he worried about my safety. Rightly, he would say now.

I stood at the crossroads outside the station, traffic racing by and pedestrians jostling in all directions, and considered what to do. I hadn't really made many friends in London, other than the couples with whom Darren and I had spent time, going to various dinner parties and gallery openings, and pleasant though they were, they were all his friends, rather than mine. Even if I had wanted to contact any of them, I didn't have their phone numbers. Darren had organised all our socialising, I just tagged along. I took my phone out of my pocket and scrolled through the numbers in my address book. I considered calling Chris. He was a musician, he'd understand, and he'd be angry if he discovered later I hadn't called him, but I couldn't face sympathy, or pity. Either emotion might break me, and then I'd be useless and unable to fix anything.

Charlotte. From the strip club.

I hadn't seen her for a year and hadn't heard from her during that time other than a few Facebook posts, but I was confident that if nothing else, Charlotte would cheer me up, and take my mind off the violin catastrophe.

I pressed 'call'.

The phone rang. A man's voice answered, sultry, sleepy, as if he'd just been woken up in a very pleasant way.

'Hello?' he said.

I struggled to hear over the rush of traffic. 'Sorry,' I said, 'I think I have the wrong number. I'm looking for Charlotte.'

'Oh, she's here,' said the man. 'She's just a bit busy at the moment.'

'Can I speak to her? Can you tell her Summer is on the phone?'

'Ah . . . Summer, Charlotte would be happy to speak to you, I'm sure, but her mouth is full.'

I heard giggling and a scuffle, and then Charlotte's voice on the phone.

'Summer, darling!' she said. 'It's been for ever!'

More scuffling, and then a soft moan through the receiver.

'Charlotte? Are you still there?'

Another moan. More scuffling.

'Hang on, hang on,' she said, 'give me a minute.' The muffled sound of a hand over the receiver and, in the background, a man's deep, throaty chuckle. 'Stop it,' she said in a whisper. 'Summer's a friend.' Then she was back. 'Sorry about that, darl,' she said. 'Jasper was just trying to distract me. How are you, honey? It's been too long.'

I imagined the two of them in bed together and felt a

pang of envy. Charlotte was the only girl I'd ever met whose sexual capacity seemed to rival mine, and she was so open about it, something I had never been. There was a ready aliveness to her. She had the energy of the air after a tropical storm, all damp heat and ripe lushness.

I remembered when we had gone vibrator shopping in Soho a few hours before she'd interviewed at the strip club near Chancery Lane. I had felt a little embarrassed and stood at her side uneasily, watching her confidently pick up dildos of all shapes and sizes, and rub them against the soft skin of her inner wrist to check their sensation.

She had even approached the bored-looking man at the counter and asked for batteries, slipping the AAs inside the base of two similar but slightly different Rabbits with a practised wrist. One of them had a flat nose, and the other was split at the end into a sort of prong, designed to encircle the user's clit as it buzzed. She ran one pulsating toy up her arm gently, then the other before turning to the man standing behind the counter.

'Which one do you think would be better?' she asked him.

He stared at her as if she were an alien, arrived in his store from another planet. I felt the earth move beneath my feet and hoped it was the ground about to swallow me up.

'I. Don't. Know,' he said, pausing between each word in case she didn't understand.

'Why not?' she replied, not at all dissuaded by his surly tone. 'You work here.'

'I don't have a vagina.'

Charlotte pulled out her credit card and bought both, figuring that she would soon earn enough money stripping to pay the bill.

We left the store and she stopped abruptly outside one of those spaceship-like public toilets, the sort that open with a push button at the side, and that I suspected were not often used for their true purpose.

'You don't mind, do you?' she said, stepping inside and pushing the door-lock button before I had a chance to respond.

I stood outside, blushing furiously as I imagined her standing in the cubicle with her knickers rolled down to her knees, pushing a vibrator first inside her and then running the tip round her clitoris.

She was out of the toilet, smiling, within five minutes.

'The flat one's better,' she remarked. 'Want a go? I bought cleaner and wipes. And lube.'

'No, I'm good, thanks,' I replied, wondering what the people on the street would think if they could overhear our exchange. To my surprise, thinking of Charlotte masturbating in the toilet had turned me on. I wouldn't tell her, but lubricant would certainly not have been necessary.

'Suit yourself,' she said breezily, popping the vibrators into her handbag.

Despite the broken violin in my case, and the ache in my heart when I thought of it, imagining Charlotte most likely naked at the other end of the telephone, her long, tanned legs spread out carelessly on the bed beneath the watchful gaze of Jasper, aroused me.

'I'm good,' I said falsely, and then told her what had happened in the station.

'Oh my God! You poor thing. Come over. I'll throw Jasper out of bed for you.'

She texted me the address and within the hour I was curled up on a swing seat in the living room of her apartment in Notting Hill, sipping a double espresso from a delicate porcelain cup and saucer set. Charlotte's fortunes had definitely been on the up since I saw her last.

'Dancing is going well, then?' I asked her as I surveyed the spacious interior, polished wooden floors and large flat-screen television on the wall.

'God, no,' she said, flicking off the coffee machine. 'That was awful. I didn't make any money, and I got sacked again.'

She wrapped a finger round the handle of her own small mug and walked over to the sofa. I suspected that her now very long and dead-straight brown hair might be the result of extensions, but I was pleased to see that she still didn't have fake nails. Charlotte was no shrinking violet, but she had class.

'I've been playing online poker,' she said, nodding towards the desk and large Mac in the corner of the room. 'Made a fortune.'

A door opened down the hall and steam drifted out, presumably from the bathroom. A languid smile spread across Charlotte's face as she watched my head turn in response to the sound.

'Jasper,' she said. 'He's in the shower.'

'Have you been seeing each other long?'

'Long enough,' she replied with a grin as he sauntered into the living room.

He was one of the most handsome men I'd ever set eyes on. Thick, dark hair, still wet from the shower, lean thighs wrapped in loose-cut denim jeans, a short-sleeved casual shirt, all the buttons open to reveal sculpted abdominals and a fine trail of hair running down to his groin. He stood silently near the kitchen, towel-drying his hair with one hand, as if waiting for something.

'I'll just see the lovely boy out,' Charlotte said to me with a wink, and pushed herself up off the couch.

I watched as she took out a wad of banknotes from an envelope resting on her bookshelf and pressed the bundle into his hand. He folded the wad over and slid it discreetly into the back pocket of his jeans without counting.

'Thank you,' Jasper said to her. 'It's truly been a pleasure.'

'The pleasure is all mine,' she replied, opening the front door and kissing him gently on both cheeks on the way out.

'I've always wanted to say that,' she said to me, dropping down onto the sofa again.

'Is he an . . . ?'

'Escort?' she finished for me. 'Yes.'

'But surely you could . . . ?'

'Pick anyone up?' she finished again. 'Probably. But I like paying for it. Puts the shoe on the other foot, if you know what I mean, and then I don't need to worry about all the other bullshit.'

I could certainly see the appeal. At that moment, or indeed at almost any other moment, I would have killed for a guilt-free, complication-free, painless fuck.

'Do you have any plans tonight?' she asked suddenly.

'No,' I said, shaking my head.

'Good. I'm taking you out.'

I protested that I wasn't in the mood and didn't have any suitable clothes to wear or any money. Besides which, I hate nightclubs, full of young girls batting their fake lashes for a free drink and seedy men trying to cop a feel.

'It'll take your mind off it. I'm paying. I have an outfit for you. And this place is different. You'll love it.'

*

A few hours later, I was standing aboard a large boat moored on the Thames that doubled as a fetish-themed nightclub once a month over the autumn.

'What exactly does that mean, "fetish"?' I asked Charlotte nervously.

'Oh, nothing really,' she said. 'The people just wear fewer clothes, but like they mean it. And they're friendlier.'

She grinned and told me to relax in a manner that suggested I do exactly the opposite.

I was now dressed in a pale-blue boned corset, frilly knickers and stockings with a blue seam running down the back of my legs from thigh to ankle to meet a pair of silver heels. Charlotte had teased my hair into a thick mass of curls, doubling the already large volume of my red locks, and had then balanced a top hat on my crown at a jaunty angle. She had lined my eyelids carefully with liquid eyeliner, thick and dark, painted my lips a vivid, glossy red and stuck a little silver glitter to my cheeks with Vaseline. The corset was a couple of inches too big and had to be cinched all the way in to tighten round my waist, and the shoes were a touch small, making it difficult to walk, but the effect overall, I hoped, was pleasing.

'Wow,' said Charlotte, looking me up and down once she'd finished decking me out in all her finery. 'You look hot.'

I moved awkwardly over to her mirror. Damn, my feet were going to hurt by the end of the night. The shoes were pinching already.

I was pleased to see that I couldn't disagree with Charlotte's description, though I wouldn't say so aloud, obeying the presumed rules of behaviour and putting on a show of modesty. The girl in the mirror didn't really look like me. More like a rebellious older sister in a burlesque costume. The corset, though loose-fitting, forced me to stand straighter, and though I was inwardly nervous about leaving the apartment like this, in my new skin, I guessed I would look confident, my shoulders back and throat bared, like a dancer.

Charlotte had stripped off completely in front of me and rubbed her body with lube, before asking for my help to shimmy into a tiny bright-yellow rubber dress with two red lightning bolts running up either side of her waist. The dress was cut low at the front, so that nearly all of her plump breasts and a tantalising hint of her nipples were visible, pressed tightly against the scooped neck. The lube was cinnamon-flavoured, and for a moment I had been tempted to give her a lick. I noticed that she didn't wear any knickers, although the dress barely covered her arse.

Charlotte was brazen, that was for sure, but I admired her confidence and, after a day spent in her company, was beginning to get used to it. She was one of the few people I knew who did exactly what she liked without giving a damn what anyone else thought.

In my too-small five-inch heels and Charlotte in her enormous red platforms, we'd had to cling on to each other's arms, giggling, as we tentatively scooted down the steep metal ramp and onto the boat.

'Don't worry,' Charlotte said, 'you'll be on your back before you know it.'

Would I?!

We arrived at about midnight and the club was in full swing. I was a little self-conscious about removing my jacket and joining the party with more than my usual amount of flesh on public display, but Charlotte insisted that I would fit right in. We presented our tickets in exchange for a stamp on the wrist at the front desk, checked in our coats and then teetered up the stairs, through the double doors and into the main bar.

My senses were assaulted immediately. Everywhere men and women were dressed in eye-popping outfits. Latex abounded, but also vintage-style lingerie, top hats and tail coats, military uniforms, even a man wearing just a cock-ring, his flaccid penis bouncing happily as he walked. A short woman wearing a voluminous skirt and nothing else, her full breasts hanging freely, walked through the crowd holding a lead with a very thin, tall man attached to the other end, his back and shoulders hunched heavily so that she could pull him along without straining. He reminded me of Mr van der Vliet.

Alone on one of the couches sat a petite man, or possibly an androgynous woman, wearing a full rubber body suit and face mask. Charlotte hadn't been entirely right about the fetish crowd wearing fewer clothes. Of course, many of them were wearing next to nothing, and wearing it well, but a large number wore elaborate costumes that covered every inch of flesh, yet still managed to look sexual. Cheap fancy dress and street clothes were both banned, a finer detail that elevated almost all of the boat's occupants from tacky to theatrical.

'What are you drinking, honey?' asked Charlotte, taking my attention away from the crowd. I tried with all my might not to stare at anyone, but I felt as though I had been dropped into an adults-only movie set, or had stumbled through a corridor into a parallel universe where everyone was like Charlotte and didn't give a damn about what the rest of the world thought of them.

She'd been right at least about my outfit. Not only did I fit right in, but I was one of the more modestly attired revellers in attendance. They probably thought I was downright demure. This thought relaxed me. Normally, in any group of friends or social gathering, I worried I was the weird one, with my relaxed attitude to sex and relationships. No one had ever labelled me demure.

'Just water for me, thanks,' I replied.

I didn't want to take advantage of her generosity, and I wanted to absorb all this with a clear head, so I wouldn't wake up in the morning thinking it was just a dream.

Charlotte shrugged and returned a few minutes later with our drinks in hand.

'Come on,' she said. 'I'll show you round.'

She took me by the hand and led me through another set of double doors, this pair leading to the uncovered prow of the ship, where a handful of smokers and men dressed in thick, hot-looking military jackets were standing, either smoking or cooling down, or both. The women, who were generally wearing far fewer clothes, were huddled around the two gas heaters standing in the middle of the space. Two of them wore latex skirts with the backsides cut out and their pale buttocks shone under the gas light like low-hanging twin moons.

I walked over to the side and stood still for a moment, holding Charlotte's hand and staring at the Thames stretched out into the night like a long, black ribbon, nestling gently between the two halves of the city. The water looked thick and viscous, and made a soft slapping sound as it lapped at the base of the boat. Waterloo Bridge joined the two sides behind us, Blackfriars Bridge in front, the lights on Tower Bridge barely visible in the foreground, like a dark promise of things to come.

I felt Charlotte shiver.

'Let's go,' she said. 'It's cold out here.'

We walked back through the double doors and into the main bar, and then through another set of doors and onto the dance floor. I watched, open-mouthed, as a dark-haired, beautiful, vampy-looking woman covered herself with gasoline and then blew fire into the air over her head, while grinding round a pole to the sound of a heavy rock song. She reeked of sex. In the company of Charlotte, and in the presence of so many others who seemed unashamed of their bodies and proud, even, of their sexuality, I felt, for the first time in my life, as if I might not be a freak. Or at least, that if I was a freak, I had company.

A tall man standing at the edge of the dance floor caught my eye. He was wearing a pair of tight, bright-blue sequinned leggings, long riding boots, a red and gold military jacket and a matching hat. He held a riding crop in one hand and a drink in the other, and was chatting happily to a gothic-looking girl wearing latex hot pants. She had long, black hair with a single white lock at the front. The man's leggings barely concealed a large bulge at the crotch, and I stopped still for a moment, mesmerised. I thought I'd seen a similar pair of leggings in the window of a women's fashion store, but on him the effect was decidedly masculine.

Charlotte tugged my hand. 'Later,' she whispered into my ear, eyeing the man with the leggings. 'The show's on. That means it'll be quiet downstairs.'

She led me through a small, red velvet-curtained

corridor, then into another, smaller bar, filled with similarly clad partygoers, and then down a flight of steps.

'This is the dungeon,' she said.

The room didn't look how I expected a 'dungeon' to look, although I really had no concept of how a modern-day dungeon would look or even that such a thing existed. I stopped in my tracks and looked around, soaking it all up, in case I never saw anything like it again.

The décor was just like the bar above, only with a few extra pieces of strange-looking furniture. There was a large, padded red cross in the shape of an X rather than a crucifix. A woman, naked, was leaning against it with her legs and arms spread, while another woman beat her with an instrument that Charlotte called a 'flogger'. I couldn't see the handle, as it was covered firmly by the woman's hand, but instead of one single strand, like a whip, it had several pieces of soft-looking leather attached. The woman doing the flogging took turns at whipping then stroking the other woman's arse with the palm of her hand, and sometimes running the strands of leather softly over her body. The woman on the receiving end moaned with pleasure and twitched unintentionally throughout, and the woman flogging her often bent forward and whispered what I imagined were sweet nothings into her ear. She was smiling, laughing and leaning her body towards her partner on the cross. They were surrounded by a small group of interested onlookers, but appeared to be in a world of their own, almost as if an invisible screen stood between them and the people watching.

The sight would have shocked me if I had seen it in a photograph, or read a salaciously worded description of it in a newspaper. I'd heard of this sort of thing, of course, but filed such activities away in my head, in the same place that I put stories of people rushing to hospital after an unfortunate accident with a hamster and a vacuum-cleaner pipe – I supposed some people might get into it, but I thought it was mostly either an urban legend or the prevail of the very strange. The people involved here all looked quite nice and normal, though they were kitted out in the same dramatic costumes that filled the rest of the boat. I moved in a bit closer to get a better look.

Yes, the person on the whipping end was definitely having a good time. I would have given a limb, right then, to know how that felt. And the beating itself, the rise and fall of the flogger, looked precise, rhythmic, expertly orchestrated. The whole thing was rather beautiful.

Charlotte, noting my interest, approached a man who was standing near the cross and tapped him on the shoulder, then beckoned to me.

'Mark,' she said to him, 'this is Summer. It's her first time here.'

Mark looked me up and down, though in an appreciative rather than predatory way.

'Nice corset!' he said, kissing me on both cheeks, European style. He was on the short side, a little fat and balding, but he had a friendly face and an attractive gleam in his eyes. He wore heavy flat boots and a rubber apron and vest. The apron had several pockets, which held a number of different implements, each, at first glance, similar to the flogger that was in use on the cross.

'Thank you,' I replied. 'Do you come here often?'

'Not nearly as often as I'd like,' he replied, laughing as I blushed.

'Mark is the dungeon master,' Charlotte inserted.

'Basically,' he said, 'I make sure everything is OK down here and no one's being a dickhead.'

I nodded and shifted from one foot to the other. Despite being taller than me, Charlotte was a shoe size smaller and my feet were really beginning to hurt.

I looked around for an empty chair, but didn't see anything, aside from a metal frame with a padded flat section at roughly waist height that I suspected wasn't a seat.

'Am I allowed to sit on that?' I asked, motioning towards the frame.

'Not really,' said Charlotte. 'You're not supposed to sit on the equipment. Someone might want to use it.' Then her face lit up. 'Oooh!' she said, giving me a wicked grin and nudging Mark in the ribs. 'You could give her a spanking, Mark. Then she could rest her feet.'

Mark looked at me. 'I'd be delighted,' he said, 'if the lady would like that.'

'Oh, no . . . Thanks, but I'm not sure.'

Mark politely replied, 'No problem,' in the same breath that Charlotte insisted, 'Go on – what are you afraid of? He's an expert. Just try it.'

I glanced over again at the woman on the cross, who now appeared to be in a state of ecstasy, unconcerned what sort of spectacle she provided to onlookers.

I wished I was like that, I thought, so brave and uncaring. If I had given less of a damn about the opinions of others, I'd probably never have ended up spending more than one night with Darren.

'I'll be right here with you,' added Charlotte, no doubt watching my resolve falter. 'What's the worst that could happen?'

What the hell. Nobody here would think any less of me and I'd get to lie down for a bit, and besides that, I was curious. If it was all bad, this many people wouldn't be doing it.

'OK,' I said, mustering a smile. 'I'll try it.'

Charlotte wriggled with delight.

'Which instrument would you prefer?' Mark asked, waving his hand in front of the tools held in his apron.

I followed his hand as it waved. Though he wasn't a tall man, he had big, sturdy hands. They looked tough, the kind of hands that were engaged in some sort of physical work throughout the day, not hovering over a computer, typing and getting flabby.

Charlotte watched the line of my gaze with interest. 'I think she's the bare-handed sort, you know,' she said.

I nodded.

Charlotte took my hand again and led me over to the bench.

Mark gently turned me away from Charlotte to face him. 'Right,' he said. 'I'm going to start very, very gentle. If you're uncomfortable at any time, just put your hand up into the air and I'll stop straight away. Charlotte is going to stay right there next to you. Do you understand?'

'Yes,' I said.

'OK, good,' he replied. 'This really isn't going to work through frilly knickers. Would you mind if I took those off?'

I held my breath. Christ. What had I got myself into? But I knew this was coming; it wouldn't be the same, clearly, through thick frilly underwear, and the room was full of nudity, so I would hardly stand out.

'Sure.'

I turned to face the bench and leaned forward against

the padded frame, lifting my weight off my shoes and giving my feet blessed respite. My waist and torso rested against the flat, padded section of the middle of the frame, and there were two further padded sections for me to lay my arms against, and handles to wrap my hands round.

I felt a finger hook round the waistband of my frilled panties and gently pull them down over my thighs and then down my stockinged legs. Mark cradled one foot and then the other in his hands, helping me to step out of them. My legs were spread wide apart and I guessed that, crouching at my feet as he was, he had a clear view of every part of me. My cheeks flushed with warmth, but I could already feel myself begin to surrender, and a pleasant, tingling heat suffused my lower body. He pushed himself up to standing, and Charlotte squeezed my hand.

For a moment, I felt nothing, just the slightest caress of air against my bare buttocks and the imagined gaze of strangers on my naked flesh.

Then a strong palm cupped my right arse cheek, gently circling clockwise, followed by the tiniest of breezes as the hand pulled away into the air, then smacked down again, first on one cheek, then the other.

A sharp sting.

Now the soft touch of his cool hand on my hot flesh, soothing, stroking.

Another brush of air as the hand travelled away from me again.

And a jolt as the hand slapped down on my arse, harder this time.

I gripped the metal bars with my hands, arched my back, pressed my thighs into the padding, felt another blush burn across my face as I realised I was soaking wet and I imagined Mark must be able to see my excitement, must be able to smell it. He would be able to feel that my body was becoming pliant under his touch, the curve in my back deepening so that I could thrust myself closer towards him.

Another smack, this time much harder, genuinely painful. The sharp sting made me jump and for the briefest moment I considered asking him to stop, but then his hand was on me again, resting on the cheek that he'd just hit, taking the sting away and replacing it with a strange sort of warmth that travelled all the way up my spine to the nape of my neck.

Leaving one hand cupping me, he ran the other gently up my back to my neck and into my hair, spreading his fingers, tugging my hair softly at first, then harder.

Now I was somewhere else. The room fell away; the imagined stares of strangers faded; Charlotte disappeared; there was nothing but me and the feeling of his hand pulling my hair as I bucked my body on the bench and moaned as he kept slapping.

Then I was back again. There were two hands on my stinging cheeks, just resting, gently, and Charlotte squeezing my hand. The noise of the room began to filter back into my consciousness. Voices, and music, ice cubes chinking in glasses, and the sound of someone else being slapped.

'You OK, honey? You still with us? Wow,' she said, I presumed to Mark, 'she was gone like a rocket.'

'Yes,' he says, 'she's a natural.'

I craned my head back to smile at them and then attempted to stand, but found I couldn't walk. I felt as jittery as a newborn foal, and I was so clearly aroused, my legs were slippery. I was embarrassed by the level of my response, but neither Mark nor Charlotte, nor any of the spectators, seemed the least bothered or surprised. This was a normal weekend (or perhaps everyday) event for them.

'Easy there, tiger,' Mark said, wrapping a firm arm round my waist and leading me over to a chair only vacated as the combined gaze of Mark and Charlotte had caused the occupant to leap up and walk away.

I slipped down onto the seat and Mark stroked my hair, holding my head gently against his thigh. His rubber apron felt cool and strange against my face, and one of his paddles pressed uncomfortably against my arm.

I felt myself drifting away again as he ran his hands through my hair, and their voices came to me as though floating through a tunnel.

'I think you're going to have to take her home,' he said to Charlotte. 'Has she had too much to drink?'

'Not a thing. Been guzzling mineral water all night. You've broken in a virgin.'

'How wonderful,' he chuckled.

'She looked like she was having a pretty good time to me,' Charlotte remarked, 'and I didn't even get to show her the couples' room.'

I fell asleep on Charlotte's shoulder in a cab on the way back to her flat and woke up in the morning still wearing the pale-blue corset, though Charlotte had loosened the strings. The pillow was covered in glitter and streaks of black eye make-up. I felt as though I had a hangover, although I definitely hadn't had a drop to drink.

'Morning, sunshine,' Charlotte called from the kitchen. 'Made you a coffee.'

I stumbled to the kitchen, immediately more alert at the promise of caffeine.

'Wow,' said Charlotte, 'that outfit looked better on you yesterday.'

'Thanks,' I replied. 'Can't say the same for yours.'

Charlotte was standing in the middle of the kitchen, holding a small china saucer in one hand and a cup of espresso in the other. She was completely naked.

'I don't wear clothes if I can help it,' she said.

'And when would that be?' I asked.

'When I'm deep-fat frying,' she replied, 'or when I have gentlemen callers. I put clothes on so they can take them off again. Blokes seem to like that.'

When she said 'blokes', I remembered that Charlotte was from Alice Springs and was amazed again that anyone as cosmopolitan as her had been raised in the outback of Australia.

'You're in a good mood.'

'Made some money already today,' she said, glancing over at her computer, 'and I slept well knowing that I expanded your mind last night.'

She was grinning, but I felt a little strange about the whole thing. Nothing, other than music, had ever made me feel that way – that epiphany of both detachment and pleasure filtering its way through the pain. I pushed the feeling out of my mind.

'Your phone's been ringing off the hook. You could get a better ringtone.'

'It's Vivaldi, you philistine,' I said. She shrugged.

I fished my phone out of my purse and check the 'missed call' list. Darren. Ten times last night, another dozen times this morning. He must have heard about the violin somehow. I glanced at the clock above the oven in the kitchen. It was 3 p.m. I'd slept most of the day.

'Stay another night,' Charlotte said. 'I'll cook for you. I haven't even turned the oven on in this place.'

She left me in the apartment to shower and rest, while she went to the shops to buy food for dinner. I had a bath and then spent thirty minutes combing out the knots in my hair. Eventually, I grew tired of waiting and texted Charlotte to check if I could use her computer.

'Of course,' she replied. 'There's no password.'

I waved the mouse until the screen appeared. Checked my Gmail account. Ignored the messages from Darren and the inevitable spam. Logged on to Facebook. One message in my inbox. I hovered the mouse over the inbox screen cautiously, expecting it to be yet another missive from Darren, but the message was from a profile that I didn't recognise with no picture attached.

I clicked on the message with mild curiosity.

A polite introduction.

Then:

> I am willing to gift you with a new violin.
> Do you accept my challenge and my terms?

I clicked on the profile, but it was almost completely bare, just the location 'London' in the personal details. The name of the profile was just one initial: D.

Of course I thought of Darren, but this just wasn't his style.

What else could the 'D' stand for? Derek? Donald? Diablo?

I ran through a mental Rolodex of people who might know I was missing a violin and might be inclined to do something about it, and I came up with nothing. The only person who had all the details of the incident was the fat-handed London transport officer, and he seemed about as romantic as his profession suggested – that is, not at all. If the violin had been stolen, or worse, left strangled on my doorstep, I might have feared that I had an Internet stalker, but the message didn't appear malevolent to me.

A spark had been lit, and try as I might, I couldn't extinguish it now.

I stared at the screen for a further ten minutes, none the wiser, until Charlotte burst through the door, her arms full of shopping bags.

'You better not be vegetarian,' she called out, 'because I got nothing but meat.'

I assured her that my predilections were firmly in favour of steak and beckoned her over to read the email.

Charlotte stared at the screen, raised an eyebrow and smirked.

'What challenge?' she asked. 'And what terms?'

'I don't know. Should I reply?'

'Well, that would be a start. Go on – write back to him.'

'How do you know it's a him?'

'Of course it's a him. It's got alpha male written all over it. Probably someone who's seen you playing, got the hots for you.'

I deliberated, then pressed the 'reply' button. I rested my fingers gently on the keyboard and replied:

> Good evening,
> Thank you for your kind words.
> What is your challenge? And your terms?
> Regards,
> Summer Zahova

A reply came back within minutes.

I would be delighted to respond to your queries in full.
Meet me.

A question mark was conspicuously absent from his request.

Against my better judgement, and with Charlotte egging me on, I arranged a date with the stranger, for noon precisely the following day.

I was ten minutes late.

He had suggested we meet at an Italian coffee shop in St Katharine Docks. I pretended I knew the place, although I didn't; it saved me having to suggest a location.

When I arrived, I discovered that it was right in the middle of the water. Walking one way round the boardwalk at the sides of the dock, I realised the path was closed for repairs and had to turn and walk back again the other way. I was the only person on the docks, walking back and forth, lost like an ant who discovers a crumb in its path, and I imagined that the mysterious stranger was watching my movements from the comfort of the cafe all the while. I was wearing the least sexual outfit of Charlotte's that I could find so as not to give him the wrong impression. I had overslept and hadn't had time to pop back to my own flat and change.

Charlotte had found me a navy dress, part wool and part stretch, that she had stored from a very brief interlude working as the receptionist at a law firm before she began her career in online poker. It was lined, sat just past the knee and had a very modest scoop neck and four buttons placed evenly over the chest, military style. It was a little tight on the hips, but loose on the waist, and I wore it with a thin cream belt, my lace-up ankle boots, which I had fortunately been wearing the day of the Tube brawl, and a pair of skin-coloured hold-up stockings. The packet read 'Lightly oiled – bare-legged look'.

'He's going to think I want to fuck him if he sees I'm wearing these,' I said to Charlotte.

'Well, maybe you will want to fuck him,' she replied.

Then she told me not to be silly as I would have to be bending all the way over for the split at the back to reveal what I had on underneath. The split was fortunately set low, which meant that it was a little hard to walk, but also meant that hopefully nobody would know that I wasn't wearing any underwear. As the fabric of the dress immediately highlighted my pantyline, Charlotte had refused to let me leave the house with my knickers on. I surrendered them to her at the door like a soldier surrendering a flag.

She had lent me her cream wool coat also, with a warning not to leave it behind as it was expensive. The coat smelled strongly of perfume, a musky variety that was not of my style, and of cinnamon-flavoured lubricant from the night she'd worn it over the latex dress.

By the time I arrived, I was glad of the coat as it was pouring with rain. Charlotte had also loaned me her red umbrella, and I felt like a scarlet woman as I held it open, as if I were inviting attention, the one spot of colour among a sea of black and grey.

I surveyed the interior of the cafe. Nothing special, but from the look of the Italian man behind the counter, I guessed the coffee would be good. The coffee they serve at airports in the rest of Europe is better than anything you'd find in England. Another fact I wouldn't mention to anyone English. A nation of tea drinkers.

A counter, a few tables and chairs. A freestanding set of stairs leading upwards into a second area. I looked out of the windows. A clear view across the docks. He had undoubtedly seen me coming, if he was here. I didn't see anyone downstairs, so I took the steps upwards to the first floor of the cafe. No one there either, just a middle-aged woman with a newspaper and the remains of a cappuccino. My phone buzzed. We'd exchanged numbers in case of any delay or mix-up en route.

'I'm downstairs,' said the message.

Dammit. I walked down again, trying not to look flustered, and spotted a table behind the stairs with a clear view running under the open wooden slats. The man sitting at the table, given the right angle and degree of attention, would most likely have had a perfect view up my dress. I felt a stab of arousal at the thought, that I had just given this stranger a vision of me, completely naked under my dress. A flash of shame quickly followed. I had better compose myself, quickly.

He smiled without a hint of displeasure at my tardiness or any indication that he'd just been watching my stocking-tops flash by overhead during my awkward ascent.

'You're Summer.' It wasn't a question. His eyes glittered, but they gave nothing away.

'Yes,' I replied, extending my hand to meet his, business-like. I remembered the confident air that the corset had given me and purposefully straightened my shoulders.

He extended an arm and briefly shook my hand in a formal fashion. His grip was firm.

'My name is Dominik. Thank you for coming.'

His hands were warm and solid, larger even than Mark's from the other night. I reddened at the thought and quickly sat down.

'Can I get you a drink?' he asked.

'Flat white, please, if they've got it. Or a double espresso,' I replied, hoping my words would not betray my nervousness.

He moved past me, walking towards the counter, and as he did so, I caught a whiff of him. He did not smell at all of cologne, just a very faint odour of musk, the smell of warm skin. I find something very masculine about an unscented man, skin unadulterated by products and perfumes. He was the sort of man who I imagined might smoke cigars and shave with an old-fashioned razor.

I watched him order our coffees at the counter.

Dominik was moderately tall, about six foot, I guessed, and lean, but not overly muscled. He had the strong arms and back of a swimmer. A very hot guy, despite his cool demeanour. Or maybe because of it. I'd always preferred men who didn't simper or try too hard to impress me.

He asked the barista very politely for a sugar bowl.

His voice was deep and rich, public-schooled, my favourite kind, but it had an irregular lilt to it, and I wondered if he was, in fact, English. I have a real thing for accents, perhaps a natural result of having come from someplace else. I tried to push the thought out of my head, to not let on that I found him attractive and give him the upper hand.

He was wearing a dark-brown, ribbed, high-collared jumper that looked comfortable and soft to touch, cashmere maybe, a pair of dark denim jeans and recently polished tan leather shoes. Nothing about his dress or manner suggested anything in particular, other than that he seemed pleasant enough and not dangerous. At least, not dangerous in a psychopathic way. Perhaps dangerous in other ways.

I reached into my bag and texted Charlotte to tell her that I hadn't been chopped into bits yet.

He returned with a tray and I began to stand, to help him unload the cups, but he waved me away, balancing the tray on one hand and sliding a cup of coffee in front of me. As he did so, he leaned a fraction closer than was strictly necessary to offer me sugar, brushing his hand against my arm, his touch lingering almost long enough to necessitate a response from me, of either approval or disapproval, but he removed his hand and I pretended I hadn't noticed.

I shook my head, no, waited for him to make the obligatory 'You're sweet enough' remark, but he didn't.

We sat in a strangely comfortable silence as he delicately stirred first one, then another, then another, then yet another cube of sugar into his cup. His fingernails were neatly manicured, though square in shape, so the effect was manly rather than effeminate. He had a slight olive tone to his skin, whether from ethnicity or a recent holiday, I couldn't tell. He withdrew the teaspoon from his cup very gently and laid it neatly on the saucer, watching his own hand as he did so, as if his gaze could prevent any stray drips from leaking off the spoon and onto the tablecloth. A silver wristwatch sat on his right wrist, the old-fashioned, not the digital, sort. I've always found it hard to determine age, especially in men, but I guessed that he was in his forties, probably no older than forty-five unless he looked young for his years.

If he had a violin, it wasn't anywhere near the table.

He leaned back in his chair. Another moment of silence.

'So, Summer Zahova.' He rolled the syllables in his mouth as if tasting them, one by one. I watched his lips.

They looked extraordinarily soft, though the set of his mouth was firm. 'You are probably wondering who I am and what this is all about.'

I nodded and took a sip of my coffee. It was even better than I expected.

'Good coffee,' I said.

'Yes,' he replied. A bemused expression spread over his face.

I waited for him to continue.

'I would like to replace your violin.'

'In exchange for what?' I asked, leaning forward with interest.

He responded by leaning towards me also, his palms now flat on the table, his fingers spread, nearly grazing mine, a gesture that invited me to run my hands inside his. I caught a faint whiff of coffee on his breath, and as I had when Charlotte smeared herself with cinnamon lube, I felt a sudden urge to lean closer and lick him.

'I would like you to play for me. Vivaldi, maybe?'

He leaned back again, lazily, a slight smile playing on his lips, as if he had noticed my attraction to him and was teasing me for it.

Two could play at this game. I straightened my shoulders again and met his eyes with my own, pretended to be oblivious to the heat rising between us and arranged my features so that I must seem merely lost in thought, considering his bizarre offer as one would any professional contract.

I remembered the last time I had played *The Four Seasons*, the afternoon after the fight with Darren. That was the day someone had deposited the fifty in my case. Probably Dominik, I now figured.

I felt him shift his weight under the table and saw his eyes flash. Satisfaction? Desire? Perhaps I didn't look as collected as I had hoped.

A hot flush spread across my cheeks as my leg brushed his and I realised that I'd been sitting with my knees spread apart under the table like a man. I hadn't had sex for over a month now and was almost ready to mount one of the table legs, but he didn't need to know that.

He continued, 'Just the once, to begin with, and you shall have your violin. I will decide on the venue, but you will understandably have safety concerns. You should feel free to bring a friend if you so prefer.'

I nodded. I had by no means decided that I would go along with his plan, but I needed to buy some time, to mull it over. The undertones of his suggestion were obvious, and his arrogance irritating, but – despite my best intentions to the contrary – I did find Dominik attractive, and I desperately needed a violin.

'Well, Summer Zahova, does that mean that you accept?'

'Yes.'

I would think it over later and decline by email if necessary.

He ordered two more coffees without asking if I wanted one. His assumption annoyed me and I was about to protest, but I did want another and would look a fool if I turned his away and ordered my own on the way out. We sipped them, talked about the weather, briefly discussed the minutiae of our ordinary lives. Not that mine felt ordinary any more, violinless as I was.

'Do you miss it? The violin?'

I felt a strange and sudden sweep of emotion, as though without a bow and an instrument to release all the sensations held within my body, I might tear apart from the inside out, explode, self-combust.

I remained silent.

'Well, then, we should make it soon. Next week maybe. I'll be in touch to confirm the location and will procure the instrument for the occasion, and if all goes to my satisfaction, we can go shopping for a more permanent instrument.'

I agreed, again ignoring the almost disrespectful degree of arrogance in his tone, and, keeping my reservations under wraps for the moment, took my coat from the chair. We walked out of the cafe together until our paths separated and we exchanged polite goodbyes.

'Summer,' he called out to me as I walked away.

'Yes?' I replied.

'Wear a black dress.'

4

A Man and His String Quartet

Dominik had always been an attentive reader of spy thrillers and had memorised some of the basics of spycraft from the many books he had eagerly devoured. As a result, he had sat himself in the cafe in an obscured position on the ground floor, in a corner by the stairs where he had a clear view of the door but could not necessarily be seen because of the glare of the outside light. In this instance, though, there was no need for an escape route.

He saw her enter, just a few minutes late and slightly out of breath, and perfunctorily look around the almost deserted cafe where the heavy smell of coffee drifted seductively from wall to wall and the espresso machine chugged away. He noted her missing him in the recessed area behind the stairs, and seeking him out. She then made her way up to the first floor, her tight blue pencil dress stretching across her hips with every ascending step and affording him a clear view up her dress before the darkness between her legs obscured any further exploration. Dominik had always been something of a private voyeur and this involuntary all-too-brief glimpse of her secrets was a delight and an exquisite promise of better things to come.

Without her violin and the hypnotic effect of her music, he could now concentrate on her physical appearance. There was the burning bush of her hair, a waspish waistline, an almost manly allure to her movements. Not quite as tall as he remembered her under the low ceiling of the busy Tube corridor, he noted. She was not a traditional beauty in the fashion-model sense of the word, but she stood out, whether in a crowd or alone, rushing through the cafe or approaching across the docks outside. Yes, she was different, which appealed to him a lot.

He called up her number on his phone and texted her, advising her of his whereabouts, redirecting her. She walked down the stairs, her face ever so slightly flushed from the embarrassment of having missed him first time round.

She now faced him.

'You're Summer,' he said, and introduced himself, inviting her to sit down opposite him.

She did.

A faint whiff of cinnamon reached him. Somehow not the fragrance he expected of her. He would previously have thought that the pallor of her skin would conjugate better with a perfume with a strong green note, dry, discreet, sly. Oh well.

He looked Summer in the eyes. She held his gaze, defiant but curious, firm and just a little amused. She evidently had a strong mind of her own. How interesting this could prove.

The coffees were ordered as they examined each other in silence, observing, judging, weighing, speculating. Like chess players before the battle, they probed for their adversary's weak spot, the breach through which the opposite number could be broken, invaded.

Dominik rose to fetch the tray on which the barista had placed their espressos while she quickly sent a text to someone, presumably reassuring a friend she was safe and he was no regulation-issue serial killer or championship-standard creep at first glance. Dominik allowed himself a faint smile. It seemed he had passed the initial test. Now the ball was in his court.

He confirmed his proposal, outlining the bare lines of a seemingly straightforward initiative, while all along a more complex plan slowly grew in his mind. Fantasies unrolling, visions coming to life like a Polaroid emerging from a dark mass of clouds. How far could he go? How far would he take her?

Half an hour later, as they parted, a touch of uneasiness still lingering between them for all the things unsaid, Dominik realised he was hard, his erection tenting the front of his jeans as he watched her sashay away across the walkways of St Katharine Docks towards Tower Bridge. She never turned back, but Dominik knew she was aware of his eyes following her.

Ah, this was going to be a worthy challenge . . . Risky and exciting, but . . .

For someone who had spent most of his life in the kingdom of books, Dominik was both a fount of knowledge – however theoretical it might sometimes appear – and a man of action. Back in his university days, he had almost simultaneously spent hour after hour in libraries and then switched with ease to the racetrack and shorts to compete in athletics. He had proven a strong high- and long-jumper, as well as an exceptional middle-distance and cross-country runner, although he was less successful when involved in team sports, as he never quite succeeded in blending in or synching with others. He saw no contradiction in these two distinct sides of his life.

For years his sex life had been both conservative and traditional. He'd never been at too much of a loss for bed partners, even in his younger years, when he'd been prone to idealising some women and falling in love with those he could not get with puzzling regularity. As a lover, he reckoned he was just about average, not wildly imaginative, but tender. Being something of an introvert, he was never truly concerned by how he rated in the eyes of the women he bedded. Sex was just another occupation, a necessary one, but just part of the busy fabric of life, on a par with books, art and food.

Until the day he had met Kathryn.

He had of course read the Marquis de Sade and many of the modern classics of erotica. He consumed pornography (and enjoyed it to recurring ejaculatory climaxes) and knew about BDSM, domination, submission and the palette of perversions on offer, as well as the paraphernalia of the fetish life, but it had never truly intersected with the day-to-day reality of his own life. It was something else, abstract, remote, something others did, indulged in. He observed with intellectual interest, but this other parallel world didn't call him, beckon for him to participate.

She was also an academic, albeit in a different discipline, and they had met at a conference in the Midlands, a quizzical exchange of glances across the floor during the course of one of his keynote lectures, followed by an uneasy conversation at the crowded evening bar. Back in London, they had become lovers, although she was married and Dominik was at that time in a long-term relationship with someone else.

Most of their carnal encounters took place in daytime hotel rooms or on the carpeted floor of his small office at the college between the happy hour and the last train from Charing Cross to the southern suburbs.

Every minute counted, and the sex was an eye-opener for both Dominik and Kathryn, as if all their previous sexual experiences had been leading to this moment. Hurried, hard, desperate, compulsive like a drug.

Knees rubbing against the thick pale-brown carpet squares, her body beneath him, both panting, on the edge of breathlessness, his erection digging harder and deeper inside Kathryn with every successive thrust, her eyes closed in lustful communion, Dominik had taken a mental pause and frozen the moment in his mind. Storing memories. Wondering whether, one day in the future (how far along?), he would have to resort to evoking this particular image to gratify himself in the loneliness of his solitude.

He examined the pink flush spreading from her neck to the onset of her small breasts, listening to the licentious sounds of their lovemaking, the physical friction amplified to obscene levels by the emptiness of the office. The gasps emerging from her pursed mouth as her lungs exhaled her breath in staccato fashion. The sheen of sweat on her forehead, a mirror image of the beads now rising through his own pores across his chest, his arms, his legs and all known and active parts of his body as he laboured joyously above and within her.

'Jesus,' she moaned.

'Yes,' Dominik acquiesced, steadying the rhythm of his pelvic assault, every breathy whisper of Kathryn's willing acceptance of the dire consequences of their lust. She closed her eyes, sighed deeply.

'Are you OK?' he asked, slowing, concerned.

'Yes. Yes . . .'

'Do you want me to take it easier? Be more gentle?'

'No,' Kathryn said, her voice hoarse and stretched. 'Go on. More. Please.'

Dominik adjusted his position to relieve the pressure on his knees, briefly lost his balance and almost fell down on her, instinctively throwing his hands forward to find some support, his fingers brushing against Kathryn's wrists. He took hold of them.

A nervous twitch coursed like electricity through her body under the effect of the additional contact.

'Hmm . . .'

'What?'

'Oh . . . nothing . . .'

But her eyes said something else. She looked at him, digging deep into his soul with questions? No, a demand, begging? A supplicant nailed to the cross of their fuck.

In response, he gripped her wrists as hard as he could and dragged her arms up behind her head, his hips still grinding repeatedly into her, pinning her like a butterfly to the hard floor. Now her cheeks were crimson red. It must be hurting her, he realised, but her soft moans of pleasure seemed to invite the increased pressure, the abuse of her body.

Another lengthy look into his eyes, wordless but nonetheless self-explanatory. It meant 'more'.

He moved his thumbs away from her thin wrists, fearing he might be leaving her marked, bruised, and let them glide downwards until they were pressing against her neck and his hands circled the skin like a necklace, a choker. Her pulse radiated outwards, moving from the surface of her skin to the hard tips of his fingers. Her life signal.

She took an insanely deep breath and cried out, 'Harder.'

He was both scared and aroused to rock hardness sheathed inside her, expanding still as his erection grew to seemingly abnormal proportions, pressing against her soft, wet inner walls, just as his fingers were now pressing against her neck, beginning to cut off the circulation, and the colour in her pale face went into overdrive across the spectrum of the rainbow.

Kathryn came with a loud, guttural moan, an almost masculine sound of triumph. He loosened his grip on her neck and with the animal sound came a savage outpouring of breath.

All the time he had been fucking her, the incessant come and go of his cock fracturing against her, like a machine, pitiless, cruel, unshackled. He closed his own eyes and at last allowed himself to come; it felt as if his whole being was bursting into flames. Elemental. Primeval. Possibly the most intense fuck of his life.

Later, bodies still bathed in sweat, half-eyeing their watches and thinking of last train times, she said to him, 'You know, I'd always wondered what it would feel like, harder, like that. You knew how to do it.'

'I've never tried that before. Read about it, of course, but it was all just theory, just words, concepts on a page.'

'I knew I could trust you, that you wouldn't take it too far.'

'I didn't want to hurt you. I would never hurt you.'

She leaned closer, resting her head on his still-slick shoulder, and whispered, 'I know.'

Thus began weeks of sexual experimentation in which Kathryn slowly unveiled her innermost desires, her fantasies at their most basic, the fire within that betrayed her submissiveness. It wasn't that she was a masochist, far from it, but the craving for pain, for the breaking of limits, was undeniably present, had been for many years, dormant under the surface veneer of civilisation and breeding, and had never been given the opportunity to break loose. Dominik was the first person to recognise this trait in her, instinctively channelling it in the right direction, dominating her, liberating her.

He'd read the novels, knew the stories, but this was no master-and-slave, dom-and-sub situation according to the clichéd rulebook. They were both in this together, peeling away layers, getting down to the foundation stones of lust and sexual attraction. There was no need for all the paraphernalia that they had once associated with this new land of joyful excess: the latex, the leather, the baroque and cruel implements.

Their eyes had been opened, and Dominik, for one, knew he would never be able to close them again.

It was also, inevitably, the beginning of the end for their furtive relationship. With every step nearer to the abyss of no return, with every new improvisation and move away from the conventional river of sex, he could see the seeds of doubt being planted in Kathryn's mind. The fear of where all this might be leading.

Eventually, Kathryn succumbed to the burden of reality, a middle-class upbringing, a Cambridge literature degree and a dull marriage to a man who was kind but had no imagination, and she opted to break up. They never spoke again and were both careful not to bump into each other at functions or events, until she and her husband moved out of town and she gave up teaching.

Dominik, however, had opened Pandora's box and the

whole wide world had become a jungle full of delicious temptations and the knowledge that, with Kathryn, he had reached another level, that there was more to life than he had previously assumed, would never leave him.

•

First, Dominik knew he had to test Summer, ascertain her willingness, her propensity for play. He was already comfortably aware that she had a mind of her own and would not respond to crude manipulation or blackmail. He wanted her to enter the adventure, the experiment, with a full knowledge of the risks and consequences. He was not seeking a puppet whose strings he could pull at leisure, a blind participant. He wanted a partner in crime whose trepidations would pulsate in unison with his.

From the brevity of their encounter and the many words unsaid, she must know already that the violin was just a bait to ensnare her, that he would require more than the gift of music in the long term. Maybe not a deal with the devil – he didn't see himself in that Machiavellian role – but a game in which both participants could play each other to the end. Not that he had a clue as to what end he wanted to reach. Yes, there was a darkness he wished to probe, but he didn't yet know how deep it could be.

He phoned an acquaintance who worked at a music college in the City and had a somewhat shady reputation. He was willing to answer his queries. Yes, there was a store where he could hire a reasonably good-quality violin by the day, the week or even monthly, and indeed his acquaintance knew the best place to advertise for classical musicians in search of a gig.

'It's for a very private party, mind,' Dominik established. 'Would they be likely to object to wearing blindfolds?'

At the other end of the phone line, his interlocutor guffawed. 'Damn! I think I'd love to be a guest at such a party!' he replied. Then, more thoughtfully, 'If they knew the piece they are hired to play and the money was good, I'm sure you could reach a satisfactory agreement. Maybe best not mention that particular requirement in the initial advertisement, though?'

'I see,' Dominik said.

'Let me know how it goes,' the other added. 'I'm now eminently curious.'

'I'll keep you informed, Victor. Promise.'

The following day, he visited the music store he had been recommended. It stood halfway down Denmark Street in London's West End, just off the Charing Cross Road. From outside, like most of the other stores on this street that had once been called Tin Pan Alley, they appeared to be doing a roaring trade in electric guitars and basses and amplifiers; no other instrument was on display in the window. Thinking that he been advised wrongly, Dominik took a tentative step inside and was quickly reassured by the presence of a bulky glass case with half a dozen violins on display.

A young woman behind the counter greeted him. She wore her jet-black, evidently dyed hair down to her waist, skinny jeans like a second skin, and her face was heavily made up with full crimson lips to the fore. A heavy piercing dangled from her nose, and her ears bore the weight of countless earrings made of a variety of metals. For a moment, Dominik amused himself by watching her and imagining the rest of the piercings she most likely sported. He'd always wanted to go to bed with a woman with a genital piercing of some sort, or a nipple-ring or two, but so far had only enjoyed navel adornments at best, which he felt sadly didn't convey the right level of eroticism for his own sensibility. Surely there was something downmarket – nay, proletarian – about bellybutton piercings.

'I'm told you also hire instruments,' he said.

'We do, sir.'

'I require a violin,' he added.

She pointed to the cabinet and its glass front. 'Take your pick.'

'They can all be hired?'

'Yes, although we'd need a deposit secured either in cash or by credit card, and a proper form of photo ID.'

'Of course,' Dominik confirmed. He always carried his passport in his inside jacket pocket, an old habit he'd never lost. 'Can I take a closer look?'

'Certainly.'

The goth girl liberated a key from an assortment dangling from a long chain attached to the cash register and unlocked the cabinet.

'I don't know much about violins, I fear. This is for a friend I'm helping out. Mostly plays classical music, though. Do you know much about them, by any chance?' he asked her.

'Not really. I'm more a rock, electric sort of girl,' she replied with a smile. Her lips were like beacons.

'I see. Well, which of these is considered the best?'

'I reckon the most expensive.'

'I suppose that makes sense,' Dominik remarked.

'It's not a science,' the sales assistant said with a flirtatious smile.

'Indeed.'

She handed him one of the violins. It looked old, its wood brushed orange by seemingly generations of previous owners, burnished and shiny, catching a reflection of the store's fluorescent strip lights.

Dominik pondered a while, all the time holding the violin. It felt so much lighter than he had expected. He reckoned its musicality would depend on whoever played it. He was momentarily annoyed at himself. He should have done some homework about violins before coming here. He must look like a total amateur.

His fingers stroked the side of the violin he had been given to hold.

'Do you play anything?' he asked the young woman with the jet-black hair. Her T-shirt had slipped slightly over her right shoulder and he saw the faint outline of a large tattoo.

'Guitar,' she answered, 'but when I was a kid, I had to take cello classes. Maybe one day I'll go back to it.'

From the mental image of her imagined piercings, Dominik quickly drifted to a private movie of her on a stage with a cello between her legs. He smiled at the thought and abruptly said, 'I'll take it. Say for a week?'

'Great,' the assistant said. She pulled out a pad and began her calculations as Dominik kept on gazing at her bared shoulder, following the black, green and red flowers of her tattoo, then noticing she also had a minuscule tattoo of a teardrop inked below her left eye.

While he waited for her, other customers streamed in and out of the store, attended to by a male assistant in matching principally black goth attire with a minimalist geometric haircut.

Finally, she looked up, giving her column of figures a final glance.

'So what's the damage?' Dominik asked.

The violin came with a case.

Back at his house, he carefully deposited the expensive instrument on one of the sofas, went to his laptop and checked the seven-day weather forecast. For the first episode of the adventure he had in mind, he would rather not be inside. That would have to come later, when discretion would become the better part of valour and events might branch out into somewhat more illegal-in-public manifestations.

The forecast was good. No rain was expected over the next four days at least.

He texted Summer and informed her of the day, time and place of their next meeting.

Her answer reached him within the half-hour. She was available, and still willing.

'Do I have to bring a partition?' she queried.

'I don't think so. You'll be playing Vivaldi.'

The sun was out on Hampstead Heath, the sound of birds chirping as they criss-crossed the tree-lined horizon. It was still early in the morning and there was a bit of a nip in the air. Summer had alighted from the tube at Belsize Park and made her way down the hill, past the Royal Free Hospital, the Marks & Spencer store that had been built on the site of an old cinema, the small shopping parade on South End Road, the fruit and vegetable stall by the entrance to the overground railway station, finally reaching the car park where they had arranged to meet. She'd been here before, some months previously, with friends intent on a weekend picnic.

There was only one metal-grey BMW parked there, and from a distance, she recognised Dominik's silhouette in the driver's seat. He was reading a book.

As instructed, Summer was wearing her black velvet dress, the one that bared her shoulders, and, to keep the chill away, Charlotte's coat, which she had not been asked to return yet.

He saw her approaching, opened his door and stood waiting by the side of the car as she made uneasy progress in her heels across the rough sand and stone surface of the improvised municipal car park, which doubled during holidays as a fairground.

He looked down at her feet, noticing the high heels. Her regulation formal stage footwear. He was all in black. Crew-neck cashmere sweater and black trousers with a sharp front crease.

'Maybe you should have worn boots,' he remarked. 'We have to trek over the grass a little to get where we are going.'

'I'm sorry,' Summer said.

'There's still a lot of dew on the grass at this time of the morning. Your shoes will get wet, damaged maybe. You should take them off for the walk. I see you're wearing tights or stockings. Do you mind?'

'No, not at all. Stockings, actually.'

'Good.' He smiled. 'Hold-ups or suspenders?'

Summer felt her cheeks warm. A streak of impudence provoked her to answer back. 'Which would you have preferred?'

'A perfect answer,' Dominik replied, but did not elucidate further as he opened the door behind the driver's seat and pulled a dark, shiny violin case from the back seat. Summer shivered.

He clicked on his fob to lock the BMW and indicated

the vast expanse of grass, the field ahead beyond the low-hanging car-park fence.

'Follow me.'

Summer took her shoes off when they moved onto the grass. He was right: it was wet and spongy under her almost bare feet. Within minutes the sensation became pleasurable enough. Dominik led the way, past the ponds, across a small bridge facing the outdoor swimming area and up a path. Here she had to slip the shoes back on because of the wilderness of pebbles digging into her soles. The squelching sensation of soggy nylon against the unyielding leather felt awkward, but they soon reached an expanse of grass again and she was able to resume her stocking-footed progress behind him as he held a steady, determined pace, holding her shoes by the straps in one hand. She wondered where they were heading. This part of the heath was unknown to her, but there was something about Dominik she trusted. Gut instinct. She didn't believe he was luring her into some dark cranny in the woods to take advantage of her. Not that the thought of such a fate was in any way disturbing.

For a few hundred yards, the canopy of trees hid the blue of the sky and the warmth of the sun, and then they emerged into the light. A circular field totally open to the sky. An infinity of green, like an island emerging from a busy sea, a slight inclination and, at the top of the mound, a bandstand. Old-fashioned Victorian wrought-iron columns, rusting in places, overlooking a blissfully empty field.

Summer gasped. This was beautiful, an absolutely perfect setting, oddly deserted and eerie. She now understood why he had chosen such an early time in the morning for them to come here. There would be no spectators, or at any rate very few, unless the sound of her playing began to attract some from further afield across the heath.

Dominik bowed, indicating the bandstand, which they had now reached.

'Here we are.' He handed her the violin case and she mounted the stone steps leading to the bandstand's stage.

Dominik positioned himself in one corner, leaning casually against one of the supporting metal posts.

Summer, for a fleeting instant, experienced a pang of rebellion. Why was she obeying his damn orders, being so docile and obliging? Part of her wanted to put her foot down and just say, 'No', or, 'No way', but another part of her that she didn't know had existed until recently seductively whispered in her ear to go along with the game. Say 'Yes'.

She froze.

Then, composing herself, Summer moved to the centre of the stage and opened the violin case. The instrument looked exquisite, so much better than her old battered and now useless instrument. She caught his eyes as she greedily ran her fingers across the burnished wood, the neck, the strings.

'This is just a temporary instrument,' Dominik said. 'Once matters are settled to our mutual satisfaction, I will procure you a permanent violin, a better quality one.'

Right now, Summer couldn't imagine ever holding a finer instrument than this one. Its weight, its balance, its curves just seemed downright perfect.

'Play for me,' he commanded.

She slipped off Charlotte's coat and allowed it to slide to the floor. By now, the morning cold on her uncovered shoulders was no more than a gentle breeze as she travelled into the zone, oblivious to the place where she stood, the unnatural and isolated situation, the undertones of the relationship – yes, she knew it was going to be a relationship – with this curious and dangerous man.

She leaned over to retrieve the bow from the case she had set down on the bandstand floor, allowing Dominik, she was aware, a brief glimpse of her breasts. She never wore a bra with the black dress.

Summer looked back at him as he stood there, patiently waiting, expressionless, and began to tune the violin. Its sound was so full and rich, it bounced across the bandstand, every note floating towards the roof and back again like a silent echo.

And began playing Vivaldi.

By now, she knew the concertos by heart. Always her party piece whether busking or playing for friends or even just rehearsing. The centuries-old music just made her heart sing, and as she played it, eyes ever closed, she could evoke the landscapes of the Italian Renaissance she had seen in so many paintings, the unrolling life of nature and the elements. Somehow there were seldom actual people in her musical reverie inspired by Vivaldi, although she'd never bothered to find an explanation for this curious fact, this possibly Freudian omission.

Time came to a standstill.

The sounds she was now extricating from the violin were truly blissful and she felt she was finding a whole new undiscovered dimension in the music. She had never played this well before, relaxed, finding the truth at the core of the melody, navigating its waves, losing herself within its maelstrom. It was almost as good as sex.

By the time she reached the third concerto, she briefly

opened her eyes to check on Dominik's presence. He was still there, in the same place, motionless, pensive, his eyes hypnotically fixed on her. She remembered someone once mentioning to her that the shape of her body was not unlike that of a violin: small-waisted, generously hipped. Is that what he saw in her right now beneath the billowing folds of her black velvet dress?

She noticed a handful of bystanders at the outer edge of the clearing, no doubt attracted to the sounds of the music she was playing. Anonymous spectators.

Summer took a deep breath, both gratified and disappointed that this was no longer a concert for one only. She completed the third concerto and finally ceased playing. The spell had broken.

A couple of women in jogging gear in the distance applauded.

A man got back on his bicycle and continued his journey across the heath.

Dominik coughed gently.

'The fourth concerto is technically a bit more awkward,' Summer said. 'I'm not sure I could get it all right without having to consult the partition,' she excused herself.

'No problem,' Dominik said.

Summer waited for his judgement. He kept on staring at her.

A heavy silence began to weigh down on her. Once again, she could feel the coolness of the morning lap against her bare shoulders. She shivered. He failed to react.

Dominik watched as Summer grew visibly more nervous. The music and her playing had been sublime, everything he could have hoped for. Getting her to play for him here had been a brilliant idea, and the solo performance had elicited so many strong sensations inside him, a sense of terribly intimate connection. Now he wanted to know what the feel of her skin would be like, the smooth curve of her undressed shoulder against his fingers, his tongue, the million secrets beneath her dress. He could already conjure up the shape of her body. He had always regretted not having learned to read or play music on any instrument when he had been younger, and knew it was now too late in life to begin, but Dominik sensed that Summer was an instrument, one he could play for hours on end. And he would.

'That was quite beautiful.'

'Thank you, kind sir.' She couldn't help herself teasing him. Maybe it was because right now she felt supremely happy.

Dominik frowned.

He noticed the relief spread across her face as he delivered his verdict, but she was still tense – he could see from the straight line of her shoulders and the hard set of her jaw. Perhaps she knew that this was only just the beginning. There would be more.

'You will have your violin,' he indicated.

'And you're certain I can't have this one?' she protested, stroking its long, smooth neck with a possessive hand. 'It's a wonderful instrument.'

'I'm sure it is, but, like I said, I will find you a better one. You deserve it.'

'You're sure?'

'Yes.' Dominik's tone was firm; he would brook no further argument.

He walked over to Summer, picked up her coat from the

ground and helped her into it. They walked back to the car, where she returned the violin to him.

Summer was full of questions, but didn't know where to begin.

He pointed to the passenger seat.

'Sit with me,' he ordered.

Summer obeyed.

She had been fearful that the inside of the car might reek of tobacco – somehow Dominik looked like a smoker – but it didn't. It was slightly musky, but not in a disagreeable way.

Dominik felt her closeness as he sat behind the wheel. She had lost her smell of cinnamon and all he could intuit was the scent of the soap she had used when washing this morning. Somewhat sweet, hygienic, reassuring. He could feel the warmth of her body inside the coat radiate outwards towards him.

'Next time you play for me, it will be with your very own violin, the one I am now going to find, one that will fit you like a glove, Summer. Price will be no object,' he said.

'OK,' she opined.

'Now, tell me about your first time with a man, sex.'

For a brief moment she seemed taken aback by the abruptness of his demand, and Dominik thought, for a second, that he had guessed incorrectly; perhaps she wouldn't go through with it.

Summer paused, gathering her thoughts and memories. In a novel way, she had already been intimate with this man and there was no point holding back now.

The car's front window was misting up a little and Dominik switched on the air-conditioning.

She told him how it had happened.

*

The instrument had been built by someone called Pierre Bailly in Paris in 1900 and cost Dominik in the low five figures. It had initially caught his eye in a specialist dealer's catalogue. The wood veered towards yellow more than orange or brown, a peaceful shade that evoked serenity and patience, but the patina in his mind held over a century of melodies and experience. The salesman in the small Burlington Arcade boutique was surprised he did not wish to play it before purchasing it, and didn't appear to initially believe him when he declared he was buying it for an acquaintance. He knew he had long fingers, a musician's fingers – many friends and women he had known had mentioned the fact to him – but did he look like one, let alone a violin player?

With the expensive antique violin came a certificate of provenance, listing all its owners over the past 112 years. There had been only five, most of their foreign names betraying past winds of war and continental drifts along the tides of history. The last owner had been called Edwina Christiansen. After her death, he was told, her heirs had sold the instrument at auction, where it had been acquired by the dealer, alongside other items of lesser note. No, he replied when asked by Dominik, he wasn't in a position to supply further information about the late Miss Christiansen.

The Bailly violin came without a case and he purchased one online, a brand-new one, as he felt it would be best for Summer not to advertise the vintage status of her new instrument in a similarly visibly aged case. Dominik had always been eminently practically minded as well as cautious.

Once the case was delivered, he transferred the rusty-yellow violin into its new habitat and carefully wrapped it before handing it over to a courier service who would arrange for the package to reach Summer Zahova at the apartment she shared with others in East London. The instructions were clear: she had to sign for it personally. He warned of its impending arrival and requested an acknowledgement.

When her text came, it consisted of a single word: 'Beautiful.'

In the letter he had written to her accompanying the expensive package, he had insisted she spend as much time as possible playing, rehearsing on it until the moment he would advise her of the new challenge, and he had given a precise instruction not to take it out in public yet, let alone busk in the Underground.

Now arrangements had to be made and enquiries conducted.

His advertisement on the freelance jobs display board at the music college sought three musicians, under thirty by preference, used to playing in a string quartet, willing to undertake a one-off performance with a minimum of rehearsal time and in unusual circumstances. And whose discretion would be adequately recompensed. A photograph was required with the application.

One answer he received filled all the boxes: a group of second-year students who had performed throughout their first year as a quartet but were now short of a member, the second violinist having returned a few weeks before to her native Lithuania. The two young men, who respectively played violin and viola, looked presentable, while the cello player, a young woman with a mass of curling blonde hair, was actually rather pretty.

All the other applications that landed in his letterbox as a result of the call-out were from solo musicians with minimal experience of playing with others, so it proved an easy decision.

Before organising a formal interview, Dominik sent them the questionnaire he had assembled for the occasion. Once the responses came back all positive, as he expected them to be considering the substantial fee he was in a position to offer, he arranged to speak to the trio on Skype and answered their remaining questions, assessing their reactions to some of his more unusual demands and requirements.

They would have to dress all in black, they would be able to rehearse with the fourth musician for a short period of time, but then they would be blindfolded for the main performance. They would sign a document with penalty clauses if news of the private concert they would be playing leaked out. They would not seek to contact him or the anonymous violin player again after the performance was completed.

All three of them appeared puzzled by the offer, but the monetary rewards visibly overcame their doubts.

The cello player, the blonde, even suggested a rehearsal place he could hire for the occasion, a crypt in a deconsecrated church where the sound resonated just that side of perfect for strings, and which 'offers total privacy for whatever you have in mind', she said. As if she had known all along that Dominik's house was unsuitable for the occasion.

How could she even guess what I have in mind? he wondered, noticing an amused twinkle in her eye.

The music was agreed on and he took their particulars before ending the call. Now all the elements were in place and a date could be set. He picked up his phone.

'Summer?'

'Yes.'

'It's Dominik. You will play for me again next week,' he informed her, advising her of the location and the time. He also mentioned the music she would be performing for him and the fact she would be one of four musicians, the final element in a quartet, and would have the opportunity of two hours' rehearsal with her fellow musicians before the actual private concert.

'Two hours is not a long time,' she pointed out.

'I know, but it's a piece the other three already know well, so that will make it a little easier.'

'OK,' Summer accepted. Then added, 'The Bailly will sound divine in a crypt.'

'I have no doubt it will,' Dominik said. 'And . . .'

'And?'

'You will perform nude.'

5
A Girl and Her Memories

Dominik had asked me about my first time.

It was odd, I thought later, that I agreed to tell him the story, but playing *The Four Seasons* had put me into a dream, as it always did.

That's what I blamed it on.

And this is what I told him.

'I spent my first sexual experiences alone. Masturbating. I began when I was young. Younger than my friends, I think, though I didn't ever talk about it with anyone. Always felt a little ashamed. I didn't know what I was doing, really. I didn't ever come – at least not for a few years.

'Maybe you noticed when I was playing back there, I reach a certain point in the music where I'm in a sort of trance – I'm off in a world of my own – but as soon as I stop, everything comes flooding back. Playing the violin, you see, has always had a physical effect on me. A release of sorts, but it also seems to heighten sensation.'

I glanced over at Dominik to check his reaction.

He had lowered the driver's seat down and lain back, relaxed. I did the same, inhaling the scent of his car, a clean, fresh smell, typical in my opinion of BMW drivers. The interior was spotless, personality-free, no hint of a recently consumed snack, gun holster or suspicious package in sight, just a book he had been reading earlier resting on the dashboard. An author I had never heard of.

Dominik didn't look at me, just stared straight ahead through the windscreen. His expression was that of a man completely comfortable, as if he were on the verge of meditation. Despite the irregularity of the situation, his response, or lack of one, relaxed me. I was sharing secrets that I hadn't shared with anyone, but the way that he blended into the car like that, it was almost as if I was talking to myself.

I carried on. 'I played nude sometimes, with the window open, enjoying the cold air on my body. I left the lights on and the curtains open, imagined that the neighbours could see me playing my violin naked. If they could, they never mentioned it.

'This carried on for a while, and I ended up spending so much time alone that when I was in high school, my mother became concerned that I was getting unbalanced, obsessive, and she tried to get me to join a school sports or a drama team. She wanted me to do something "normal". We fought over it and eventually she won, though she let me choose the sport.

'I chose swimming, mainly to irk my mother, as I knew that she really wanted me to do something more sociable, like hockey or netball, but I won that round by arguing that my violin-playing would benefit from stronger arms.'

A small smile crossed Dominik's face as I shared this detail, but he remained silent, patiently waiting for me to carry on.

'Swimming, as it turned out, had virtually the same effect on me as violin-playing. I liked the feeling of the water, and the way that time disappeared as I swam one lap after another. I was never very quick, but I could go on for ever. I swam for so long, so easily, that my swimming coach would have to tap me on the shoulder to tell me that the training session was over and I could go home.

'He was a good-looking guy and had been a professional athlete for our region when he was at school. Gave it up when he stopped winning. Started teaching instead, but still had the body for it. Wore the whole lifeguard-look ensemble – short shorts and T-shirt and a whistle to show it off. I ignored him most of the time. Thought he rated himself a bit much, and it didn't suit him somehow. As if he was putting the authority on for show. All the other girls fancied him. I don't know how old he was. Older than me.

'It was him, in the end. My swimming coach. The first time.'

I looked over at Dominik again. His expression remained impassive, bemused.

'Go on,' he said.

'One afternoon, he didn't stop me. Just let me swim and swim. I broke out of it, after I don't know how many lengths, because I suddenly noticed it was getting dark and I was the only one in the pool. Everyone else had left already. He said, when I finally got out of the pool, that he wanted to see if I'd carry on swimming until he told me to stop.

'I picked up my towel and went to the changing rooms, and when I started to dry myself, I found that I was . . . well, I was horny. I'm not sure why, really, what it was, but the feeling was so strong I couldn't wait until I arrived home. I was touching myself when I saw him looking at me through the changing-room door. Maybe I had forgotten to close it. I hadn't noticed him push it open.

'I didn't stop. I should have, I suppose, but the way he looked at me . . . I carried on. And that was the first time I ever had an orgasm. With him watching.

'He walked in then, after he saw me come. And when he then got his cock out, I couldn't stop staring at it.

' "You haven't ever seen one of these before, have you?" he said.

'I replied that I hadn't.

'Then he asked if I'd like to feel it inside me, and I said yes.'

I turned to Dominik, checking to see if he wanted me to continue, to tell him more. He snapped out of his reverie almost immediately.

'Good,' he said, bringing his seat up to a driving position. 'That's all I wanted to know. Perhaps you could tell me more another time.'

'Sure,' I said, and pulled the lever to bring my own seat back up again. Perhaps the experience of retelling my story to this man ought to have made me uncomfortable, but it hadn't. If anything, I felt a little lighter, the weight of past secrets transferred from my mind to Dominik's.

'Can I drop you anywhere?'

'Just the station, please.'

'No problem.'

He might have the details of my sexual history, but I wasn't quite ready to show Dominik my front door, and I still wasn't sure whether he wanted me to do so anyway.

I needn't have bothered with the attempt to retain any privacy from him. Within a week Dominik had requested my home address, and provided a date and time for me to stay in and sign for a package. I hesitated before I gave him the address. Besides the pizza-delivery guy up the road, he'd be the only man in London with my personal details, and I liked it that way. He had something to post me, though, and I'd only sound churlish, or paranoid, if I refused to tell him where I lived.

The package, as I'd half expected, was the violin Dominik had promised. Based on the quality of the violin that he had provided for the Vivaldi performance, I had guessed he would choose something nice, but I had never imagined that he would offer me an instrument so beautiful. It was a vintage Bailly, the wood a soft yellow, almost caramel, the colour of a jar of manuka honey held to the light. It reminded me of home, of the soft golden tones of the Waihou river when the sun catches the water.

According to the certificates enclosed, the last owner was a Miss Edwina Christiansen. Ever curious about the stories held within my violins, I tried Googling her, but found no clues to her history. Oh well. My imagination would have to do.

The case was brand new, black with a deep-red velvet lining. A little morbid for my tastes, and it didn't suit the warmth of the Bailly, but Dominik seemed a smart guy and not romantic in the foolish sense of the word, so I supposed that the new case was just a way to disguise the value of the contents.

He had enclosed instructions: that I must acknowledge the arrival of the package, and then spend as much time as possible rehearsing with it, though not in public. And that I was to await his next instruction. Rehearse and wait.

Rehearsing with the Bailly was a joy. She fitted me perfectly, as though my own body had evolved to hold her. I had asked for a leave of absence from the busking gig, and under the circumstances, after the tube brawl, the organisers were very understanding. I played the Bailly every moment of every day, better than I had ever played before, the music pouring from my fingers as though the melodies had been trapped inside me and Dominik's violin was the key that released them.

Waiting was another matter. I'm patient by nature, and have always preferred endurance sports. However, I wanted to know exactly what I was signing myself up for. Firmly of the belief that life gives no free lunches, I presumed that Dominik would be wanting a return on his investment, and until I understood what the payment terms would be, I decided to think of the violin as a loan rather than a gift. He had suggested an agreement, a contract of mutual satisfaction, not offered to be my sugar daddy. I would have turned him down flat if he had. But still, until I knew what he wanted, I wouldn't be able to decide whether I wanted to give it to him.

I wasn't looking for another relationship so soon after Darren. I was hoping for some single time. And Dominik didn't seem like a man looking for a girlfriend. He was aloof, a loner; he didn't have that desperate air of someone on the lookout for a partner. I mulled over his initial email contact. A bit of a geek maybe, probably with a large, arty porn collection on his PC, but not someone with a profile on the Guardian Soulmates website.

If he didn't want to date me, what did he want?

I looked at the violin again, ran my hands over the graceful cut of the neck, guessed that it must be priced in the tens of thousands.

How big a return, and what sort of return, I wondered, would Dominik expect? What would satisfy such a man?

Sex? It was the obvious answer. But not, I thought, the correct answer.

A man who wanted sex would have just invited me to dinner. A wealthy classical music aficionado looking for a beneficiary would have sent me the violin without all the dramatics.

Dominik's approach had something more to it. He didn't have the air of a psychopath, but he seemed to be enjoying whatever game it was that he was playing. I wondered if he had a point, an endgame, or if he was just rich and bored.

I could have sent the violin back, of course, and maybe that would have been the proper thing to do. But it wasn't just the violin that interested me; frankly, I was curious.

What would Dominik do next?

A few days later, my phone rang.

He spoke before I had even had a chance to say hello. Under other circumstances, I might have been annoyed, but I decided to hear him out.

'Summer?'

'Yes.'

He advised me, coolly, that I would be playing for him next week, in the afternoon. String Quartet no. 1 by the Czech composer Smetana – fortunately, a piece I liked and was reasonably familiar with, as it had been a favourite of Mr van der Vliet. I would be playing with three members of a quartet who knew the piece very well, as the violinist and viola player had, it appeared, performed it on previous occasions. I need have no concern over my privacy or the discretion of the other musicians involved in such an affair, as they had sworn never to reveal any details of the event.

Which was fortunate, as I would be performing nude.

The other players would be asked to don blindfolds before I disrobed, so my nakedness would be apparent only to Dominik.

As soon as he had said the words, a hot rush spread throughout my body. Again, I supposed I ought to say no. He'd just asked me point-blank to take my clothes off in front of him. But if I refused, I'd never know what it was that he was scheming. And, I thought idly, it would technically be our third date. Considering that I sometimes went home with men on a first date, this wasn't really any different, except that I had agreed to do so up front.

Or had I?

Dominik hadn't said that he wanted to fuck me.

Perhaps he just wanted to watch me.

The thought filled me with trepidation, but despite my best efforts to ignore the feeling, I found myself aroused and wet.

No surprise really – I had been so caught up in the loss of my violin, skint and now tied to the Bailly, I hadn't had a chance to date anyone, and hadn't had sex since the last time with Darren. Irritating, though, that thoughts of Dominik should have this effect. It put him a step ahead of me in whatever negotiation it was that he had in mind.

Naked, with him watching, I worried that he would know what effect he was having on me. After my revelations in the car to him, that day on Hampstead Heath, I doubted that he would be surprised. I was probably about to provide him with exactly the response that he was hoping for.

If this was to be a battle of wills, then I had given him all the ammunition he needed.

*

A week later, I made my way to the location that Dominik had hired, this private crypt in Central London. I did not know the place, though I wasn't surprised to hear of its existence. London is a city full of surprises. He had given me the address during our phone call, but advised me not to scope out the venue in advance, in order to keep the performance fresh. I had considered checking it out anyway, but felt strangely compelled to follow his instructions to the letter. He'd bought the violin, so the recital at least was his gig, after all.

The crypt was tucked into a side street, the only clue confirming its location a small brass plaque on the left-hand side of the wooden door. Gingerly, I pushed it open and walked inside, finding a set of steps leading steeply down into a pool of darkness.

I had swapped my flat shoes for heels a block earlier, which now caught on the uneven stone floor, causing me to lose my balance and nearly plunging me head first down the stairs as I fumbled unsuccessfully against the wall on my right for a handrail.

My breath caught in my throat. Not with fear, though common sense dictated that I should be nervous, should have told someone where I was going, arranged a safety call. I hadn't told anyone, even Charlotte, about the Bailly or the crypt. This new turn in my life seemed too odd to share. Besides, I shrugged, if Dominik had wanted to kill me, he'd had ample opportunity to do so already.

The constriction in my stomach, the rapid beat of my heart, wasn't wholly nerves. I was excited. Playing with three new musicians would be a challenge, for sure, but I had practised the piece until I could play it note perfect under any circumstance. And I knew Dominik would take no pleasure in an afternoon that did not run to his satisfaction. Whatever he had in store, I was sure that he had planned every detail with a view to achieving perfection, including my performance.

There was the added matter of my impending nakedness, of course, but the thought of performing nude for Dominik actually excited me more than it antagonised me. I had always been something of an exhibitionist, a nugget of information that he had evidently stored away from the details I had provided to him of my first sexual experience.

Still, I was little reticent, and part of that, I supposed, was the thought of being on such public display. I was comfortable walking naked around my own living room, but deliberately undressing for a virtual stranger was another matter altogether. I wasn't sure that I could go through with it. My mind was at war. If I refused, I'd show him that he'd got to me, ruffled my feathers, but if I agreed, he'd still be the one calling the shots. Then there was that thought in the back of my head that I just couldn't shake. The entire situation turned me on. But why? What was wrong with me?

I decided to at least ready myself for the possibility of taking off my clothes. Then I could decide when the moment came.

My preparations for the event today had been intensive, beyond rehearsing the music. I had showered slowly that morning, carefully shaved my legs and then hovered briefly over my bikini line. To shave, or not to shave? That was the question. Darren had preferred me completely bare, and consequently I had grown it out, my own small rebellion. He had hardly ever gone down on me anyway.

What would Dominik prefer? I wondered.

He was an unusual man who had so far demonstrated a taste for richness, for detail, and I suspected that his sexual tastes would run to the exotic. Perhaps he would like my hair. The slight musky smell, the covering. My mind danced ahead, down dark pathways, thoughts sharply curtailed by my sense of reason. I pushed my fantasies out of my head. Dominik had enough of a window into my soul already. Thank God the rest of the quartet would be blindfolded and unable to bear witness.

In the end, I decided just to trim and tidy a little, opting to keep my pubic hair as a curtain, just an inch or two of privacy. I would not be completely naked for him, yet.

I made my way slowly to the bottom of the steps, found another wooden door, pushed it open. My senses were immediately assailed by the almost cloying, thicker nature of the air in the crypt, the feeling of being underground, entombed. The ceiling was high, but the room narrow, and a sweep of arches overhead made it seem closed, claustrophobic. I was reminded, momentarily, of the dungeon in the fetish club that I had visited with Charlotte. The crypt fitted much better with my idea of a dungeon.

The walls were bathed in a low, electric light, which contrasted oddly with the ancient feel of the place, and the smell of recently lit candles. It was a little cold, though I was sure that if there was a light switch, there must be some method of heating down here. Perhaps Dominik had ordered the heaters switched off, for authenticity. Or perhaps he wanted to watch the response of my skin as the cool air brushed my body. I gripped the case of the Bailly tighter and banished the thought from my mind.

Spotting the three musicians on the slightly raised front dais, I headed towards them, my high heels skittering across the stone floor, echoes bouncing back, musically. My earlier trepidation was replaced suddenly by joy: the acoustics were indeed incredible and the Bailly would sound amazing in here. Dominik would soon experience the recital of his life. That, at least, I could guarantee.

The rest of the quartet was in position, waiting for me, but as promised, I saw no sign of Dominik. I made my introductions, communication a little awkward at first, the situation being really rather extraordinary for all of us.

They were each dressed in black suits and crisp white shirts, offset by black bow ties. Two of them, the violinist and the viola players, were men, and rather quiet. The cellist, who introduced herself as Lauralynn, appeared to be the leader of the pack, and she talked for all three. She was confident, though not annoying with it. American, from New York, studying music in London. She was tall, with long legs, Amazonian in shape and had dressed like the men, in a shirt and tie, and a black jacket with tails, cut short in the body to emphasise her waist and hips. With her flock of blonde hair and delicate features, she made a curious mix of both masculinity and femininity in the traditional sense of the words, and was very attractive with it.

'So do you know Dominik?' I asked.

'Do you?' she replied coyly.

Her fleeting expression of wicked amusement made me wonder if Dominik had told her more about his plans than he had let on to me, though she continued to deflect all of my questions. Eventually, I gave up asking and got on with the business of rehearsing. We didn't have much time.

It's a fairly intense piece, a little dark, but an excellent choice for the setting, and Dominik was right: Lauralynn and her two shy partners did know it well.

I heard Dominik's footsteps before I noticed him coming, his shoes tapping sharply on the stone floor, a staccato drumbeat juxtaposing the sustained harmonic E in the last movement that I was coaxing from the Bailly as he approached the stage.

He nodded to me in acknowledgement and then signalled to the musicians that they should put on their blindfolds.

They did.

Evidently he had not let them know that I would be nude throughout the actual performance, as he stepped up onto the stage and whispered a soft instruction into my ear. His lips nearly brushed my lobe and my face warmed in response.

'You may undress.'

I had worn my shorter black dress this time, rather than the long velvet one, as it attracted less attention during a daytime commute. It was a one-shouldered affair, shaped to fit my body, with a hidden side zip. I had purposefully not worn a bra, so that when I disrobed, if I disrobed, my skin would be free from strap marks. I had nearly not worn underwear for the same reason, but changed my mind at the last moment, and was glad I had when the short dress rode up as I navigated the wide step from tube platform to train at Bank station.

Dominik stepped back down again onto the main floor and took a seat in the single chair placed facing the stage, staring at me, expressionless under his ever-present façade of politeness, sheltered by a thin wall of reserve that I reckoned hid a much more animal nature than he at first let on.

Whatever it would take to break him of that, I would like to try.

I took a breath and resolved to do it.

I slid a hand to my side, held Dominik's gaze and pulled at my zip.

It stuck.

Dominik's eyes flashed as I struggled with my dress. Damn. And was that another grin spreading across Lauralynn's face? Could she see me through that thick blindfold?

My cheeks burned as I imagined her gaze on my body also.

I must be the colour of a fire engine now. I had hoped at least that I would manage to drop my dress in one graceful movement, the way leading ladies always do in films. I should have practised disrobing at home. I'd die before I asked for Dominik's help. Finally, I kicked the dress off, then reddened further as I realised I would have to bend over to remove my underwear. I turned a little, to hide the freefall of my breasts, before realising how foolish my reticence must look, as I knew I would have to play for him front on.

I picked up my violin, fought a sudden urge to use the instrument to hide the completeness of my nudity from him a moment longer and then turned back, placed the Bailly under my chin and began. Fuck nudity, and fuck Dominik. A flash of irritation shook me before the music took over.

Next time, if there was a next time, he would not see me vulnerable when I undressed.

Finally, the music drew to a close and I loosened my grip on the neck of my violin. I brought it down, away from my chin to rest against my side, not in front of me. I faced

Dominik as he deliberately, slowly clapped his hands together, an enigmatic smile spreading across his face. I noticed my bow hand was shaking, I was panting a little, and my forehead felt damp, as if I'd just finished a five-mile run. I must have been really going for it, though I had realised none of this while playing, my mind full of thoughts of Eastern Europe, Edwina Christiansen and the wealth of stories that must be held within the Bailly.

I wondered when I would next be able to afford a city break. Financial constraints being what they were, I hadn't travelled in Europe nearly as much as I would have liked.

Dominik interrupted my daydream with a gentle cough.

'Thank you,' he said.

I nodded in acknowledgement.

'You may go now. I would see you out, but I need to say my goodbyes to your fellow players and settle their remuneration. You can find your own way to the exit safely, I trust?'

'Of course.'

I slipped my dress back on, faking a purposeful nonchalance this time, although I felt anything but, and ignored his quip about making a safe exit.

Perhaps he'd somehow known I'd nearly catapulted down the stairs on my way in.

'Thank you,' I said to my three accompanying musicians, all still seated and blindfolded, awaiting Dominik's next instruction. It was evident he had previously furnished them all with very precise instructions as to the sequence of events and their conduct.

I wished, not for the first time, that I knew exactly what he had done to secure their compliance. What was this effect that he had over people? Especially the girl.

Lauralynn didn't strike me as the obedient type. Quite the reverse.

I had noted the way that her thighs hugged the cello, and remembered how despite the initial apparent gentleness of her grip round its neck, she had played it almost viciously, as if she were wringing out melodies against the instrument's will.

She smiled wickedly again, directly at me; this time I was sure she was in on the game or could somehow see me through her blindfold.

I picked up my case, turned and strode to the exit, my posture as businesslike as I could manage. We had both fulfilled our sides of the bargain; I had my violin, he'd had his naked recital.

I pushed open the door that led from the crypt to the base of the stairs and stopped, leaning against the cool stone wall to collect my thoughts.

Was that really it, our deal complete? I should have been pleased, but couldn't shake a lingering sensation of regret. As if I hadn't given him enough in return for the instrument. Charlotte would say I'd done well out of it, but I felt incomplete somehow.

I took a breath and headed up the stairs without looking back.

I arrived home at my flat in Whitechapel, thrilled to find the hallway and shared bathroom empty. My neighbours were out. Good. I wouldn't need to make the usual polite small talk, or worry about them suspecting what I was up to, as I disappeared into my bedroom to relieve the now almost painful throb of arousal that had distracted me all the way home.

I had my hand between my legs the moment I kicked my bedroom door closed, dipping my index finger inside myself to collect some lubrication before running the pad of my fingertip in quick, clockwise circles. I eyed my laptop briefly, considered watching a YouPorn clip to speed things along a bit.

Darren had hated me watching porn. He had caught me at it once with a magazine that I found under his mattress, and he had sulked all evening. When I asked him what upset him so much he said that he knew women masturbated, he just didn't think they did it like *that*. I never did work out whether he was jealous or just thought me unladylike, but since our break up I had taken a particular thrill out of my new freedom to do whatever I liked. Still, in the state that I was in now, it wouldn't take long to reach orgasm, and finding a clip that would work for me would take longer than it was worth. I replayed that afternoon's adventures in my head instead.

I remembered, suddenly, the way my nipples had hardened in response to the cool air in the crypt – or had it been in response to Dominik's gaze? And Lauralynn's? I flipped up the catch on my window with my left hand, without easing the pressure of the fingers on my right, still busy with the task at hand. I unzipped my dress, easily this time – typical – and kicked it off. I had slipped my underwear into my purse rather than wriggling into it again in front of Dominik and was now completely naked, other than my high heels, enjoying the brush of cool air from the open window that now caressed my body.

I closed my eyes, and instead of falling back onto the bed as I usually did, I spread my legs and fingered myself in front of an imaginary audience by the window.

It was the memory of Dominik's last command that finally sent me over the edge, the tone in his voice as I had bent down to undo the ankle straps of my shoes.

'No. Leave them on.'

It was not even a challenge; there was no question at all in his voice, no thought that I might not do as he said, even though I didn't think I seemed in any way to be the meek sort. That sense of authority, for some reason that I just couldn't explain, sent me into waves of ecstasy.

I came in a rush, wonderful spasms coursing through my pussy and then the resulting aftershocks warming the rest of my body nicely.

I had always been that way, now that I thought of it. I remembered how Mr van der Vliet had turned me on, the pleasure I had taken in adhering so closely to his lessons, though he wasn't good-looking in any traditional sense. How I had been so aroused when my swimming coach told me that he wanted to see how long I would swim for if he didn't tell me to stop. The way I had felt as the dungeon master had slapped my arse at the fetish club.

What did it mean?

I lay down on my bed and tried to banish these thoughts from my mind, falling into a troubled slumber.

I awoke in the evening, still troubled. And still horny. I tried to push the feeling away but just couldn't seem to think about anything else. Even playing with myself again did nothing to ease my frustration.

Thoughts of Dominik's imperious tone, his habit of providing such precise instructions ran through my head. Even the way he had given me the address of the crypt had turned me on. I considered calling him and disregarded the idea immediately. What would I say?

Please, Dominik, tell me what to do?

No. Aside from the ridiculous nature of such a notion, I had more power this way, not letting on how much he had got to me. I knew that he would call, eventually, that brief flash of hunger in his eyes; he wouldn't be able to resist coming up with some new scheme. And though it irked me a little to be on the back foot, I would enjoy it when he did.

For now, I would need to find some other way of satisfying this new urge.

Again I considered calling Charlotte, but I still wasn't ready to share this portion of my life.

The fetish club. It was a crazy thought, but maybe I could go alone, check it out again, just to see. I wasn't sure what had come over me, this new sense of fearlessness, on the one hand, frightening, but on the other, exhilarating. I could always leave if it didn't work out.

I had felt safe there. Not that I couldn't look after myself, but West End clubs were tiresome, full of drunken, groping lads in packs closing in on every girl who tried to make her way solo to the bar or the ladies' room.

Despite, or perhaps because of, the open-natured crowd at the fetish club, the patrons had seemed respectful, not sleazy.

Yes, it was the sort of place that I could go alone.

A quick Google search indicated that the club I'd visited with Charlotte was only open on the first Saturday of every month, and it was a Thursday night. None of the larger fetish clubs was running, but I found a link to a small club, not far from Whitechapel in a taxi, that boasted a dungeon space and elusive-sounding 'play areas' as well as an intimate, friendly vibe. It would do. The dress code indicated that certain strict rules were enforced. I would have to find an outfit that would fit the bill. I didn't want to seem out of place.

It was now 11 p.m. The party would be just getting going. I booked a cab, then hunted through my wardrobe and pulled out something that I thought would be suitable, put it on and surveyed my reflection in the mirror. I had chosen a high-waisted, form-fitting navy pencil skirt, with large white buttons at the front and back that held in place thick braces, with straps that criss-crossed at the back and, at the front, ran in a straight line over each of my breasts. I'd bought it on sale from a 1950s-styled boutique on Holloway Road in North London and worn it with a high-necked white blouse, a cheap, though not tacky sailor hat and red velvet pumps to my neighbour's uniform-themed fancy-dress birthday party earlier that year.

Tonight I was wearing a red bra to match the shoes, and no blouse. Would that pass as fetish wear? I remembered the outlandish outfits from the night I'd been out with Charlotte and thought, Probably not. I wanted to fit in, and in this case, I would attract less attention if I had fewer clothes on. I took one final look in the mirror and ditched the bra. The braces sat tight against my breasts, holding them in, and covered my nipples, and besides, I'd already spent a good part of the day in the buff, hadn't I?

I wore a jacket in the taxi and felt a rebellious, heady rush of freedom at the thought that I was half naked beneath it.

*

A young, friendly dark-haired girl with a pierced nose took the small cover charge at the front desk. I noticed she had a tiny teardrop tattoo under her left eye as she asked for my wrist, then applied an entry stamp. I wondered what other secrets she might have hidden under her long-sleeved tuxedo-style latex jacket.

Latex. Perhaps I'd save up and invest in some, if I was going to make a habit of this, though I wasn't sure that the shiny rubber was really my thing. Charlotte had found it terribly difficult to get in and out of her dress, and an inability to undress would be problematic for me and my desires, I felt.

I prefer to face new and uncertain situations sober, but stopped at the bar for a drink to get my bearings.

Bloody Mary with just the perfect touch of spice in hand, I strode straight across the small dance floor, occupied not by dancers but just a few patrons chatting, and headed for the dungeon. The entrance was open, another room off the bar, without a door, but hidden from view of the dance floor by a couple of green medical screens, the kind you find round hospital beds. Interesting.

Most of the patrons were in the dungeon. Some, sitting in seats round the outside, were talking quietly; others were standing closer to the action but a few steps back from the participants. A few signs, printed on plain A4 paper, were dotted around the walls of the room. 'Don't interrupt a scene,' read one, and another, just two words, said, 'Ask. First.' The signs made me feel strangely comforted.

Several pairs of 'players' and one trio were engaged in acts of varying degrees of, I assumed, consensual violence, involving different instruments and pieces of equipment. My attention was immediately caught by the sounds in the room, the steady thwack of a cane, the softer slap of a many-stranded flogger, like the one Mark had used, the way that the sound and rhythm changed according to the movements of the wielder and the ferocity applied by each individual.

I didn't even realise how close I had moved to the trio, two men beating a third person whom initially I thought to be a man, due to the person's square body and completely shaved head, but then I thought I noted the curve of breasts pressing against the padding on the cross, and heard the higher-pitched sound of a feminine moan. Man, woman, perhaps neither, perhaps a bit of both. A beautiful creature, and what did gender mean, anyway? Not a lot here. I forgot the signs on the walls and crept in for a closer look. It was still shocking to me, in a way, but utterly engaging at the same time.

I felt a hand stretching forward from behind me to very gently touch my shoulder, then a voice in my ear.

'Lovely, aren't they?' whispered the voice.

'Yes.'

'Don't get too close. You might snap them out of it.'

I looked again at the trio. They did each seem to be lost in some other dimension, a place that was somehow still in the room, but not quite a part of it. As if each of them was in the middle of their own private journey.

Wherever it was that they were, I wanted to join them.

The owner of the voice perhaps sensed my desire.

'Would you like to play?' the voice said.

I hesitated for a moment. We hadn't even been introduced, and he, or she, was so direct. Then again, perhaps this was exactly what I needed, and no one would ever know.

'Yes, I would.'

A hand took mine and guided me over to the one vacant piece of equipment in the room, another cross.

'Undress.'

My body responded to the command immediately; it was almost the same instruction Dominik had used, and in response I was flooded with desire, straight-out lust, but also the desire for something more than that. What, I still wasn't sure.

I snapped off the braces, freeing my breasts, and eased down my skirt, feeling once more the thrill of knowing strangers were watching me, enjoying the show. I spread my arms and legs out on the cross, fully naked again for the third time that day. This was becoming a habit.

A leather strap was buckled round each of my wrists and pulled tight, though not uncomfortably so. No 'safety word' or gesture was given to me this time. Oh well. My mystery partner seemed experienced enough if confidence was anything to go by, and if it got too much, I would cry, 'Stop'. I'd had only one drink, my mental faculties were fully functioning, and I was in a room full of people who could intervene if necessary.

I relaxed against the cross and waited for the blows to rain down.

Which they did.

Harder this time, much harder than my last 'spanking', and without the reassuring caress on my arse that Mark had made with each strike, muting some of the pain. I gasped, my body jolting under each burst of force that arrived not just on my arse but the sides of my back too. He, or she, I wasn't sure which, and hadn't tried to find out, preferring to keep this experience anonymous, must have been using a device, an instrument of some sort, but I couldn't be sure what. It sounded like a flogger but felt so solid and hard, much harder than the soft, limp lengths of leather looked on the short handle.

My eyes watered, tears ran down my face, and I realised that the more I tensed my body, fought the impact, the more it hurt.

So I relaxed. Tried to find that place, wherever it was that the others seemed to go. Imagined my body melting into the hand, or the flogger, or whatever it was striking me. Listened to the steady whack, whack, the rhythmic beat of my partner's music, and eventually, the pain dulled, a sense of peace descended as I became a part of my player's dance, not a victim to it.

Then the buckles on my wrists loosened. Gentle caresses stroked the beaten parts of my skin, stinging a little with each touch.

A soft laugh, another whisper in my ear, and then the voice was gone again, into the crowd.

I stood there, stretched immobile on the cross for I don't know how long, until I finally managed to peel myself off, dress and call a cab home.

I'd got what I came for.

Hadn't I?

That sense of peace, of disappearing into another dimension, this other consciousness that had been my refuge, my home one way or another, for as long as I could remember.

Back in my flat I fell into bed and, despite my throbbing skin, slept better than I had in weeks.

It wasn't until the next morning, in the bathroom mirror, that I noticed the bruises.

An almost beautiful pattern of marks in varying shades

lined my lower back and sides, and closer inspection in the full-length mirror in my bedroom revealed the faint outline of a handprint on one of my buttocks.

Fuck.

I hoped Dominik left it a good few days before he called again.

6

A Man and His Lust

Dominik drove in a daze, his mind journeying back on a loop through every single moment of the afternoon. On automatic pilot, he navigated the grey BMW through the labyrinth of roadworks surrounding Paddington, inching his way towards the Westway.

The colour of her skin.

The supernatural pallor. The thousand shades travelling at sub-atomic speed between white and white, with microscopic shades of pink, grey and a dull form of beige calling out in unison to be allowed their day in the sun. The intricate geography of moles and minor blemishes scattered across the landscape of her skin. The way the artificial light of the crypt had highlighted her curves, dancing over her surface, highlighting the areas of darkness, the shimmer of her muscles under the thin protection of her flesh, the sinews in her calves as she shifted imperceptibly to reach another note, the way the rounded edge of the violin ground against her neck, the speed of her fingers navigating across the strings while her other hand vigorously deployed the taut bow as it attacked the instrument like a warrior in flight.

He almost missed the exit and had to switch his memories off for a brief moment as he took a sharp turn, attracting the klaxon of a nearby Fiat driver who disapproved of his last-minute manoeuvre.

Dominik had always been told he had something of a poker face, seldom betraying his feelings in public, let alone in more intimate situations. He had watched the recital in a state of silent prayer, his face a mask, watchful, attentive to the music and all its subtle nuances. Recording the movements of the musicians as they went about their exquisite business, clothed in black and white and, of course, unclothed. Summer.

It had been like a ritual. A symphony of contrasts between the dark evening suits and formal white shirts and the audacious nudity of Summer's body as she literally fought with her instrument to extract every note, every shard of melody from the music, riding it, taming it. At one point, a tiny bead of sweat had rolled down from the tip of her nose, cascading past one of her hard, pale-brown nipples and then ending its brief lifespan on the hard stone floor of the crypt just a few inches away from her shoes, the high heels he had ordered her to keep on.

Maybe the ritual would have been even more arousing, Dominik thought, if he had asked her to wear a pair of hold-up stockings. Black, of course. Or then again, maybe not.

He had watched it all with a mixture of fiery desire and restraint coursing beneath the shield of his own skin. Like a grand inquisitor at a special feast, supremely detached in appearance had you asked any hypothetical onlooker, but feverishly involved, his mind racing in all directions, his thoughts a mad, unformed jumble, gazing, examining, probing, wondering. All to the gracious accompaniment of those immortal melodies the improvised quartet had been so good at playing, evoking both visions and words as the best music always does.

The shape of her breasts, the delicacy of their size, the ever so slight valley separating them, the crescent of darkness below their underhang like a promise of further secrets, the miniature crevice of her navel, its vertical cavern pointing like an arrow to the territory of her sex.

He liked the fact that, unlike so many other modern young women, she was not fully shaven down there, her thin thatch of pubic curls shaped, trimmed, in dark shades of reddish brown like a necessary barrier to her most private possession. One day, he had already decided, he would shave her. Himself. But he would keep this for a very special day. A ceremony. A celebration. The Stygian river beyond which she would forever be even more naked for him. Open. Bare. His.

The solidity of her thighs, the length of her calves, the infinitesimal scars across one of her knees – no doubt the vestigial inheritance of some childhood playground scrap – the surprising narrowness of her waist as if she had just been poured like liquid out of a Victorian corset into the sweet prison of her flesh.

The road now led uphill through Hampstead, the car diving through a canopy of low-hanging trees spilling from the heath extension. Dominik took a deep breath, mentally filing away every single sound and each seductive vision he had experienced, creating a memory album of emotions for rainy days.

Now on familiar roads, he distractedly remembered the thin smile on the lips of the blonde cellist, whose name he could no longer recall, as she had adjusted her black velvet blindfold and had given him a final look before plunging into personal darkness. The sparkle in her eye, as if she knew what was about to happen, had guessed at the nature of his plans. He had even briefly thought she had winked at him, complicit, mischievous.

Also, how Summer's face had travelled through a spectrum of pinkness when the time had come to undress, once the other musicians' vision had been impaired, the way she had turned her back on him to slip her panties off, displaying the roundness of her pale arse in all its majesty, the crack of her buttocks as she bent forward, revealing a thin valley of shadows. Then she had turned round to face him and had quickly moved the violin momentarily across her genitals as if to hide herself from Dominik, although she knew only too well that she would have to play standing up and wouldn't be in a position to shelter her privacy from him for much longer.

Already Dominik knew he would feast on these fragments for a long time to come. As he parked on his drive, he looked down at his trousers. He was hard.

Dominik poured himself a glass of sparkling water and sank into his black leather office chair, thoughts of Summer flooding his mind.

He sighed, took a sip from his glass, the water deliciously cool on his tongue.

Images of Summer performing naked blended seamlessly across his imaginary screen with visions of Kathryn below him on a bed, on the floor, against a wall. Of lovemaking, of fucking, of the sheen of sweat on skin, the memories, the pain and the pleasure.

How, once, a guttural sound of both disgust and expectation had passed her lips as he ploughed into her from behind, his focus as ever pornographically fixed on the flower of her arsehole and thoughts of sodomy clouding his already troubled mind. The sound had acted as a trigger and he had smacked her buttock hard, twice in row, so hard that barely a few seconds later, the reddening imprint of his hand had emerged like a Polaroid bursting into life, across the delicate white skin of her behind. She'd screeched in surprise. So he'd repeated the assault, this time across her other cheek as he felt her cunt muscles tightening like a vice around his probing cock, an all too obvious betrayal of the effect the spanking was having on her.

Thing was, he had never spanked a woman before, neither in jest or in anger. He had never felt the need or even given it any thought. Nor had he been spanked himself in the interests of sex or minor kink. He knew that the practice was popular. So many Victorian novels of upstairs-downstairs, man-and-maid nature were full of the stuff, and it hadn't escaped his attention that hard-core porn performers would on a regular basis take a hand to their partner's arse in the throes of fucking, but he had somehow assumed this was all a convention, something many of them did for effect when facing the camera if only to relieve the monotony of the piston-like in and out of their warring genitals.

Later, he had asked Kathryn, 'Did it hurt?'

'Not at all.'

'Really? Did you like it, though?'

'I . . . don't know. It was part of the moment, I suppose.'

'I'm not sure why I did it,' Dominik had admitted. 'Just did. On the spur of the moment.'

'It's OK,' Kathryn had said. 'I didn't mind.'

They were on the floor of his study, sprawled over the carpet, still catching their breath.

'Turn round,' he'd asked. 'Let me see.'

She shifted her body, settled on her flank, offering him the sight of her regal, square arse. Dominik peered. The mark of his hand over Kathryn's lunar surface had almost faded away. The way the imprint of sex disappears so rapidly from a person's features and you never know once they are dressed and assuming their conventional civilian persona what they had privately been doing; this had always baffled him. As if, deep down inside, he wanted people to be marked by the sex they had shared, for it to be for ever written on their face. Anyway, the outline of his outstretched fingers was now just a memory across Kathryn's rear.

'It's almost gone, the mark of my hand.'

'Good,' she had said. 'It would have been pretty awkward for me to explain to my husband had it still been present!'

Later, during the course of their short-lived affair, on the one occasion he had managed to steal Kathryn away from her marriage for a whole weekend, and they had found a pretext to squat a room in a Brighton seafront hotel and never seen the light of day or beach, he'd marked her arse with added savagery and she'd complained of a dull, persistent pain when she had to sit down to eat in a nearby restaurant overlooking the seafront. Dominik had been surprised by the compulsive nature of the way he had spanked her, hit her and briefly felt shame – violence against women disgusted him. He had never even thought of hitting a partner before. Spanker and spankee, is that what they were becoming? Where did this compulsion to dominate, to express the depths of his desire in violent fashion, come from?

But Kathryn had never objected.

It puzzled him long after they had parted. The unanswered question in his mind as to what she actually felt when he was doing this to her, in the moment.

He unzipped his trousers, freeing himself at last, noting the thin pattern of veins coursing up and down the stem of his rock-hard cock, the ridge below the penis head, the scar tissue from his childhood circumcision and darker shades of flesh embroidering the upper reaches of his trunk. He thought of the pale glimpse of Summer's shapely, fragile buttocks as she had undressed before diving into the music.

He wrapped his fingers round his cock and pulled on it again. Up, down, up, down.

He silently imagined the slap of his balls against Summer's firm arse, and the sound his hands would make with every sharp, dry contact, the way her skin might shudder under every repeated impact, what private melodies it would forcibly extract from her lungs to roar past her pursed lips.

He closed his eyes. His imagination was now in overdrive and filling the size of an Imax screen.

And came.

Yes, Dominik knew, when the time came, he would most definitely spank Summer Zahova, violin player of this parish, but then you only spank the women you still lust for after the initial fuck. Those you want badly. The special ones.

Dominik only waited forty-eight hours before he made contact with Summer again. Over and over, he reflected on their previous encounters. Gut feeling told him that she had not quite embarked on this ambiguous adventure merely for the sake of the violin, the expensive vintage Bailly he had gifted her with and whose crystal tones had dominated that late afternoon in the crypt with such intense and melodious clarity. This, or at any rate, what this was fast becoming was not just a transaction between benefactor and beneficiary, client and customer, a man full of lust and a young woman with a flexible attitude to morality. He had seen something in her eyes from the very first time they had met. A curiosity, an unspoken challenge, a willingness to take unreasonable risks in the quest to keep the fire inside going. At least, that's the way Dominik explained her words and gestures to himself, and her easy acceptance of his unconventional demands. She was no amateur whore doing this for the money, or the violin.

Of course he wanted her. Badly, at that. The way she had played for him, naked, with just that hint of blush spreading across her cheeks when she had finally undressed, until the divine flow of the music had abolished her final reservations and she had stood playing with exhibitionistic pride. It was undeniable. The faint curve of her lips throughout the special performance had betrayed the fact. She had felt at peace with herself, floating in some strange private mental place throughout, oblivious to surroundings or circumstance. It had excited her.

Dominik now knew that he wanted more than to just take her to his bed.

That would only be the beginning of the story.

He finally called her late on Saturday morning when he knew she would be working at her part-time job at the restaurant in Hoxton. He wanted the conversation to remain brief, not to give her the opportunity to ask further questions. It would no doubt be a busy time there.

The phone rang several times before Summer picked up.

She sounded rushed.

'Yes?'

'It's me.' Dominik knew he no longer had any need to give his name.

'I know,' she said calmly. 'I'm at work. Can't speak long.'

'I realise that.'

'I was expecting you'd call.'

'Did you?'

'Yes.'

'I want you to play for me again.'

'I understand.'

'You will make yourself available Monday. Let's say early afternoon.' Dominik, secure in her likely availability and willingness, had already secured the crypt. 'Same place.' They agreed the time.

'On this occasion, you will be playing alone.'

'OK.'

'I look forward to it.'

'So do I.'

'Must I prepare any particular piece?'

'No. You choose what you wish to play. I wish to be enchanted.'

'Good. What must I wear?'

'Again, your choice, but wear black stockings underneath. Hold-ups.'

'I will.'

'And your black heels.'

The images in his mind were already materialising.

'Of course.'

He'd picked up the keys to the crypt the previous evening and paid a generous bribe to the caretaker to ensure that, once again, there would be no staff in attendance beyond the closed door throughout their stay.

Rushing down the steep and narrow stairs, Dominik pushed the door open and the musty, enclosed smell of the underground area washed over him, followed by a delicate substrata of wax, faded memories of burned-out candles and long-forgotten devotions. Peering into the darkness, he brushed his hand against the cold stone wall on first his left- and then the right-hand side and finally found the light switch. He'd forgotten from the previous recital that the switch was on the wrong side of the door. He slid the plastic knob upwards through its narrow allotted channel until the crypt was shrouded in a delicate veil of light, not at full power, but discreet, velvety, just the right level for the occasion. Dominik had always been an orderly sort of person, precise, attentive to details, and this was a ritual he had rehearsed endlessly in his mind since his brief conversation with Summer on Saturday when today's arrangement had been concluded.

Checking on his watch, an expensive silver Tag Heuer, he hurriedly carried some isolated chairs that had been scattered across the crypt and pushed them up against the back wall. It had to be just right. He looked up at the ceiling and noted a bar of small spotlights. He walked back and picked up one of the chairs, brought it to the centre, climbed on it, wary of its somewhat unsteady grip on the irregular stone floor and adjusted the position of the central spotlight so that it shone onto a particular area. To emphasise the effect, he slightly unscrewed two of the other lights at either end of the rail. Yes, this would now work much better.

He glanced at his watch. Summer was a couple of minutes late.

Briefly he flirted with the idea of reproaching her for this and the possibility of heaping some form of punishment on her for this infringement, but decided against it just as he heard her quiet rap on the wooden door.

'Come in,' he shouted out.

She was wearing her little black dress again, with a grey knitted woollen top covering her shoulders and arms, firmly gripping the handle of her violin case in one hand. The heels made her look taller.

'I'm sorry,' she blurted out. 'There were delays on the Jubilee line.'

'That's fine,' Dominik said. 'We have all the time in the world.'

He looked into her eyes. She held his gaze, pulled her top off, looked for somewhere to leave it, unwilling to let it drop to the floor.

'Here,' Dominik suggested, and held out his hands.

Summer passed it over to him. The wool was still warm from its continued contact with her body. He unashamedly brought it to his nose, sniffed it, hunting for her scent, something green and pungent far away in the fragrance's background. As she watched, Dominik turned his back on her and carried the light garment away to set it down on one of the chairs he had left against the crypt's back wall.

He stepped towards her. 'What will you be playing?' he asked her.

Her response was hesitant. 'Actually, it's something of an improvisation, based on the *Fingal's Cave* overture. I'm a great fan of Mendelssohn's violin concerto, but it's very technical and I haven't quite mastered all its intricacies yet.

This has similar wonderful melodies, so over the years I've been playing around with it, although it's written for a full orchestra and not a violin on its own. I hope you don't mind me not sticking to a strict classical repertoire?'

'That will be fine,' Dominik remarked.

Summer smiled. For the past day she had agonised over her choice of music to play.

Still just a few metres from the wooden door that allowed passage into the crypt, she glanced ahead of her and noted how Dominik had positioned the lighting, the way the spotlight threw a circle of incandescent white across the stone floor, and realised this was to be her 'stage', where he wanted her to play today.

She took a couple of steps in that direction. Dominik followed her with his eyes, alert to her movement, the way her legs elegantly danced across the ground in spite of the evident unsuitability of her high heels across the rough stone surface of the crypt.

Just as Dominik opened his mouth to convey his next set of instructions, Summer gently set the violin case down on the ground and unzipped the side of the little black dress.

Dominik smiled. She had anticipated his command, had guessed he wanted her to play naked again, albeit this time with no other musicians by her side. On this occasion, he would be the sole person dressed.

The dress slipped down, uncovering her torso, and then with a rapid movement of her hips, Summer shuffled so that it moved all the way down her legs to land, crumpled like an accordion, on the floor at her feet.

She was not wearing any underwear.

Just the dark-black stockings that stopped halfway up her creamy thighs.

And the five-inch designer high-heel shoes. He idly guessed Summer owned a fair few classy shoes.

She looked up, straight at Dominik.

'This is what you wanted.'

It was not a question, merely evidence.

He nodded.

In the circle of light, she stood, straight-backed, proud, conscious of the way she was brazenly displaying herself. On her terms more than his.

Again, the cold buried within the crypt's old stones began to shroud her body, her nipples hardened, her cunt grew humid.

Dominik caught his breath.

'Come here,' he ordered her.

Summer hesitated, for the briefest of moments, then stepped out of the narrow circle of light where she had been on unmistakeable display and edged her way towards him. As she moved slowly, Dominik noted, peering at her through the diminished visibility, a thin line running against her flank, a hint of redness, connecting the curve of her rump with her thin waist. He squinted, thinking at first it was just a shadow conjured up by her stepping out of the zone of limelight he had set up earlier into a more welcoming form of penumbra. No, definitely some form of blemish on her skin he hadn't noticed on the previous occasion when she had turned her back on him to disengage from her dress once the musical students had donned their blindfolds. Today, she had been standing full frontal all the time.

Dominik frowned. 'Swivel round,' he said. 'I want to see your back.'

Summer caught her breath. She knew there were still

visible marks on her buttocks from the club. She had caught sight of them in the mirror earlier when showering in preparation for the recital. She hadn't realised they wouldn't fade in time for today. This was why she had been so careful not to expose her rear to him when she undressed. She experienced a strong flash of apprehension, unsure what his reaction would be, although part of her wanted to brazenly show off her well-earned marks of personal infamy.

She sighed and executed the order.

'What are those?' he asked.

'Marks,' she replied.

'Who did them to you?'

'Someone.'

'Has someone even got a name?'

'I don't even know. Would a name mean anything to you? I didn't introduce myself. I didn't want to.'

'Did it hurt?'

'A little, but not for long.'

'Are you a masochist?'

'Not usually. I . . .' Summer paused, stuttered, thought. 'I didn't do it for the pain.'

'Why, then?' Dominik continued his questioning.

'I needed the . . . rush . . .'

'When?' he enquired, although he thought he already knew the answer.

'Straight after my playing for you the other day, with the quartet,' she confirmed.

'So you're a pain slut?' he asked.

Summer smiled at the description. She had heard Charlotte use that phrase, when she was describing some of her acquaintances at the club on the boat.

She stopped, thought, considered. Was she a 'pain slut'?

She had tolerated, even enjoyed it at times, but pain had on that occasion just been the vehicle, the means to transport her into that other dimension, not the motivation for her experience.

'No.'

'So just a slut?'

'Maybe.'

As she said this, even though it was partly in jest, Summer felt she had crossed a metaphorical Rubicon and knew that Dominik felt the same way. Instinctively, she straightened her back, her firm breasts on full display. She could feel him examining the thin lattice of lines and faint bruises strewn across her arse, the temporary tattoo that betrayed her inner wanton.

Dominik pondered, the steady rhythm of his breath a gentle hiss blowing through the crypt's heavy atmosphere.

'That was more than just a spanking,' he remarked.

'I know,' Summer said.

'Come closer.'

Summer tiptoed back a few more inches until she was standing right behind him, the warmth of his body reaching her through his clothes.

'Bend over.'

She obeyed, conscious of the spectacle she was offering.

'Spread your legs.'

Now he could see not only the marks but also her intimacy.

She felt his hand touch her left buttock, at first like a gentle caress as he explored the surface of the skin, like a rough glove gliding along her curves. His hand was so hot.

But then again so was her skin.

He lingered awhile, following the parallel lines of pinkness that criss-crossed her buttocks, probing the scattered, isolated pale-brown and yellow bruise islands.

A finger then trailed slowly down along the crack of her arse, skipping along her exposed and pulsing sphincter as she held her breath, sliding across her perineum, which made her jump, and with slow deliberation reaching her slit. She knew how humid she already was there and felt no shame at being so obviously exposed in this way both physiologically and mentally. So she found Dominik's touch, his words, his manner arousing. So what?

The hand withdrew.

For a moment, the loss of contact was unbearable. Surely he was not going to stop, was he? Could he be that cruel? Did she yearn for such cruelty?

'You like that, don't you?'

Summer remained silent, at war with her desire to tell him how much she did, indeed, like it.

'Tell me,' he said again, his voice barely a whisper, soft in her ear.

'Yes,' she said at last. 'Yes, I like it.'

Dominik stepped back, circled her again. He would take his time over this one. He watched her body closely, noted the raw heat that emanated from her. She was almost sweating, despite the cold. He noted the way his words seemed to affect her.

Interesting, thought Dominik.

'Why?'

'I don't know.'

He pressed her further.

'Tell me what you desire.'

Summer's legs ached now, but she didn't move. She

stayed in position, enjoying the tiny currents of air that swept across her body as Dominik continued to circle her, moving ever closer but never touching her skin.

'Tell me what you want, Summer.'

'I want you to touch me.'

She spoke quietly, but Summer knew that Dominik could hear her.

Was he really going to make her beg for it?

'Louder. Say it louder.'

Yes, it seemed that he was.

Her body moved imperceptibly in response to his words. The most minuscule signs of arousal, but unmistakeable, he thought. She would ask him to fuck her.

Of that he was almost certain. And he was in no rush.

Dominik waited.

'Touch me. Please.'

At last.

He stepped back, satisfied by the desperation, the need, in her voice.

'First, you will play.'

Summer's body shook with thwarted desire. She straightened, slowly, knowing he was toying with her and helpless to defend herself.

She moved back to the circle of light and finally turned to face him.

'An improvisation on the themes of Mendelssohn's *Fingal's Cave*,' she said, taking a delicate bow in his direction. Then Summer bent her knees and, with all the grace she could summon in such a state of undress, extended her hand to pick up the violin case she had settled on the ground. Still partly crouching, she opened it and took out the Bailly.

She knew his gaze was fixed on her genitals, as if the voyeur inside him was hoping that as she crouched, her cunt lips might yawn open ever so slightly and betray her growing wetness. At the mere thought of this, her whole body temperature rose, banishing the returning cold of the crypt.

The yellow-orange varnish of the vintage instrument almost shimmered under the concentrated ray of light in which Summer was bathed. She adjusted her grip on the bow, launched into the piece, her eyes closed.

In her imagination, every time she played this particular music, it evoked waves breaking against a rocky shore of Scandinavian-fjord ruggedness, spume rising like mist in the air against a background of grey and windy skies. For Summer, every piece of music owned its own landscape and it was to these places she was often transported when she played, born on exotic winds on journeys of the mind. She knew the real-world Fingal's Cave was associated with the Giant's Causeway, but she had seen neither place in real life. Sometimes the imagination was reward enough.

She felt her ragged breathing slow, her body relax. Time came to a halt.

Beyond the hypnotic wall of the music and her self-chosen blindness – for which she required no blindfold – she could sense Dominik's presence. The loudness of his silence, the muted distant sound of his breathing. She knew he was watching her, not only listening to every note she was bringing to life, but aware that his piercing eyes were travelling across the geometry of her body like an explorer investigates unmapped lands, pinning her to his imaginary map like a lepidopterist takes ownership of a butterfly, enjoying the vulnerability of her nudity, the gift of her body.

Finally, with a superfluous wrist movement full of showmanship, Summer came to the conclusion of her improvisation. There was a further instant of sound, as the echo of the melody kept on bouncing between the stone walls, before the utter silence returned, a silence so deep that she briefly thought she was now on her own in the crypt. When she opened her eyes, however, she saw Dominik, rooted to the same spot where she had last seen him, immobile, with a faint smile of pleasure colouring his lips.

His hands rose and he clapped slowly, with deliberation and appreciation.

'Bravo,' he said.

Summer nodded, accepting his compliment as if she were on a stage.

She leaned over to set the precious violin down on the stone floor, conscious of the fact her breasts would sway, come alive.

She looked at Dominik again, awaiting further words, but he remained silent.

Her lips were dry and she passed her tongue across them. She thought the heat radiating from her body must form some sort of halo around her, like an extra-terrestrial in a science-fiction movie or a nuclear scientist who'd just been irradiated by leaked radioactive waste following some atomic catastrophe.

'Exquisite,' Dominik finally remarked.

'Me, or the music?' Summer asked tartly.

'Both.'

'That's kind of you,' she said. 'Can I dress now?' she asked.

His gaze was unwavering. 'No.'

With the grace and latent danger of a panther stalking its prey, Dominik moved towards her. Summer looked up, her eyes met his. Face to face she refused to cede her position, felt once more waves of excruciating heat pass through her at their closeness.

Dominik gripped her shoulder, spun her on the spot and pushed her forward past him, so that she now faced the crypt wall. He set a hand down against the small of her back to accentuate the arch formed by her pelvis and her jutting arse.

His touch sent a lightning bolt of pleasure rocketing through her body.

She wanted to turn her head to look at him, but knew he would disapprove. Her eyes were fixed on the stone floor, a fuzzy upside-down vision of the delta of her open legs, and the protruding lips of her cunt in the periphery of her vision.

She heard a shuffling movement, tried to interpret it and, before she knew what was happening, felt the heat of his cock against her opening, so close, almost touching, he must be no more than a hair's breadth away.

If Summer adjusted her position, just ever so slightly, pushed back a fraction, she would feel him inside her. But he had not yet asked her to.

'Is this what you want?' Dominik said. 'Tell me.'

'Yes,' she whispered. She was uncertain of her ability to hold back a moan if she spoke any louder.

'Yes, what?'

Summer would not wait any longer. She pressed her

body back against him, but she had barely moved, had scarcely felt his head pulse once at her entrance, when in one swift movement Dominik had his hand wrapped in her hair and was jerking her forward again, away from his shaft.

'No,' he said hoarsely. 'I want you to ask me for it. Tell me what you want.'

'Fuck me. Please fuck me. I want you to fuck me.'

His hand gripped her hair and he pulled her back again, breaching her in one swift, rapid movement. The heavy lubrication she had been secreting made it all too easy for him to invest her to her full depth in an instant.

She surrendered to the sensation, enjoying the way he filled her, wondering whether he was already fully extended or would grow larger and harder inside her as some men often did. At any rate, he felt quite wonderfully large already.

He began to thrust.

The fit was perfect, she reflected idly, abandoning herself to the sensations beginning to flood her whole body, while his hand on her waist maintained her exposed position.

'Say it again,' Dominik said, feeling the way she tightened round him in response to his instruction, spearing her again with one hard, almost brutal push, hitting her inner walls like a battering ram.

'Oh,' was the only word she could find in response.

'We're fucking,' he said.

'Yes,' she sighed, 'I know.'

'And is this what you wanted?'

She nodded her head in acquiescence, just as a further hard thrust almost propelled her forehead against the crypt's stone wall.

'Answer,' he said.

'Yes.'

'Yes, what?'

'Yes, it's what I wanted.'

'And what did you want?'

Yes, he was growing inside her, stretching her, stuffing her. Forcing her inner walls into retreat.

'I wanted you to fuck me.'

'Why?'

'Because I'm a slut.'

'Good.'

His intensive rhythm accelerated. There was nothing subtle about this, they both knew; it was animal lust at its most basic, but it was right for the moment.

For their first time.

The rush, the hunger that had stood between them these past few weeks was finally out in the open, expressing itself.

He took hold of her hair again, aggressively pulling it back with one hand, riding her, mounting her as one would a horse. Summer gasped. Uncommon feelings were rushing across her mind, full of confusion and even a sense of panic. The encounter was scary but also welcome. In a flash, she realised he was not wearing a condom. She was being used raw, bareback. Even with Darren she always insisted on his cock being sheathed. But it was too late for that now, and she had known, had felt the bare skin of his cock waiting for her to respond. It could always be remedied later; there were pills for that, she knew.

She felt Dominik's breath grow halting, irregular.

As he came like a torrent inside her, he also slammed his open left hand against her arse cheek with terrible strength. The violence of the sting was instant and painful, until the sensation quickly settled, although she knew that the mark of his fingers across her pale butt cheeks would linger for hours on end.

He stayed inside her for an added minute or so and then withdrew. Summer felt as if she was now hollow, no longer invaded, filled to the brim. Incomplete even. She began to straighten herself, but the firm touch of his hand against the small of her back indicated that Dominik wanted her to remain in the same position, still wide open and on display.

Summer wore an inner smile: Dominik was a man who came in silence. Summer made a clear distinction between the quiet men and the chatterboxes. She'd always preferred the former kind. In the throes of lust, there was a right time and a wrong time for words.

At which point, Dominik said, 'I can see my come dripping out of you, down the inside of your thighs, dotting your pubic hair, painting your skin shiny . . . It's the most exhilarating of visions.'

'Isn't it obscene?' Summer ventured.

'On the contrary, it's beautiful. I will never forget it. If I had a camera right now, I would photograph it.'

'And blackmail me later? Bruises and all?'

'Maybe the marks add to the effect,' Dominik remarked.

'Would you have . . . wanted me had I not displayed the bruises?' Summer asked.

'Absolutely,' he indicated. 'Get up now. Gather your stuff, and the violin. I'm taking you back to my house.'

'What if I had other plans?' Summer asked, scrambling for her dress.

'You don't,' Dominik said, and out of the corner of her eye, Summer saw him tightening his black leather trouser belt. She'd been fucked but still hadn't seen his cock.

*

Dominik's house smelled of books. Past the front door, following him down the initial corridor lined by shelves, all Summer could note were the parallel rows of books packed close together and the rainbow of colours from the spines facing outwards racing by in her wake. Passing a succession of open doors on both sides of the corridor, she noted that every other room was lined with bookshelves. Outside of bookshops, she had never seen so many books in one place in her whole life. She wondered if he had read them all.

'No,' he said.

'No what?'

'No, I haven't read them all. That's what you were thinking, wasn't it?'

Could he read her mind, or was that the first thought anyone had who entered this house?

Before she could ponder this point any longer, she felt an arm under her legs, and another supporting her back, as Dominik lifted her into the air. He carried her down through the hall to his study, kicked the door open and went straight to his desk, setting her down in the middle of its large wooden surface, completely clear of clutter other than a pot filled with pens, a pile of papers in one corner, and a desk lamp, a conical light on a moveable stem.

She sat facing him, nervously, the smells of the crypt and their rough fuck still lingering on her body under the crumpled fabric of her black dress.

'Pull up your dress,' he said, 'and spread your legs apart.'

Summer complied, now acutely aware of her bare arse on his desk, and her unwashed state, of the secretions that filled her, which he had not yet allowed her to wipe away.

He grabbed hold of each of her thighs around her buttocks and pulled her towards him, so that her bum rested just on the edge of the desk. Then he turned to the low bed behind them, against the wall (A bed in the study, thought Summer, strange man), and took a pillow, lifted her head gently and placed it beneath her. He pulled the desk lamp over, switched it on and set it directly over her cunt.

Summer drew a breath. She had never been so open, so on display. She was no prude, insisting on darkened rooms, lights switched firmly off, but this was another level of exhibitionism entirely.

He pulled up his office chair, sat in it, stared at the wetness of her sex, still open, relaxed after his previous attentions.

'Play with yourself,' he said. 'I want to watch.'

Summer hesitated. This was infinitely more intense, more personal, than fucking. She barely knew this man, but it aroused her so much, at the same time, her legs so obscenely spread, a spotlight on her most intimate parts.

Dominik leaned back, his eyes fixed on her, his expression a combination of concentration and interest, as her fingers expertly navigated the intimate geography of her inner and outer folds, the firm, quick circles of her clitoris, the movement of her hand as skilful and precisely orchestrated as it had been on her violin.

He observed with interest as she responded to his comments and his instructions, requests for her to speed up or slow down, promises of what he was going to do to her. It was one of these promises that made her come in a rush, a soft moan escaping her lips and her body, shuddering. From his perfect vantage point, he could see the muscles of her vagina spasming, could tell she wasn't faking it, not that he had thought that she would.

He lifted her up again, into an embrace, wrapping her legs round his waist, her wet pussy hot against his still clothed body.

'Kiss me,' he said.

His lips were soft, unusually so for a guy, she thought.

While his tongue gently created a passage for itself past her lips, grazing the barrier of her teeth, until it reached her own tongue and she felt herself interlacing with his, Summer felt his hand tugging on the black dress's zip and loosening its constraint. The kiss continued and now she could taste him, a jumbled cocktail of impressions with no dominant note, the lingering Tic Tac-mint wind on his breath, the masculine vigour of his closeness. There was no trace of perfume or aftershave to tickle her nose. Like entering a new territory, a strange country she had never explored before.

'Arms up,' he demanded,

He pulled the dress up over her head, ruffling her tousled hair in the process, tilted her backwards so that she was forced to lower her legs to stand on the floor again as his hands began to travel across her now bare skin, caressing, testing, leaving no inch untouched across her back, her shoulders, her bruised arse.

As he did this, his other hand held her chin in its loose grip, bringing her lips back into contact with his for a second kiss, but had the first kiss even stopped, been interrupted? She hadn't noticed.

He pushed her down on the bed.

Summer flopped back, watching as he undressed. Shirt first, followed by his trousers, which he kicked away, and then his black boxer shorts. Summer caught a sight of his penis, thick, extended, veiny.

He pulled her to the edge of the bed, where he kneeled down, parted her legs at an acute angle, and ran the tip of his finger slowly from the inside of her ankle up to her inner thigh and deliciously close to her cunt. Her body quivered in response to his touch. Dominik placed his lips on the smooth skin of her upper leg, teasing her with kisses placed everywhere but where she wanted them. Summer moaned in anticipation, arching towards him. He pulled back, made her wait an agonising moment before burying his face in her mound. She sighed with ill-disguised ecstasy, shuddering as his tongue began to navigate her lips.

For a brief moment, she recoiled from his steady ardour. She was dirty, had just been fucked, had not yet had the opportunity to clean herself, but then remembered he was the one who had mounted her, and if he wasn't bothered, then why should she be?

The buzz his tongue was providing intensified until it was all she could concentrate on, all thoughts of the world, her situation, faded into oblivion, floating, flying, out of control, hovering between night and day, life and death, the zone where nothing else but sensations mattered, where pleasure and pain merged in blissful forgetfulness.

Finally, he emerged from the dark triangle of her cunt, rose above her on the bed and positioned his cock above her.

'Yes,' she said, and, still silent, Dominik entered her, and once again she was filled to the brim, the hardy girth of his cock stretching her cunt lips apart, bruising her walls wide with his steady assault.

This continued for an eternity while his hands kept on roving shamelessly across every nook and cranny, public and daringly private, of her body, orchestrating the progression of their desire. His tongue darted one moment inside her ear, and the next moment in the hollow of her neck, teeth delicately nibbling a lobe, a finger tugging a loose hair, another hand gripping her buttocks, and then two (how many hands did he have?), holding her butt cheeks briefly apart. In and out of her Dominik travelled, and with every stroke it was just like another stair to an unknown but alluring destination conquered.

There was no doubt in her mind that Dominik was skilful, a man who could take her rough or play with her slowly as he was doing now. How many other faces would he reveal?

Finally, Dominik came. With a loud roar. Just a sound from a distant jungle, no particular words she could seize.

Summer sighed as his movements inside her and outside her gradually slowed and he caught his breath again.

So not Mr Silent any longer . . .

7
A Girl and a Maid

It was early evening now, and the late seasonal sun cast a warm glow over Dominik's face, bathing him in a light that didn't suit him. Haloed unnaturally by the last pale rays drifting down from a steadily darkening sky, he gave the impression that he didn't quite fit into the normal world, though by all accounts he seemed to operate perfectly well in it. Maybe it was just that his dark, earthy features aligned better with cooler weather. Dominik was attractive, no doubt about that, but he had looked better, I thought, in the pallor of the crypt.

He was leaning casually against the doorway, his body casting a long shadow over the front porch, where I now stood, one step below him, preparing to make my departure. I had told him that I had to work that night, although I didn't, circumnavigating any awkwardness that might arise if he invited me to stay over. Or didn't invite me to stay over.

A soft breeze blew across the lawn, and with each gust of wind I smelled the faint scent of books that lined his front hallway, and the rest of the house. They seemed so much a part of him that I imagined his skin might feel like parchment, but of course it felt just like the skin of every other man, though his lips had been pleasantly soft.

The books, though they did suit him, weren't what I

expected. I had always associated book collections with messy people, with mad lecturers and more obviously academic types. I had figured Dominik would be a hotshot in the City, a bank trader, someone in finance, not a university professor, as he had told me, when I asked why his house looked like a library.

Judging by the shine of his shoes, and the money I presumed he must have, allowing him to purchase the violin and make all the other arrangements, I'd expected him to take me back to some monochrome apartment in Bloomsbury or Canary Wharf with stainless-steel fittings and décor in varying shades of silver and black, the colour of his car. I hadn't expected this, a proper house, a home, even, with a study and a real kitchen and books everywhere, in all colours and sizes, a literary kaleidoscope lining the walls. At first, I thought he must have a cat too, who was likely curled up, observing my presence from the safety of the shelves, but I deduced shortly after my arrival that Dominik was not a pet person. He wouldn't be able to put up with an animal, uncontrolled, winding its way round his legs, even a creature as independent as a feline.

He wasn't unduly secretive, didn't seem to be consciously hiding anything, but nonetheless had offered very few details about his life, the day-to-day routine of his existence outside of our meetings. He liked his privacy, I suppose, and I could understand that, reticent as I was to invite anyone into my own home. I was surprised he had taken me here. Though his books gave him more humanity, somehow. At least, if he didn't have a story of his own, he seemed to enjoy collecting the stories of others. Perhaps not dissimilar to the way that I liked to imagine the stories in my instruments, and the music I played, each piece with its own distinct imagery and adventure.

The thought made me like him more. We weren't so different, this man and I, though we must seem so to any casual observer.

I remembered the way that he had so expertly touched me, after he had insisted on watching me masturbate. I shivered again at the thought. I'd had sex with no small number of men, that was true enough – I'd had more than my fair share of casual encounters and Internet dates arranged in the throes of horniness or loneliness – but no one had ever examined me like that, gazing so intently at the way I ran my finger round my clitoris, under the bright heat of his desk lamp, like a doctor but without the air of medical disinterest. He had no shame, Dominik, and he seemed to enjoy peeling my shame away, one layer at a time. It was as if he was watching a demonstration that he planned to re-enact precisely later. He had asked me to slow down or speed up, to increase or release the pressure. Not, to turn me on this time, I thought, but so that he could gauge my response, see what it was that made my body react and what didn't work so well. He had had me on display for him like a scientist examining a new specimen. I had half expected him to start taking notes.

'One day,' he had said, 'I'm going to watch you do this again, and I will tell you to put your own finger in your arsehole.'

That was what had finally sent me over the edge. I don't come all that easily, particularly with a new lover, but the thought of him watching, and the direction that his mind seemed to travel, the dirtiness of his requests . . . Dominik pressed buttons I didn't even know I had.

He had said that he didn't play an instrument, but I thought that he would likely be rather good at it.

Yes, I thought, I would definitely like to see him again.

I shifted my weight to my other foot and loosened my grip on my violin case. He didn't seem ready to let me go yet. I waited patiently for him to speak.

'I think I'll leave you to plan the next time,' Dominik said.

I stood silent for a while, thinking. Another change of tactic. Just when I thought I had him figured out.

'What if I plan something that is not to your taste?' I replied.

Dominik shrugged. 'Would you take any pleasure in an arrangement that I didn't enjoy?'

I considered this. No, I wouldn't. If we were going to have another date, then of course I would want both of us to have a good time. Wouldn't anyone feel that way? Even so, I still wasn't sure what exactly it was that he wanted from me, or what I wanted from him, and that would make planning the next time difficult.

I shook my head, suddenly lost for words.

'I didn't think so,' he added. 'I will wait for your call.'

I agreed, bade him farewell and then turned to leave.

'Summer,' he called out, just as I reached his gate.

'Yes?'

'You choose the date and place – here, if you would like that – but I will choose the time and iron out some of the finer details.'

'Agreed.'

I allowed myself a small smile as I turned away again.

He couldn't resist taking over.

And I was surprised to find that I preferred it that way.

*

My mind was a whirl all the way home. It would soon be dark, so I dismissed the thought of taking a walk through Hampstead Heath to clear my head, though the exercise and fresh air were exactly what I needed.

The sex had been great. Hot as anything. My muscles ached a bit now, especially my calves. Probably the way that he had bent me forward in the crypt. I had stood there with my legs burning for an age as he had walked around me before we fucked. My reward, I suppose, for being so stubborn, refusing to let on that I was uncomfortable.

Then the way he had gone down on me, straight after I'd made myself come, with his come still inside me, before I'd had a chance to shower. I hadn't even been able to use the bathroom to wipe myself beforehand. I recalled how he'd picked me up and carried me to his study as soon as we got to his front door, plonked me down on his desk and spread my legs. I'd had to choke back a laugh when I realised that he was actually carrying me over the threshold.

It was, ironically, the most romantic sex I'd ever had, although we hadn't used condoms, a point that as a general rule I am paranoid about. I'd have to go and get tested. A flash of shame crossed my mind as I pictured telling the doctor or nurse on duty that I'd had unprotected sex. It was a stupid thing to do, but the heat of his cock had banished all sensible thought from my head, and the way he had fucked me so hard, like a man possessed, and kept pulling my hair back as if he was riding a horse.

No wonder I ached.

Dominik might be a little on the cocky side, but he was great in bed, and not selfish. His bedroom behaviour did not have the customary hallmarks of arrogance so prevalent in men of his kind.

I headed for the shower as soon as I got in the door, continuing to think as I rinsed off all trace of the day's adventure.

Almost all trace, I thought, as I caught a glimpse of the faintly apparent bruises in the bathroom mirror.

Had Dominik added any of his own?

At least – thank heaven for small mercies – none of the marks were on my wrists or upper arms, but on areas that I could cover most of the time, and none looked so violent that clumsiness – a story of walking into a door or falling over – wouldn't work as an excuse.

I wondered how this worked for the people I'd seen at the fetish clubs. How did they manage to fit their nocturnal (and perhaps daytime) hobbies around their ordinary lives. It was just a night out for some of them, I was sure, but going by what Charlotte had said, that wasn't true for all of them. If she was to be believed, there were men and women all around London, at home with their respective partners in front of the television with a curry in one hand and a whip in the other.

Would I soon be one of them?

Not with Dominik, I didn't think. He hadn't so far produced any paddles or handcuffs, though I had wondered if he might, considering the interest he had shown in my bruises. I had been slightly disappointed when he hadn't tied me up, suspended me from the ceiling or buckled me to some piece of equipment that I thought he might have lying around the house. I had only seen his study and his kitchen so far, though, not his bedroom. Odd that he would have a bed in his study. He said that it was for thinking.

Thinking about what? Ways to further confuse and entice me, I imagined.

The more I thought about it, the more I found myself in a tangle with no discernible exit strategy. Aside from the trouble I was having working out my own personal sexual revolution and how I fitted into this new world of deviancy that I had stumbled upon, I didn't know what to do about Dominik.

The thought of calling him to arrange our next meeting perplexed me. It was a simple enough task, but the more I ran over it in my head, the more I concluded that despite the irregularity of his behaviour up to this point, I had enjoyed the way that he ordered me about. I had appreciated the simplicity, and the surprise within his instructions. I missed the excitement of discovering what he would plan next. But even admitting the fact in my own mind made me imagine the suffragettes turning in their graves. And that was before I added my whipping and spanking experiences.

This wouldn't do.

I considered phoning Chris, from the band. He'd been working all hours of the day on recording the group's first EP and I hadn't seen him for months, though we'd exchanged a few emails. Darren had always been jealous of our friendship, and to keep the peace, I'd gradually decreased our contact. I regretted it now. Chris had always been my go-to guy, my wingman, my refuge when I needed someone to understand the eccentricities and difficulties inherent in following a creative path.

There was no way I could explain all this to him, though. He was protective; I knew that he would be suspicious of a man who gave me expensive gifts and asked me to undress in front of him in secret underground locations. I would be suspicious of Dominik if I heard the story second hand.

Instead, I called Charlotte. This was a problem that was right up her street.

'Hey, honey,' she said. 'How you been?'

She was alone this time. Good. It was hard enough describing my story to one person. I didn't want another overhearing.

'Remember that guy who sent me the email? The one with the terms and conditions?'

'Yeeeesss,' she said, suddenly all ears.

I told her the full story, the Bailly, the crypt, the nakedness, everything. Described Dominik and all of his puzzling instructions.

'No surprises there, then,' said Charlotte.

'What do you mean, no surprises? The whole thing is crazy.'

'No, it's not crazy; he's just some dom.'

'A dom?'

'Yeah. They're all like that – cocky, want to control everything. Sounds like you're liking it, though.'

'Hmm.'

'What did you say his name was again?'

'Dominik.'

Charlotte laughed. 'Well, that's just typical,' she said. 'You couldn't make it up.'

'What shall I tell him, then? About the date?'

'That depends entirely on what you want to get out of it.'

I considered. I truly didn't know what it was I wanted from him. Something, yes. I couldn't get him out of my head, but why?

'I'm not sure,' I replied. 'That's why I called you.'

'Well,' she said, ever the pragmatist, 'you need to work out what you want or you'll never get it.'

Sensible enough advice.

Charlotte continued. 'It won't hurt to make him wait. Maybe a week or two. Suggest you play for him again, naked obviously, since it turns him on so much, and at his house – saves you inviting him back to yours. Plus, he'll think you've put the ball back in his court. Which you haven't, obviously.'

I could almost hear the smirk spreading across her face.

'OK,' I replied.

'And in the meantime, you can come and serve at a little party I'm having next week, if you like.'

'Serve?'

'Like a waitress. A maid. The guests are all fetish sorts. I can introduce you properly to a few people and you can see if you really do like being dominated. I'll tell everyone you're just trying it for a night, and if you don't like it, you can drop your apron and join the party. I've got proper slaves coming too. They'll do all the hard work. You can just carry a few plates around and look hot.'

'Look hot how? What shall I wear?'

'Oh, I don't know, use your imagination. Why don't you call your rich boyfriend up and ask him to buy you something?'

'He's not my boyfriend! And no way am I asking him for anything.'

'Don't get your knickers in a twist, girl. I'm just pulling your leg. You're so sensitive.'

'Fine,' I said huffily, 'I'll do it.'

'Excellent,' said Charlotte. 'Maybe you should mention

it to him, though, see how he reacts. And I'll see you on Saturday. Bring my coat back too, would you?'

As per Charlotte's advice, I left it three days before calling Dominik.

'Summer,' he said, before I had a chance to tell him who was calling.

'Our date,' I said. 'I was thinking, next Wednesday?'

He paused and I heard the flutter of pages. Presumably checking his diary.

'No problem. I'm free. What did you have in mind? So I can make the necessary arrangements.'

'I will play for you again, at your house.'

'An excellent choice, if I may say so.'

I relaxed as he seemed pleased with my suggestion. We discussed the choice of music. I had considered trying something different on him, since he had enjoyed the improvisation in the crypt so much. I thought of playing something he wouldn't know by Ross Harris, the Kiwi composer, or maybe something outside the classical repertoire altogether, maybe Daniel D., but nerves got the better of me and I agreed his choice, a section from the final movement of the Max Bruch violin concerto.

'I'll see you then, then,' I said with forced cheerfulness. I hate phone calls.

'Summer,' he said again, as I was about to hang up, always getting in the last word.

'Yes?'

'Are you available on Saturday night?'

'Sorry, I have plans.'

'I see. No problem.'

He seemed disappointed, and I wondered if he had been

hoping to see me sooner. Then I remembered Charlotte's suggestion, that I mention her party to him.

'Actually,' I said, 'I'm going to be in attendance at a bit of an unusual party.'

'Hmm. Unusual in what way?'

He sounded amused, not annoyed, so I continued.

'My friend Charlotte is hosting, the one who introduced me to the fetish clubs.'

'She sounds like an interesting friend.'

'She is. She's . . . ah . . . she's asked me to work the night as a maid.'

'A maid? Not a waitress? Unpaid, I presume?'

'I think so. The question of money just never came up.'

'Just for the rush, as you refer to it, then?'

'I suppose so, yes.'

'How quaint.'

I wasn't sure whether that meant he approved or not.

That Friday, I received another package. From Dominik. Again, I had to sign for it, but this time he didn't check to sec if I was in.

He must have assumed I would be home, or taken the chance, but still, it was a detail that disturbed me a little. I wasn't completely comfortable with him knowing so many of my secrets.

Within the standard, nondescript cardboard box was another, smaller package, wrapped in white tissue paper and tied with a black bow. I opened it carefully, folding up the paper and putting it neatly to one side. Inside the paper was a black satin drawstring bag, and within the bag, a black corset. It was beautiful, not at all like the tacky sort I had seen on the rack in cheap lingerie stores. Fully boned, with wide, gored hips and a velvet diamond shape in the midriff to highlight the wearer's shape. Subtle velvet detailing in inch-thick strips ran down the sides of the wider satin panels, a pattern with a geometric feel to it, art deco, the kind of thing that would have suited a 1930s movie star. It was an undeniably glamorous, rather than trashy, piece of clothing. However, it did seem to be cut a little short. When I held it to myself and looked in the mirror, I realised that the cut was underbust, rather than overbust. Unless the wearer added a bra, or nipple pasties to go with it, she would have her breasts on full display.

The thought excited me, and eager to see what it would look like on, I began fiddling with the laces. Then I realised that it seemed unlikely that Dominik would want me to play for him partially clothed when he had already seen me naked. He didn't seem all that fussed about the specifics of what I wore, either, though I thought he enjoyed watching the subtle changes and variations in each outfit I chose, depending on the specifics of the occasion. The corset was more my style than his. I hunted through the box for some further clue and found two smaller packages under the protective paper that lined the box, protecting its contents from damage, and a note.

The note read, 'Wear this for me. D.'

One of the other two packages contained a pair of white frilly knickers, a packet of stockings and suspender clips. The stockings were the real sort, nylons, and seamed. I had heard of nylon stockings, of course, but had never actually seen a pair. They were slippery, slightly rough against my skin, and had no stretch in them at all, like long, thin parachutes rather than the soft, stretchy pantyhose that I was used to wearing.

The other package contained a small apron, white cotton with a black-and-white scalloped lace trim. A matching cap, about the size of a saucer, was included.

A maid costume. For Saturday. Charlotte's party.

There was no sign of shoes. Dominik had either forgotten that detail, which seemed unlikely, or assumed correctly that I would have my own pair. I did, in fact, own a pair of black stilettos with a high platform at the front and a white trim, which I had bought second hand from an ex cage-dancer in Hackney, who had given up dancing to concentrate on millinery and was consequently selling all of her footwear. They'd be perfect, if rather uncomfortably high. Still, I was prepared to make sacrifices, not necessarily for glamour, but to get the 'look' just right.

I did find one more item, buried right at the bottom. A tiny bell. The shape and style like those attached to churches, but with a stem not much bigger than my finger. It made a surprisingly clear sound when I shook it. More like the deep knell of a percussion instrument than the lighter tinkle that might accompany a pet collar or a bicycle bell.

Acknowledging the package seemed the polite thing to do, but I didn't want to encourage his gift-giving. I was in debt to him enough already, with the violin. Having said that, I had the distinct impression that he'd bought the outfit for him, not for me, so that he could imagine me wearing it, go on some kind of power trip over having me serve food with my tits out like a Hooters waitress, albeit one in a much more refined ensemble. The bell, I supposed, was for the guests at the party to use to alert me to their requirements.

In the end, I didn't let him know that I had received it.

More because I just didn't know what to say than because I wanted him to stew over it. Wouldn't do any harm, though, to let him wonder if he'd guessed wrong about me being home for the delivery and the package had been returned to the store.

I did text Charlotte, though, to check the outfit was appropriate and wouldn't offend any of her guests.

'OK to go topless?'

'Sure. Can't wait.'

I put everything back into the box that it had arrived in, shut the lid and left it sitting in the corner of my bedroom, staring at me, reprovingly, as if a lonely creature were trapped within, waiting for me to set it free.

The next morning, to take my mind off the outfit, and Charlotte's upcoming party, I went for a furious swim at the local pool, powered by my underwater headphones, playing Emilie Autumn on repeat, then went window-shopping on Brick Lane, stopping for a coffee and breakfast at my favourite cafe in this part of town, on the aptly named Bacon Street. The cafe doubles as a vintage clothing store, with racks of outfits inside dating back to the 1900s, and consequently, has that sweet, almost dusty smell of old things, a little like the scent of Dominik's books.

It was still fairly early, much earlier than I usually get up, but the street outside was packed already, each side jammed with racks of clothes, antiques and bric-a-brac laid out on blankets on the pavement, leopard-print chaises longues perched next to office furniture, food stands selling everything from barbecue ribs to fruit smoothies served in coconut shells, the air fairly crackling with the eager energy of market traders and excited tourists visiting for the first time. I had noticed, as I was walking along, picking my way through an obstacle course of zealous sellers and bargain-hunters, that my recent sexual adventures had opened my mind in other ways too. Previously, I had looked at the many stalls selling military hats, jackets and gas masks, and thought that they would be purchased by war memorabilia collectors, who must frequent markets like this one with unusual regularity, as they were always filled with the stuff.

Now, everywhere I looked, instead of collectors' items I saw fetish wear, the jackets and hats favoured by what Charlotte would call 'doms' at the clubs I had been to. The masks had been worn mainly either by submissive types with their heads covered or the punky sort with no immediately identifiable sexual quirks but an apparent interest in fetish fashion. Recognising these things in a way that I am sure other passers-by didn't, I had the pleasing sense of having been granted membership to a secret club, a society full of people who lived on the edge of the world, unbeknown to everyone else. I realised, also, with a touch of trepidation, that I would never be able to erase these things from my mind. Without even meaning to, I'd turned down a road from which I would never be able to return, even if I wanted to.

I sat in the cafe for most of the day, observing the ebb and flow of the other diners, wondering which of them, if any, were also members of this secret world. I wondered if they recognised a kindred spirit in me, if as outsiders we would be drawn to each other like a flock of geese headed inexorably south, or if I just seemed as ordinary as everyone else when I had my normal-world clothes on.

It was this feeling of resignation to the path that my feet had evidently chosen for me that led me to don the outfit that

Dominik had gifted to me for that evening, and to wear it as he had intended, with my breasts completely bared.

I spent about an hour, with the instruction leaflet close by, fiddling with the laces in the mirror. Eventually, I managed to get it on, though not nearly as tight as it should be, and I headed off to Charlotte's, catching the Hammersmith and City line from Whitechapel to Ladbroke Grove. I wore my long, red trench coat over top, enjoying the thought that beneath my outer covering, I was an entirely different person, my own person, and not subject to all the usual rules of society, like wearing a bra in public.

I wasn't so brave when I reached Charlotte's and it came to taking my coat off again. I'd purposefully arrived early, so that I could settle in and soothe my nerves before the other guests arrived. In the end, I just took a deep breath and ditched the trench coat as if I wasn't the least nervous about the party. Charlotte would have only teased me if she noticed my shyness.

'Nice corset!' she said.

'Thank you.' I didn't mention that it was a gift from Dominik.

'You can lace it tighter than that, though. Come here.'

She turned me to face the wall and then put her hand on the small of my back and pressed me forward.

'Put your hands on the wall.'

I remembered the sex with Dominik in the crypt, the way he had pushed me into almost the same position. I wished he was here, fucking me again in the same way. My nipples hardened at the thought and then grew even stiffer as I realised that it was likely I would find tonight's 'service' a turn-on, and if my nipples remained this stiff, it was unlikely that I would be able to hide the fact. Had Dominik considered that point? He was observant and I knew that he had noticed my triggers of arousal, but I wasn't sure if he had meant for me to find the maiding and, particularly, wearing the outfit he had chosen for me arousing. Did he want me to be horny tonight, without him? With the possible consequences that might ensue? Or had he just meant to exert his control, to see if I would follow his increasingly bold instructions? The topic of exclusivity hadn't arisen. It was far too early for that. I wasn't even sure if we were technically dating.

'Enjoying that, are you?'

I was so lost in thought I hadn't noticed Charlotte pulling my laces tighter.

'Breathe in.'

I gasped as she put her foot on my back and then pulled with all her might.

The corset was now laced nearly all the way up, just a couple of inches spare at the back. The sensation was completely different from the corset of Charlotte's that I had once borrowed, which had been too loose and simply felt a little stiff. Dominik had selected the perfect fit, though I knew the laces did allow for a little flexibility in the size. Laced tightly, my breathing was constricted and my back perfectly straight. I found it surprisingly pleasurable, a bit like being encased in a very tight hug. I was glad that I had put my matching heels on earlier, as now I couldn't bend over at all. If I had to pick anything up from the floor tonight, I would have to crouch down somehow, with my back straight. The thought turned me on, I was certain that Charlotte would be able to smell my arousal as she squatted in front of me to straighten my stockings.

*

I spent most of the evening in the kitchen, arranging plates of food and enjoying for once an opportunity to be more creative than I was at work – the chef there was insistent that his orders be followed to the letter. When the bell rang, I responded immediately, and with each trip to the dining area and back to the kitchen again I caught glimpses of the party unravelling, Charlotte's colourful guests moving closer together and becoming less and less clad with each fresh top up of their glasses. There was roughly an even number of men and women present, dressed very much like the partygoers on the boat, most in a mixture of latex and lingerie. One of the men was dressed as a maid, in a short bubble-gum pink frock with a white frilly apron over the top, though his manner suggested that he was not in a service role. Despite Charlotte's assurance that I would have company in the kitchen and wouldn't be doing any heavy lifting, I was the only guest working.

All night, each time I had difficulty breathing or had to bend or crouch awkwardly, restricted by the tight grasp of the corset, I felt as though Dominik was controlling my movement, as though he had the power, even, to alter the way my chest rose and fell, pressed tight as it was against the satin panels and steel boning that surrounded my torso. Every time the bell rang, and I hurried to take a plate away, or refill a wine glass, I imagined that Dominik was the bell ringer, and myriad images flooded my mind, images of all the ways that I hoped he would take me and use me, as though a mental flood of violent desire had been unleashed in my head.

Charlotte watched me curiously.

'I have a surprise for you later,' she whispered into my

ear, as I refilled her drink. She had rung the bell for me more times than anyone else that night.

'Really?' I replied, with a degree of uninterest. The fantasies playing out in my head were frankly more exciting than anything she might have in mind.

Dinner was finished now, and she was sitting on the lap of a man I recognised. It took me a few minutes to remember where I had seen him. He was the one in the sequinned leggings and military hat that I had noticed at the fetish club on the boat, before we had entered the dungeon. Charlotte had known I was attracted to him, I was sure. I wondered if she'd invited him on purpose, and if she was sitting on his lap just to wind me up. A little silly perhaps – I hadn't even spoken to her friend – but Charlotte had toyed with men I liked in the past. I think she just enjoyed watching me react to it, so I did my best to appear unfazed.

I was in the kitchen, spooning dessert into bowls, when I heard the clear sound of a viola playing in the living room, the voices of Charlotte's guests now hushed, listening to the music. It was a Black Violin cover, though without the usual violin accompanying the viola. Chris. It was one of the covers that we played together, one we'd played the night I had introduced him to Charlotte. She'd hooked up with him afterwards, a fact that had angered me and embarrassed him, even though our friendship had never had even the remotest sexual spark, a fact I'd always found odd: I had a sexual spark with virtually everyone, even the milkman. But it was nice to have a male friend with whom I could relax without worrying about the consequences.

What would he think of me now?

The song came to a close, and then I heard the piercing

ding-a-ling of the bell, reaching my ears over the din of appreciative applause. Charlotte, no doubt, hurrying the dessert along. I picked up as many bowls as I could carry and took them into the living room – partly because Dominik's bell called me like a siren song, and I was compelled to follow it, and partly because I knew that Charlotte was setting me a challenge and I'd be damned if I let her win. I wouldn't cower in the kitchen or attempt to hide myself, and Chris would just have to deal with it.

His eyes widened when I appeared. I glanced at him quickly and then looked down, hoping that he would understand my silent gesture and not say a word. He didn't.

It was Charlotte who spoke first. 'What do you think of our waitress?' she said to Chris.

'I think she looks lovely,' he replied, without falter.

Then he began to play again, cutting off any further conversation. I breathed a sigh of relief and disappeared back into the kitchen. Thank God for good friends. I resolved never to abandon Chris again, no matter what the opinion of any future lover on our platonic relationship.

He completed his performance and cornered me in the kitchen on his way out, clearly shocked by the behaviour of Charlotte's guests, who were now revelling in the living room as if they were coming to the final course of a Roman banquet. The air was filled with sexual tension and I suspected that an orgy might be on the menu – straight after dessert.

'Sum,' he said, resolutely maintaining eye contact without so much as a glance at my naked chest, 'do you know these people?'

'Well, not exactly, just Charlotte.'

That was true enough. She hadn't introduced me by

name to her guests, a natural function of my position for the duration of the evening. It was odd, now I considered it, the way the role she had saddled me with had consumed me completely, the moment I had the apron on and heard the first ring of the bell.

'All a bit odd, isn't it? You know,' he added in a whisper, glancing over at a now topless girl at the dining table who was openly running her hand up and down the pink-frocked man's thigh, 'if you needed money this bad, I would have helped you out, hon. You should have called me.'

My heart sank. He thought I was doing it for money. I couldn't bring myself to tell him that I was working, dressed like this, for free. How would I ever explain the sheer madness of it?

I nodded, mutely, too ashamed to meet his eyes. He gave my shoulder a gentle squeeze.

'I got to go, baby. I have a late-night gig after. I'd give you a hug, but . . . you know . . . it would be weird.'

My eyes filled with tears. Chris had always been the only person who I felt really understood me. I wasn't sure what I'd do if I lost him over this.

He stretched forward, carefully avoiding my breasts, and gave me a soft peck on the cheek. 'Call me, OK? Or come round later if you wish, once you're, um, finished here.'

'OK,' I replied. 'See you later.'

He let himself out, and the bell rang again.

It took Charlotte a moment to articulate her request, as she was busy, kneeling on the floor, naked, her face buried in the cunt of another girl. She waited until I had had a good look at the action and then asked me to bring her a spoon and another bowl of ice cream.

'Stay there,' she said. 'I want you to watch.'

I was rooted to the spot, not entirely because she had instructed me to stay there. Charlotte was daintily spooning ice cream into her partner's vagina and then ducking her head and sucking it out. The woman flinched with each transition from hot to cold, though her enjoyment was obvious. The man from the club, whom Charlotte had been sitting on earlier, was watching also, his cock straining against the crotch of his jeans. I wanted to unzip him and pull it out, but my arms wouldn't move in response to the thought, either out of loyalty to Dominik, still constrained as I was in the confines of his corset, or because it didn't seem appropriate, in my position as maid, for me to be so bold.

Charlotte turned her head to meet the eyes of the man behind her, nodded slightly in approval and then spread her long legs wide. He peeled off his jeans and his cock sprang straight out, unencumbered by underwear. He had a particularly beautiful penis, perfectly straight, evenly coloured, and a promising length and girth. It was like something you would expect to see carved in marble in an art gallery. He stopped for a moment, picking up his jeans and foraging in the pocket for a condom.

Then he bent his knees just low enough so that he could drive his cock into her from behind. As he did, Charlotte's face was washed with pure pleasure, an almost religious ecstasy. I was forgotten, lost as she was to the sensation of the thick shaft pumping into her.

I forgave her in that moment. Charlotte was no less captive to her desires than I and evidently looked quite beautiful in the throes of passion.

I picked up her now empty plate and discarded spoon,

and returned to the kitchen. The bell didn't ring again, but still I waited, locked into the corset and stilettos, my feet now throbbing. The discomfort gave me a sense of peace, not dissimilar to the way that I felt when my body ached after a few dozen lengths of a swimming pool.

Eventually, the guests left and Charlotte called me a cab.

'Was that OK for you, honey?' she asked, her arm draped affectionately around my shoulders.

'Yeah,' I replied. 'Actually, I kind of enjoyed it.'

'Good,' she said.

She stood on the front step, clutching a sheet, her only protection from the cab driver's curious gaze, and watched me disappear into the night.

Dominik called the next day, to confirm our date.

'There's something different in your voice,' he said.

'Yes,' I replied.

'Tell me.'

I thought I detected a hint of worry, but I couldn't be sure. Whether he really had been worried about me or this was just another turn in his game, I was no less compelled to answer his question than I had been to respond to his bell. I told him about the corset, and Charlotte, and how I had felt watching her being filled from behind.

He texted me, the night before our meeting: 'Come at 10 p.m. tomorrow. You will have an audience. Of more than one.'

8

A Man and His Guest

It was a room in Dominik's house that Summer had not yet encountered. On the top floor. It might well have been an attic at one time, but had undergone extensive renovation and conversion. Here and there the ceiling curved, following the path of the roof above. Only two of the walls were covered with bookshelves, mostly housing long runs of often yellowing-spined literary and film magazines, although the upper shelf on the left-hand wall was dominated with an assortment of older, leather-bound volumes of some sort, mostly with French titles. Summer was not allowed the time to take a closer look at the bookshelves and investigate further. There were no windows and the only light came from two square skylights carved into the ceiling.

The room featured nothing else, as if Dominik had deliberately emptied it of furniture or anything that might prove a distraction.

She had been asked to report at 10 p.m. This was to be an evening performance. Her first at such a late hour of the day, as all their previous encounters, as part of the unwritten contract between them, had taken place during the course of the day or in the early evening.

Dominik had greeted her at the door and given her a casual peck on the cheek. As ever, his features were inscrutable, and Summer knew she would not get any answers out of him, so she remained silent. He escorted her up the stairs and opened the door that led to the topmost level of the house.

'Here,' he said.

Summer settled her violin case on the wooden floor.

'Now?' she asked Dominik.

'Yes, now,' he nodded.

She was dying to ask who would be in attendance in addition to him, but thought better of it. Pangs of arousal were beginning to swirl inside her at the thought of the audience who would witness her recital, her service, spying on her every movement and gesture.

She undressed. She'd come to Dominik's wearing a pair of old jeans and a tight white T-shirt. He had told her there was no need to dress up today. Neither stockings nor high heels, he had indicated. She was to be totally nude. He appeared to enjoy the subtle variations of dress and undress in the continuing process of her ongoing exhibitions, the way he orchestrated her successive performances like a madcap, if thoughtful conductor.

She swiftly shed her few clothes and stood there naked, facing him. For a brief moment, she wished he would just take her right there and then, on all fours on the wooden floor, but she realised this was not his intention today, or at least not before she had conjured up the music that made him so lustful. Once again, they had agreed beforehand on the piece she would be playing: the solo from the final movement of the Max Bruch violin concerto.

His eyes kept on X-raying her. The room was warm; dying embers of sunlight filtered through the skylights.

'Is that a new lipstick?' he queried, glancing at her lips.

He was observant. She normally switched lipsticks depending on the time of day, moving to a darker shade of red when night came. She'd been doing this for years. It made her feel the transition between her day and night self so much more acutely.

'Not quite new,' she answered. 'I tend to wear a darker, warmer shade of lipstick for evenings,' Summer replied.

'How interesting,' he remarked, appearing uncommonly thoughtful. Then, 'Do you have the lipstick with you?'

'I have both, of course,' Summer said, indicating her small handbag, which lay on the floor next to her discarded jeans and T-shirt.

Dominik walked over, opened the handbag and retrieved the two tubes she kept there and looked closely at them, assessing the respective shades.

'Night and day,' he said.

'Yes,' Summer confirmed.

He jettisoned one of the tubes, took the other between his thumbs and twisted it, causing the dark, waxy, finger-shaped lipstick to emerge from its plastic casing. He'd gone for the night colour.

'Come here,' he ordered.

Summer obeyed, unsure of what he might have in mind.

'Straighten your back,' he said.

Summer did so, thrusting her breasts ever so slightly forward in the process.

Dominik approached her, his lipstick-wielding hand moving to her nipples, where he carefully began painting her hardening tips. Summer gulped. One nipple. Two nipples.

Painted. Decorated. Enhanced. She looked down. It

made her look so brazen. She smiled, admiring the perversity of his imagination.

But he wasn't finished.

He took a step back, looked Summer in the eyes and said, 'Open your legs wide,' and got down on one knee, still wielding the lipstick tube. Following her gaze, he ordered her to look straight ahead, not down.

She felt his finger separating her labia, inserting itself inside her moistness, pinching each lip in turn and holding it while his other hand began drawing the lipstick vertically along her cunt and then across both cunt lips.

Summer felt a tremor race through her whole body, and for a moment her parted legs felt wobbly. She could only imagine what she looked like right now.

Dominik rose.

She had now been made up for her coming performance.

'Painted like the Great Whore of Babylon,' Dominik remarked. 'Adorned. Perfect.'

Still shocked by what had just happened, Summer was struggling for words.

Dominik pulled a piece of black cloth from one of his trouser pockets and fastened the blindfold round her head and Summer was plunged into darkness.

'I won't know who is present?' she protested feebly.

'No.'

'Whether it's just one person or more?'

'That's for you to guess and for me to know,' Dominik answered.

Another variation in the ritual.

As the implications of the situation crowded her mind, Summer drew her breath.

'I'll leave you now,' Dominik said. 'You may rehearse if

you wish. I will be back with my guest . . . or guests . . .' She noted the deliberate touch of irony in his voice. 'When I return in a quarter of an hour or so, I will not be alone. I will knock on the door three times and then enter. Then you will play for us. Do you understand the rules fully?'

Summer signified her agreement.

Dominik left the room.

She picked up the violin and began her tuning exercises.

Dominik had asked Victor to leave his shoes downstairs, so when they entered the top-room floor, Summer was unable from the soft shuffle of socks on wood to analyse the sound with any degree of precision that might betray the number of visitors.

Seeing Summer standing in all her glory, violin in hand, her parts artificially enhanced by the scarlet shade of the lipstick, Victor beamed from ear to ear and turned to Dominik as if to congratulate him. He knew he was not allowed to speak.

Ever since he had assisted Dominik in recruiting Lauralynn's short-manned string quartet, he had been pestering him for information about what specifically he had been organising. Dominik also suspected that Victor had more than a passing acquaintance with Lauralynn, and that they were in each other's pockets. Victor had always been a shady presence on the campus and in Dominik's academic social life. He had maddeningly complicated Eastern European roots that mischievously seemed to vary according to whomever he was telling his story to. He was a guest lecturer in philosophy and a music aficionado of note, who moved between universities like a low-flying pundit and seldom lingered in one place very long, gratifying the amphitheatres with cunning brilliance, rehearsed gusto and abstruse theories he somehow always managed to get into print in rarefied publications. Victor was of average height, with salt-and-pepper hair and a short Mephistophelean beard, which he trimmed with maniac precision.

Dominik was not one who listened to much gossip, but he knew the rumours surrounding Victor were plentiful, and often wonderfully spurious. He was the man to go to when it came to intrigue and matters libertine, with, supposedly, a seraglio of student affairs on his personal résumé. A head of department had once tut-tutted and hinted that there were certain extra-curricular duties automatically involved should any postgraduate researcher of the female kind want Victor to supervise a thesis. Indeed, very few students who were not pretty were ever taken on board by him, it had been noticed.

For some time now, Victor had been wheedling Dominik for information about his 'project', as he put it, and Dominik had finally given in and admitted to Summer's existence and how the game he was playing with her had been developing, even if he kept some of the more intimate details back.

'I must see her,' Victor had said. 'I absolutely must.'

'She is quite fascinating, I agree,' Dominik had replied. 'Maybe . . .'

'Not maybe, my dear boy. You just have to allow me. If only once. Surely she would consent?'

'Well, she has consented to everything so far, or at any rate tolerated the strange detours this is taking,' Dominik admitted to Victor.

'Just as a spectator, you understand. Although not a disinterested one, naturally. Isn't there a voyeur in all of us?'

'I know,' Dominik said.

'Will you ask her. Please?'

'Sometimes her consent is not actually expressed in words. I assume it. Or it's in the eyes, the way she moves.'

'Makes sense,' Victor said. 'So would you, Dominik? I'm so fascinated by the object of your experiment.'

'My experiment?'

'Isn't that what it is?'

'Yes, I suppose it is when you put it that way.'

'Good. So we understand each other, no?'

'You watch her play, that's all, understood?'

'Absolutely, my dear boy, absolutely.'

Victor distractedly fingered his short beard in a desultory fashion at regular intervals while Summer played. Her dark-red nipples were like targets bathed in the thin moonlight racing down through the square skylights, surrounding her with an uncanny halo that seemed to reverberate to the sounds of the music as the melody unfurled, journeying through its intricate avenues and side roads before reaching the perfection of its final destination.

Her fingers were on the fret board and the smooth movement of the bow across the taut strings was like a surfer riding a wave. The music coursed through her body at a subcutaneous level, transporting her, and the men watched in soundless communion despite the music that enveloped the room; she knowing she was being watched; them gazing at her and feasting on her physical charms and vulnerability. As to who was in control, that was another matter altogether.

Standing next to Victor, Dominik could hear the other man's breath rise and fall, and realised Victor was as much transfixed as he was. Summer naked had this effect, her back so terribly straight it felt as if she was wantonly presenting herself for use, or examination, for ravaging. A mad thought flashed through his mind. Surely not? Or . . . maybe? He bit his tongue.

With a superfluous flourish of self-satisfaction, Summer came to the end of the piece. The spell broken, Victor was about to applaud, but Dominik gestured quickly to halt his movement and brought his fingers to his lips to indicate that silence was still the order of the day. Summer must not know who or how many were present.

Victor and Dominik exchanged glances. Dominik felt as if Victor was encouraging him. Or was it his imagination? Summer was waiting, holding the Bailly by her side, proudly nude. His eyes fell to her midriff, then lower. He perceived her slit behind the thin curtain of her sparse curls in the dim light now illuminating the room.

He took a couple of steps forward, took the violin from Summer's hand and gently set it on the ground behind him where it would not be harmed.

'I want you,' he said. 'You make me want you, Summer,' he continued.

She was still blindfolded, so he could read no response in her eyes. His hand settled on her breast. The nipple was hard as rock. This was answer enough for him.

He neared his mouth and whispered in her ear, 'I want to take you right now, right here.'

There was the hint of a nod, although he couldn't be sure.

'And there will be someone else watching . . . '

Her chest heaved as she took a deep breath. He felt her shiver for a second.

His left hand alighted on her shoulder, applying gentle pressure.

'On your knees, on all fours.'

And then he fucked her.

Victor watched in total silence, fascinated by the spectacle of Dominik's thick cock as it slid in and out of Summer's opening, parting her lips with implacable force, pistoning into her depths. Observing the rise and fall of her breath as she was taken, the delicate sway of her breasts as they balanced below her, moved by the regular forward motion of Dominik's body against hers, the slap of his balls against her lower arse.

Victor wiped his forehead and briefly touched himself through the material of his green corduroy trousers.

From the corner of his eye, as he kept on working himself in and out of Summer, Dominik could see how excited his colleague was, noticed him grinning wildly at him but was soon distracted once again by the way her anal opening widened under the impact of his cock inside her, like a wave taking its point of origin at the heart of her vagina and moving outwards in concentric circles, animating first her arsehole and then the rest of her body, giving life to the whole surface of her skin as the pleasure crest travelled across her.

The rear hole yawned microscopically and Dominik could not help thinking to himself that he would one day wish to fuck her there. As he did this, he missed Victor's prompt movement as the philosophy professor positioned himself ahead of him, by Summer's bowed face. For an instant, Dominik imagined Victor was about to get his own cock out and force it into Summer's mouth, the classic 'spit roast', as he knew it was called in more vulgar circles, and was about to protest, but all Victor did was take a handkerchief out of his trouser pocket and, with terrible kindness, wiped the sweat away from Summer's forehead, gifting Dominik with a beatific smile as he did so.

Realising it wasn't Dominik who was touching her there, albeit with gentleness, Summer seized up for a second and he felt her cunt muscles grip his cock with undue vigour. Thoughts racing through his brain with impossibilities, improprieties and memories galore, Dominik reflected frantically that he had once read – was it in the Marquis de Sade? – that when women died in the throes of sex, their vaginal muscles froze and a man's cock could remain stuck there, embedded like a vice, or was it in other pornographic tales involving women and K9s, as the Craigslist personal ads less than euphemistically spelled it out? The shocking reminder struck him like a bolt of lightning and he came, violently, almost disgusted by his own thoughts.

When he looked up again, Victor had left the room. Beneath him, Summer seemed to be gasping for breath.

'Are you OK?' he asked solicitously, pulling out of her.

'Yes,' she said haltingly.

She collapsed full length onto the wooden floor, as spent as he was in her own way.

'Did it turn you on to know we were being watched?' Dominik asked.

She undid her blindfold and turned her face to him. She was flushed.

'Terribly,' she confessed, and lowered her eyes.

Dominik now knew how her mind worked, how her body responded to the gaze of a voyeur, but she was still uncertain where he would take her next.

*

It was half-term at the university and Dominik had long ago agreed to attend a conference overseas at which he was one of several keynote speakers and had arranged to take time off in the foreign city following his official talk.

When Summer had asked him when they might meet next, he had informed her of his forthcoming absence. The disappointment was visible on her face. They were in his kitchen on the ground floor having some toast and butter following the top-room fuck. Summer had slipped her T-shirt back on, still obscenely leaking, and at Dominik's request had not slipped her jeans back on and was sitting bottomless on the metal chair at the granite kitchen top, where he had laid out the plates and glasses of grapefruit juice.

She felt highly conscious of her state of undress as the criss-cross pattern of the seat's slats cut into her bum. No doubt he would witness another set of provisional marks latticed across her arse when she next stood up, and he would visibly enjoy that spectacle when she finally had to walk upstairs again to retrieve her jeans, with Dominik behind her in a perfect line of vision.

Dominik was once again his distant self and seemingly unable to address any subject of importance, let alone comment on what he wanted out of her in the long run. Summer, however, was pragmatic and happy to go with the flow. He would explain when he thought the time was right, she expected. For now, he restricted himself to small talk. She wanted so much to ask him about himself, his past, in an attempt to 'read' him, understand this curious man better, but maybe this reserve, this distance, were an integral part of the game. On one hand, she felt enormously attracted to him, while on the other, there was something of the night in Dominik, a darkness that she craved but that scared her at the same time. It seemed every step in this relationship of sorts was a sly progression in some journey to a place she couldn't yet conceive.

'Have you ever been to Rome?' he asked her idly.

'No,' Summer replied. 'There are so many places in Europe I still haven't visited. When I came to Europe from New Zealand, I swore I would take full advantage and travel all over the place, but money has always been short, so it has seldom arisen. I once went to Paris for a week with a small rock band I sometimes play fiddle with, but that's all.'

'Did you like it?'

'It was wonderful. The food was exquisite, the museums tremendous, the atmosphere electric, but because I was playing with people I'd previously not been involved with a lot – I was a last-minute replacement – I spent a lot of time rehearsing, so I didn't have a chance to visit all the places I'd hoped to. I've sworn to myself that I will go back again and see and do more. One day. Do Paris properly.'

'I understand Paris has a thriving private-club scene.'

'Fetish clubs?' Summer queried.

'Not quite,' Dominik replied. 'They call them *clubs échangistes*, which translates as "swing clubs". Almost anything goes.'

'Have you ever been to one?'

'No. I've never had the right person to take.'

Was this a covert invitation? she wondered.

'There is a notorious one called Les Chandelles, the Candles. It's terribly elegant, nothing sordid about it,' he emphasised with a faint smile.

Then he dropped the subject.

Infuriating man. Just when she was full of further questions. Was he thinking of taking her there and ordering her to perform? Music only? Or also to be sexually displayed? Mounted in public maybe? Even by others? Summer's imagination was frantically racing ahead.

'So do you have any plans while I'm away? More fetish adventures maybe?' Dominik asked.

'None right now,' Summer answered, although she also knew it was unlikely nothing would happen. It was bound to. Every single nerve in her body had now been lit like a torch and she knew her arousal and curiosity were moving down a slippery slope, the momentum increasing with every day.

Dominik was obviously aware of this.

His features became more solemn. 'You do understand you owe me nothing,' he said. 'You are free to pursue your life in my absence, although I would ask only one thing of you.'

'What?'

'Whatever you do, whatever you get involved in beyond the normal banalities of day-to-day life, working, sleeping, playing with your little band, I want you to let me know. Write to me. In detail. Report to me. By email, or SMS, or even by quaint old-fashioned letter if the time allows. Will you do that for me?'

Summer agreed.

'Can I offer you a ride back to your flat?'

She declined. His house was just a few minutes from a station on the Northern line and she needed the space to think, some form of free time Dominik did not own.

*

Dominik had declined when the Sapienza University in Rome had offered to arrange for him to stay in a hotel close to the campus. He much preferred his own accommodation and had booked a room in a four-star establishment off Via Manzoni, a ten-minute cab drive from Stazione Termini, where the train from the airport would deposit him.

He would engage with the conference, give his comparative literature lecture on 'Aspects of Despair in the Literature of the 1930s to 1950s', focusing on the Italian writer Cesare Pavese, one of a long tradition of writers who had committed suicide for all the wrong reasons. A subject matter, although somewhat uncheerful, on which he had by default become something of an authority. He would socialise with international colleagues, but he also wanted time alone to reflect on these weeks with Summer. He badly needed to clarify his thoughts, analyse his feelings and decide where he now wanted matters to lead. He had a sense there were a profusion of inner conflicts to resolve. Too many. Things could get messy.

Following the keynote speech, on the second day of his Roman stay, he had joined a group of other conference speakers and attendees, and dined in a restaurant off the Campo dei Fiori, where the *fragole di bosco*, the wild strawberries, had just the right touch of pungency and tanginess, and the caster sugar with which they had been sprinkled drew the flavour out to perfection when the fruit touched the tongue.

'Is nice, no?'

Across the narrow rectangular table, a dark-haired woman he had not been introduced to earlier was smiling at him. Dominik looked up, his eyes stealing away from the succulent concerto of primary colours on his plate.

'Delicious,' he opined.

'They grow them in the mountains, on the slopes,' she continued. 'Not in the forests as it says.'

'Oh.'

'I enjoy your lecture, very much. Is an interesting subject.'

'Thank you.'

'I also like the book you write three years ago on Scott Fitzgerald. Is very romantic subject, no?'

'Thank you again. It's always a pleasant surprise to come across an actual reader.'

'You know Roma well, Professore Dominik?' the woman asked as the waiter navigated the table juggling a tray of piping-hot espresso cups.

'Not particularly,' he said. 'I've visited a couple of times previously, but I'm afraid I don't make a great tourist. Not a huge fan of churches and old stones, you see. I love the atmosphere, though, the people. One can sense the history without going on a proper cultural safari.'

'That's even better,' she remarked. 'Is good to be one's own man, not to follow common path. By the way, I am Alessandra,' she said. 'I live in Pescara, but work at Firenze University. I teach ancient literature.'

'How interesting.'

'How long are you in Rome for, Professore Dominik?' Alessandra asked.

'I have another five days.' The conference proper ended the following evening, and he had no plans beyond. He had thought of just relaxing, enjoying the food, the weather, grabbing some time for reflection.

'If you want, I can show you around. Reveal to you the real Roma, not the tourist tracks. No churches, I promise. What do you say?'

Why not? Dominik thought. Her tousled black hair was a jumble of untamed curls, and her deep tan held a promise of warmth. Had he not made it clear with Summer, back in London, that what was developing between them was not exclusive by nature? Or had he? He knew he had not asked her for any promises, and neither had she made any demands on him. Call it an adventure, not a relationship, at this stage.

'I say yes,' he said to Alessandra. 'It's a wonderful idea.'

'Do you know the Trastevere well?' she asked.

'I expect I will soon,' Dominik smiled.

Seduction is mostly a game played between grown-up men and women, when neither party is aware who is the seducer and who the seduced. That was how it turned out with Alessandra from Pescara. The fact they ended up in her hotel room was just a matter of geographical convenience, as the late-night bar they had their final drinks in (sweet Martini for her and Dominik's usual glass of cola without ice – he was teetotal by taste and not on a matter of principle, never having enjoyed the taste of alcohol when he had been younger and a normal consumer of the stuff) was closer to her homely boutique *pensione* than his spare, impersonal, expensive chain-hotel room.

His phone vibrated just as he entered her suite, holding Alessandra's hand in his and having kissed her in the elevator and been allowed to negligently fondle her arse through the thin cotton skirt that she was wearing.

He begged Alessandra's indulgence, pretexting outstanding business matters of a non-academic nature and consulted the text message that had just arrived. It was from Summer.

'I feel empty,' it said. 'I think of your twisted desires

over and over. Confused, horny, sort of lost.' It was just signed 'S.'

As Alessandra excused herself and moved to the suite's bathroom to freshen up, Dominik walked over to the balcony where the hills of Rome curtained the surrounding landscape in the hot evening air and texted her back.

'Do what you must, but tell me all when I return. Assume your nature. Consider that a piece of advice rather than an order. D.'

He swept past the floating curtains shielding the balcony as he returned to the room. Alessandra was waiting for him and had poured two glasses. Hers appeared to contain white wine, his mineral water.

She had loosened the top two buttons of her white blouse, revealing the plump hillocks of her substantial cleavage, and was sat on a narrow chair. The bedroom door to her immediate right was half open, its darkness a beckoning cavern. Dominik moved over to her level, stood behind the chair and took her hair in his hands, gripping the jungle of unkempt curls. As he tightened his hold on her and the hair began to pull at her scalp, Alessandra groaned quietly in response. Dominik let go, bent over and kissed the back of her neck while his hands circled her neck.

'*Sì*,' Alessandra said, with a distinct breathlessness.

Still standing behind her, he could feel the heat rising from her body.

'*Sì?* Meaning?' he asked.

'Is meaning we fuck, no?'

'Indeed,' Dominik confirmed, and his hands moved further down and slipped under the fabric of her blouse and seized her breasts. Her heart was pumping away, its rhythm a drum tattoo across the surface of her skin.

His thumb rubbed against the volcanic texture of her nipples. He guessed they would be dark-brown, from her colouring, and remembered the delicate symphony of beige and pink that had delineated the contour of Kathryn's nipples and the fact they seldom got hard, and then the light-brown, coarser nature of Summer's tips, and then the breasts of yet another and another of the women who populated his past, those who had come, those who had gone, those he had loved, lusted after, abandoned, betrayed, hurt even.

He tore Alessandra's blouse off rather violently, as if now consumed by anger that she was the one now in this room with him, and not another. That her skin was the wrong shade and not consumed by pallor. That her voice expressed itself with a quaint, foreign accent that only served to remind him of Summer's Antipodean lilt. He knew he should not reproach Alessandra because her body was voluptuous and didn't have a tiny waist juxtaposing her wide hips. She was just the wrong body at the right time, he felt, but this didn't make her the enemy. She held out a hand to reach his trousers and extract his semi-hard cock from his underwear, then took it into her warm, humid mouth. Damn, he realised, Summer had still not sucked his cock. Did this mean anything, or was it just that he'd never invited her to do so? Alessandra's tongue began to play with his glans, slipping and sliding in a clever dance of arousal round it, teasing, deliberately grazing his most delicate skin with her sharp teeth. With one swift movement he pushed hard into her mouth, forcing himself as deep as she could manage to host him, lodging within her. For a brief moment, Dominik felt he was going to make her choke, and the look of fear and disapproval in Alessandra's eyes as she looked up to him from her submissive vantage point froze him, but he did not stop. He knew it was merely anger speaking, dictating the roughness of his gestures. Profound irritation at the fact she was not the woman he wanted to be with right now: Summer.

Dominik relaxed, undressed, as Alessandra silently did likewise and, divorcing her mouth from his cock, lay back on the bed to await their coming together. From the look in her eyes, they both knew this was going to be a rough fuck, a hard one, a mechanical coming together with no elements of romanticism or gentility. This was fine with both of them. It would be their only fuck. A mistake maybe. Strangers holding on to some buoy in the night. Maybe she also yearned for the arms and the cock of another, Dominik speculated, which was why their coming together tonight meant nothing.

They would part in the morning with few words or endearments, going their own way again. Dominik had no plans to return to Rome in the near future. Once they were both fully naked, he threw himself against her, skin against skin, sweat against sheen of sweat, pulled her legs apart and entered her. Without a word.

In the background, Dominik's mobile phone buzzed again, but he would not read the message from Summer until the following morning.

'So be it. S.'

Summer was worried about her finances. Now that she had stopped playing in the tube, the meagre wages and tips from the part-time gig at the restaurant were stretched thin. The band were on a hiatus, with Chris improvising some new material in a cheap home studio outside of London at a friend's country cottage, and she'd recorded her brief violin parts some weeks ago and wouldn't be paid for that work anyway until the recordings actually made any money. She was having to dip into her minimal savings. Too many cabs to distant locations: Hampstead, fetish clubs and so on. Assignations and destinations that she just couldn't travel to by public transport without feeling much too self-conscious. And no way was she about to ask Dominik to help her out. Or anyone else for that matter.

She'd heard that there was a board advertising jobs or one-off studio session work or teaching possibilities at the College of Music in Kensington. When she arrived, the main entrance hall was almost deserted and she realised it was half-term. Damn. Whatever was likely to be posted on the board would be old and out-of-date prospects!

She made her way to the far wall to peruse the pinned-up notes and rectangular cards scattered across the surface of the noticeboard, took out a small notebook from her hand-bag and scribbled down a few numbers, checking on the dates they had been initially posted to avoid wasting time on anything too ancient and out of date.

Between the requests for violin lessons for suburban kids and a dearth of well-remunerated calls for string ensembles (bring your own black dress and make-up) to fiddle along in the background for TV recordings with rock groups in search of classical credibility, she caught sight of a card with a familiar ring and realised how Dominik had found the three musicians who had accompanied her in the crypt. She smiled. All roads certainly led to Rome . . . Then she experienced a moment of doubt when she noticed that the phone number listed was not in fact Dominik's. Maybe he used another number depending on the occasion or need. She filed the information away.

'Looking for a gig?' a girl's mellifluous voice said in her ear. Summer turned round to face her interlocutor.

'Yes, but there's not much to choose from, is there?'

The young woman was uncommonly tall, almost Amazonian, bottle blonde and rather spectacular in a dark leather bomber jacket and black skinny jeans ending in shiny boots with perilous heels. There was something familiar about her. It was the wry smile at the corner of her lips, the way she contemplated Summer with detached amusement and an assumed sense of superiority.

'That one is interesting, isn't it?' the newcomer said, pointing to the card that had already caught Summer's attention.

'It is. All a bit mysterious and hush-hush,' Summer remarked.

'I think it might be out of date by now,' the other said, 'but someone's forgotten to unpin it from the board.'

'Maybe,' Summer said.

'You don't recognise me, do you?' the blonde said.

Then it all came rushing back and Summer felt herself blushing. It was the cello player from the first session in the crypt.

'Oh, Laura, is it?'

'Lauralynn, actually. I'm sorry I made so little impression on you, but then I suppose your mind was on other things. The music, no doubt?'

The mischief in her voice was evident and Summer remembered the day and how she had briefly thought that Lauralynn had been witness to her nudity beneath her blindfold somehow.

'We played well together, I thought. Even though we couldn't see you,' Lauralynn emphasised provocatively.

'That's true,' Summer confirmed. They had quickly established a solid musical rapport despite the quirky nature of the performance required.

'So what are you in search of?' Lauralynn asked.

'A job. Jobs. Anything really. In music preferably. Funds right now happen to be in short supply,' Summer admitted.

'I see. Well, some of the better ones are not advertised here. You don't study here, do you? The better gigs are usually word-of-mouth stuff.'

'Oh.'

'Shall we have a coffee maybe?' Lauralynn proposed. 'There's a nice cafeteria on the first floor, and as it's half-term, it won't be crowded. We can talk in private.'

Summer agreed and followed her up the circular staircase Lauralynn made a beeline for. The contours of her arse were wedded to the fabric of her jeans like a second skin. Summer had never been attracted to women per se, but there was an undeniable aura about this blonde woman, an air of authority and self-confidence that she had seldom come across even in men.

They quickly bonded, discovering they had spent a few years in Australia at the same time, albeit in different cities, and knew a lot of places, musical haunts in common. Summer felt herself relaxing and warming to Lauralynn, despite the ambiguous overtones of manipulation she could instinctively sense in her. They'd agreed after two rounds of coffee to tone down the caffeine rush and had moved on to Prosecco. Lauralynn had insisted on paying for the bottle of sparkling wine.

'How flexible are you?' Lauralynn asked her, all of a

sudden, following on from an idle conversation about the acoustics of Sydney venues.

'Flexible how?' Summer queried, not quite sure what Lauralynn was referring to, if any double meaning should be ascribed to her question.

'In terms of where you live.'

'Reasonably flexible, I suppose,' Summer replied. 'Why?'

'I know there is a position going in a second-division classical ensemble. I think you're good enough. You'd pass the audition for it with flying colours, I have no doubt. Even blindfolded,' she laughed.

'Sounds great.'

'It's in New York, though. And they want someone who can agree to a minimum one-year contract.'

'Oh.'

'I'm in touch with the headhunter in Bishopsgate who's handling this. She's also from New Zealand, so you'd have something in common. I would have loved to spend time in New York myself, but there's no demand right now for a cello.'

'I don't know.'

'Is it because of him that you're hesitant?'

'Him?'

'Your guy, your benefactor, shall we put it? Or is he your master?'

'No way,' Summer protested. 'It's doesn't work that way at all.'

'You don't have to pretend, you know. I guessed what was happening, what the two of you were up to, in the crypt. He wanted you starkers, didn't he? Gave him a thrill to see you performing like that while we were all still clothed, no?'

Summer swallowed hard.

'Gave you a thrill too, eh?' Lauralynn continued.

Summer found refuge in silence. She took a further sip of the sparkling wine, which was going flat by now.

'How did you know?' she asked.

'I didn't,' Lauralynn replied. 'I guessed. But a friend of mine with a good background in kink posted the ad on behalf of your man – they're friends – so I had a reasonable idea the whole episode was on the left wing of kosher. Mind you, no way do I disapprove. I'm into the scene myself.' She smiled conspiratorially.

'Tell me more,' Summer asked.

9

A Girl and Her New Friend

'I can do better than that,' said Lauralynn. 'I'll show you.'

We were still in the university cafeteria, discussing Lauralynn's involvement with the kink scene.

She reached over the table with one of her long, thin arms and took my hand, running her nails softly up the back of my wrist.

I gulped.

I wasn't quite sure if she was stating a fact or making an invitation, and for what?

'Have you ever seen a domme in action?' she asked.

Her emphasis on the double 'm' made it very clear that she was referring to the female variety, more commonly termed a 'dominatrix' outside of kink circles.

'A couple of times,' I replied, 'but just at clubs. Not, er . . . privately.'

We were on to our second bottle of Prosecco now, and I was fairly sure that I had consumed most of it. Either that or Lauralynn had an extraordinary tolerance for alcohol, as I was, by now, on the downhill side of tipsy, while she still seemed stone-cold sober.

'You should round out your education by having a taste of the other side. It's not all about the men, you know.'

She raised an eyebrow as she said 'taste' and I blushed in response. I wasn't used to flirting with women and felt decidedly out of my depth. The whole situation reminded me of my first meeting with Dominik, in the cafe at St Katharine Docks. Sitting across the table, surveying each other, an unspoken battle raging between dominance and submission, attraction and pride.

'Uh, what would that involve?'

'That would be for me to know and you to find out. I wouldn't want to ruin it by spoiling the surprise.'

She had removed her hand from mine and was now resting her forearm on the table and running her index finger round the rim of her wine glass in slow, deliberate circles. She noticed me watching the path of her fingertip, its pressure firm, unyielding against the glass, and grinned wickedly.

'Thinking about your man,' she asked, 'or about me?'

I considered Dominik. True, we had agreed that we were both free to explore our desires, and I had been keeping him filled in on the details of my explorations, as he had requested, but I wasn't sure how he would feel about me being deliberately dominated by another, rather than just casual fucking, or playing around in a club. It seemed different, somehow. Particularly since the instigator was Lauralynn, who had not so long ago been in Dominik's employ, and technically probably still was, I supposed, as she must still be carrying out the task of keeping details of our recital secret.

In fact, I wouldn't be able to tell Dominik about this. There was no way to inform him of my meeting with Lauralynn without dropping her in it. He had intended for us never to have contact after the event, I was sure of that. I would have to disobey his instruction if I wanted to accept Lauralynn's offer.

The thought filled me with a thrill of rebellion. Dominik didn't own me. His power over my behaviour only extended as far as I allowed it to, anyway. Besides, he had never specifically instructed me not to have sex, or whatever else she had in mind, with Lauralynn.

I remembered the way that her jeans had seemed sculpted to her arse, and the way her ever-roving smile moved across her lips. I bet she was filthy.

Aside from a couple of snogs and a bit of tentative stroking, I had never been with a woman. It was something I had always wanted to try, but I'd never been brave enough to push any of the situations that I had found myself in to the next level, no matter how promising they had seemed at the time.

I was buoyed by the Prosecco, and Lauralynn's obvious sexual confidence. She had more than enough for both of us.

'He's not my man,' I protested, meeting her eyes with my own.

'Good.'

Ten minutes later, we were in the back of a black cab, speeding across to her flat in South Kensington.

She also seemed to be doing well for herself, I mused, when we arrived, checking out the interior of her apartment. It was old, of course, like nearly everything in London, but much larger than most one-bedroom flats that I had seen, with both an upstairs and a downstairs. The interior was what I expected, all sleek, clean lines, everything in white, minimal fuss or frippery. The effect could easily have been cold, but there was a humorous undertone to Lauralynn's mysterious persona and I thought that the ice-queen thing she had going on was a bit of a performance. There was a warmer person underneath, I bet.

She watched me looking around.

'Noise control,' she said, 'that's why I moved in here.'

'Noise control?'

'It's well insulated.'

'Oh.'

'Drowns out the screams.'

There was that wicked grin again.

'My other neighbours kept complaining, so I had to move out,' she continued, with a shrug.

I stifled a smile. I was always amused by occasions of the mundane colliding with the obscene. This world that I was now a part of seemed so darkly and effortlessly glamorous from the outside, yet perverts, like everyone else in the world, have to fit their extra-curricular activities in with the routine of the everyday, to pay rent, to explain away the presence of unusual household items to curious flatmates and landlords, to learn and practise their art in sometimes the most ordinary of places.

Lauralynn disappeared into the kitchen, and I heard the chinking of ice being tipped into a glass and the soft fizz of a bottle opening.

'Take a seat,' she said, handing me a drink in a heavy glass tumbler and gesturing to an expansive cream leather couch with a corner seat that ran nearly all the way round two walls of the living room. 'I'm just going to go and change into something more . . . appropriate.'

I nodded and took a sip. Mineral water. Perhaps she had noticed that the Prosecco had left me a little light-headed. Alcohol and the more physically demanding sexual perversions are not a wise combination, one of the reasons why I so easily trusted Dominik and his use of my body: I knew he didn't drink.

She turned to me again, just as she reached the base of the stairs.

'Oh, Summer?'

'Yes?'

'We have a friend coming over.'

She left me to stew on that for twenty minutes or so, time I spent straining to hear the doorbell ring and wondering what I would do if it did before she returned. I also took the opportunity to use the downstairs bathroom to freshen up.

Would she go down on me? I wondered, and gave myself a quick wash, just in case. Or expect me to go down on her? I was quite an experienced giver of fellatio, a task I particularly enjoyed, revelling in the power I felt when plumbing a man's depth, giving him so much pleasure that he seemed to forget everything else, a captive to my mouth, even if I was the one on my knees, but I had never applied my tongue to a woman before, and I wasn't quite sure how to go about it. I winced when I thought about how difficult it was for a lover to make me orgasm, an outcome that was only likely given a perfectly orchestrated rhythm of touch and mental suggestion, and even then by no means assured. Would I be able to make Lauralynn come? I wasn't even sure that trying to do so would be part of this scenario.

From the little that I understood, the relationship between submissives, or slaves, and their mistresses was not sexual, but rather a power exchange, a complex dance between service and worship on one side and a benevolent, theatrical sort of authority-wielding on the other. Like all of these scenes, it appeared that the dominatrix was in charge, but in fact she usually went to great lengths to understand the particular psychology of each client and give them exactly what they wanted.

It was not an easy job, by any means, though it probably was a job for Lauralynn, which would explain her upmarket apartment and why the rooms were so impersonally furnished and all the surfaces looked to be easy-clean.

I heard her heels tapping on the stairs again and hurried to finish my cleansing routine. Lauralynn was answering the door as I emerged from the bathroom.

She was now wearing a full-length latex catsuit, minus the head covering, and she looked magnificent in it. She had changed into another pair of boots, with even taller heels, skyscrapers so high that I was amazed she could walk in them without toppling over. Her hair had been straightened, and a light gloss applied so that it shone in the light, a heavy blonde curtain that swayed when she moved. She looked like something out of a superhero film.

A goddess indeed. I could understand, without any hesitation, why a man would want to worship Lauralynn. Even the heads of flowers would bow in deference to her as she walked by, I thought.

'Marcus,' she said, to the man at the door.

She had moved to the side a little, so that I could see.

He was of average height and build, with dark-brown hair, reasonably handsome but not striking. His outfit was personality-free, jeans of an ordinary cut and a short-sleeved white shirt with a collar, neatly pressed. He was completely interchangeable with any other man on the street, the sort of man who could never be identified with any certainty in a police line-up.

'Mistress,' he replied, in a tone of obvious reverence as he lowered his head to kiss her hand.

'Come in.'

She turned her back on him imperiously, and he followed her into the flat like a puppy would follow its master. She introduced us and he kissed my hand also. The action was totally foreign to me and I was embarrassed, immediately, by his show of subservience. I wanted to explain to him that I wasn't a domme, but the expression on Lauralynn's face forbade it. This was her scene and I would respect whatever part she wanted me to play in it.

Marcus and I mutely followed Lauralynn, stopping when she reached the foot of the stairs.

'On your knees,' she said to Marcus, who immediately dropped down behind me. 'And don't look up her skirt.'

So an order of sorts had been established, with Lauralynn in charge, me as a sort of accomplice, and Marcus as Lauralynn's submissive – slave or servant, I was not yet savvy enough to identify the difference, if there was one.

'Sit down, Summer,' she said to me, waving a hand at her king-size bed, adorned entirely in black, a dramatic departure from the white downstairs. Perhaps she didn't allow her men to orgasm here, I mused, or it would be difficult to keep the sheets clean.

I sat down.

'Wash her feet,' she instructed Marcus, who was still kneeling, with his body upright, awaiting Lauralynn's commands with the ready eagerness of a dog expecting a bone.

I bent down and began to remove my shoes.

'No,' she said to me. 'He'll do that.'

Marcus crawled over to her en suite, where she evidently

had a bowl and cloth waiting. I suspected that he had done this before.

He returned, still shuffling on his knees, with the bowl balanced carefully on one hand and the cloth draped over his arm, quite elegantly, like a waiter.

He picked up one of my feet, removed my shoe and began his ministrations, all the while carefully looking away from me, to the floor over his shoulder, deliberately avoiding any accidental view he otherwise might have up my skirt. His touch was gentle, practised, judging by his skill, particularly as he was completing his task blind; he could have been a beauty therapist, and perhaps he was, in his other life.

It was pleasant enough, but the whole act made me feel desperately uncomfortable. I tried to look satisfied, not wanting to give Marcus any indication that I was not pleased with his efforts, though perhaps he would have enjoyed that. Lauralynn watched me like a hawk as she paced the room, sleek as a panther in her catsuit, the latex so shiny I could see my reflection in it if she came close enough. She was holding a riding crop now, which she occasionally waved in front of us with a flourish, either as a threat or a promise.

Finally, he was finished. I breathed a sigh of relief.

'Thank you,' I said kindly to the man at my feet.

'Don't thank him,' Lauralynn interjected. She placed the riding crop under his chin, gently lifting his head. 'Get up.'

He did.

'Take off your clothes.'

He peeled off his shirt and jeans, meekly. He was a good-looking man, on the face of it. Everything added up. Features all in the right place, a reasonably lean body, but somehow there wasn't anything about him that I found attractive in the slightest.

Lauralynn took my breath away and set my pulse racing, but my feelings for Marcus floated somewhere between ambivalence and revulsion. He looked so vulnerable, standing there with his clothes off, at her command, more naked than naked, like a lion that had just been shorn by hunters.

Was that what people saw when they witnessed me being dominated? I wondered. Perhaps they did. Maybe it depended on the particular idiosyncrasies of the onlooker. It appeared that my peculiar sexual make-up did not include an attraction to submissive men. Which I guessed, considering my relationship history, should not have come as a surprise. Other people too must have their own specific quirks and triggers.

'Get on the bed,' barked Lauralynn. She was circling him now, like a cat circles its prey.

Marcus rushed to comply.

She leaned over him and tied a blindfold round his head, checking the tightness with a gentle caress as you would reassure a pet about to be punished.

'Now you will wait for us to return.'

She left him on the bed and beckoned for me to follow her into the bathroom. She shut the door and then crouched down, opened the cabinet under the sink and produced two large, black dildos from sealed zip-lock bags, each attached to a waist harness. Strap-ons. Another item that I had seen in sex shops and porno films, but never in the flesh. Of course I'd seen girl-on-girl action at the sex parties I had been to, but the penetrative fucking, now that I thought of it, had been entirely heterosexual. A bit of a shame really – I'd like to see two women, or two men, joined together like that.

Lauralynn handed one to me and then the penny dropped.

'Put this on,' she said.

'Oh, God, I can't fuck him!'

'You might be surprised by what you can do. And he loves it. You're doing the guy a favour, trust me.'

She took another look at my face and then her expression softened.

'All right,' she said, 'I'll let you pick an end. Which do you want, front or back?'

'I'll take front, please,' I replied, certain that I would rather not take either, but accepting the harness that she offered me anyway. It was surprisingly heavy and didn't look comfortable. This was going to be hard work. 'Shall I take my clothes off?'

'No. He's not allowed to see a woman naked. Keep your clothes on, just in case the blindfold slips.'

What was the point, I wondered, in that? I supposed it made Lauralynn seem even more untouchable, if he was never able to catch a glimpse of her vulnerable self, her naked flesh.

Now buckled in, we returned to the bedroom, where Marcus was waiting on all fours, patiently offering himself up to us, for our use. I swallowed. I wasn't sure I could go through with it, but I had come this far and didn't want to make Lauralynn look a fool by backing out now.

She looked great, buckled up in her dildo. She wore it with the air of someone who actually had a cock. In a sense, I guess she did. I wished I was Marcus, suddenly. I wanted to be on all fours, prostrate before her, feeling her big, black cock invading the walls of my cunt. It would stay hard for ever too, I thought, with a pang of envy, and then of anger. He had taken my place, and I didn't like it.

I wasn't able to catch a glimpse of my reflection, but I felt awkward and unseemly, foolish, with the harness strapped over my clothes. It was too bulky, and the waist strap too large for me, so it bounced absurdly when I walked.

Lauralynn was already behind him. She had turned his arse to face her, and I watched as she pulled a surgical glove onto one hand, then covered her middle and index fingers with lube. At the sound of the glove snapping lightly round her wrist, Marcus moaned with anticipated pleasure and lifted his arse in readiness, like a dog on heat, waiting to be mounted.

She inserted one, then two fingers into his anus, with obvious relish.

'What do you say, ungrateful slave,' she cried.

'Oh, thank you, mistress, thank you!'

He began moving back and forward, back and forward against her fingers, his balls slapping hard against the palm of her hand.

She gestured to me to climb up in front of his face.

'Open your mouth and suck the lady's cock, slave.'

I moved forward a little, so he could reach me, and watched as he began to greedily lap at the head of my cock. I began to thrust.

'Are you ready for my dick yet?' said Lauralynn, pulling her fingers out of his anus and carefully removing the glove, putting it to one side with a tissue. I noticed that she had laid a small towel beneath him, directly in the path of his now fully erect penis. So that was how she kept the sheets clean.

Marcus let out a low moan, a guttural marriage of pain

and pleasure escaping from his lips as Lauralynn entered his arsehole, spearing his most obscene opening with her rod, pumping back and forth like a piston.

She caught my eyes, held my stare.

'Fuck him,' she said.

I was both aroused and enraged. I wanted Lauralynn to fuck me, not this pitiful, moaning man on her bed. I should have been the one with my legs spread in front of her, not him.

I grabbed onto his blindfold and pushed him onto my shaft, choked him with the head of my cock. 'That's how it feels!' I wanted to yell. 'Do you like that, huh, you weak shit of a man?'

I could hear him beginning to gag and released my hold on his head, but he did not release his hold on my cock, continuing to drive the dildo as far as he could into his throat.

Lauralynn, at the other end, reached forward and grabbed my shoulders, ramming into his arse as she did so with one almighty final push.

He ripped his mouth off my cock and came with a scream, spurts of white semen shooting out from his head and onto the towel, narrowly missing my skirt. Lauralynn delicately released herself from the tight grip of his sphincter and watched as he collapsed on the bed in a heap. She leaned down and removed the blindfold, giving his head an affectionate stroke.

'Good boy,' she said. 'Did you like that?'

'Oh, yes, mistress.'

'Mistresses,' she said firmly, emphasising the plural.

I frowned, then followed her into the bathroom, leaving Marcus to recover.

'So, Summer Zahova,' she said to me with a smirk as she unbuckled her harness, 'not so submissive after all, eh?'

Two hours later, I was home again, curled up on my bed and staring out of my window at the decidedly unpanoramic vista of the brick-walled building next door, as if I could glean some wisdom from the ever-present certainty of brick and mortar.

The Kiwi recruiter whom Lauralynn had recommended had left a message on my voicemail to discuss arranging an audition for the position in New York. I hadn't actually applied. Lauralynn must have forwarded my details to her anyway, right after I'd left.

I had wanted to visit New York for as long as I could remember, and I'd dreamed of getting a big break like this for years, but I was only just beginning to feel at home in London, creating a life that I fitted into at last, albeit still a confused one, what with Dominik and now Lauralynn.

I didn't know who I was any more, or who I wanted to be. The only thing I was certain of was my violin, my beautiful Bailly, and even that didn't seem entirely mine. I'd never be able to hold it without thinking of Dominik.

My violin case stood in the corner, its presence now not just a joy but an accusation.

I felt terribly guilty about my adventure with Lauralynn. The only thing Dominik had asked of me was that I be honest with him, and I hadn't, or at least, I consciously planned not to be. How would I ever tell him about my experience with Lauralynn's slave and the strap-on? It was such a departure from everything he knew of me. He would think that he hadn't known me at all.

My shift was due to start in a couple of hours, and I

couldn't afford to be distracted. I knew I hadn't been my usual cheerful and bright self for the past few weeks, caught up as I had been with all the happenings in my personal life. I had been given an informal warning a few weeks ago, the day after the last recital at Dominik's, and the event had left me feeling so mixed up that I had dropped and shattered a couple of glasses and evidently given someone the wrong change, as at closing time, the till was down twenty pounds and it had been me, mainly, working the register that day.

To brighten my mood, I pulled on my trainers and workout gear, and went for a jog, running from my house down to Tower Bridge and then along the Thames path, cutting over the Millennium Bridge to complete the circuit on the other side. Today I was listening to something American, to help me make my decision, the latest album by the Black Keys. They were one of Chris's favourite bands. Chris and I had met in the front row of their concert at the Hackney Empire, during my first week in London.

I called Chris when I got in from my run, just to hear the sound of his voice, but he didn't answer. I hadn't seen him since Charlotte's party, and the deeper I got into the fetish world, the more I worried that I'd never be able to bridge the gap, to marry the two sides of my life together, and manage to keep our friendship alive without having to hide from him the parts of my life I thought he would disapprove of.

The run had helped soothe my mind a little, but I was still a touch frazzled when I arrived at work. I tried to switch off, to cut everything out of my focus besides the steady hum of the coffee machine, the clack, clack as I flicked the attachment that held the coffee grinds into place, then the soft whine of the milk frothing in the milk jug.

It didn't take long for my peculiar power of self-hypnosis to kick in, so I was completely consumed by a long queue of tickets for flat whites and lattes, when the group of men came in and sat down without waiting to be seated. Bankers or sales consultants, I guessed, when I finally did notice them, by their sharp suits and air of arrogance.

'Summer, can you give us a hand, please?'

I broke out of my dreaming, realising that one of the other waiters was still on his break and my boss was stuck taking a bill payment from another table. He gestured over at the table of newcomers and I put the coffee orders on hold for a moment, just to take them their menus. A couple of them were already boozed, I noted, alerted to the fact by their loud guffaws and sweaty faces. A bucket of champagne in the office, maybe, to kick off the celebration for winning a big deal.

The apparent leader of the group grabbed my wrist as I turned to leave the table.

'Hey, darling, it's our friend here's birthday,' he said, gesturing at a sober and embarrassed-looking man across the table. 'Maybe you could get us a little special somethin', if you know what I mean?'

I discreetly pulled my arm out of his grasp and gave him my sweetest smile. 'Sure,' I said. 'Your waiter will be along in a few minutes to tell you all about our specials.'

I began to back away. My coffee orders were no doubt piling up, and most people were pretty impatient about getting their caffeine hit, especially if it was to take away.

'Oh, no,' he replied, 'why don't you stay and tell us about the specials, darling?'

The birthday boy noticed my embarrassment and tried to intercept.

'She's not on our table,' he hissed to his drunk friend. 'Give the poor girl a break.'

The sound of his voice set off a dim echo of memory, struggling to surface in the recesses of my mind.

Then it hit me. Birthday Boy was the anonymous person who had flogged me at the fetish club in East London that I had visited alone, after the first time I'd played naked for Dominik. I'd recognise that voice anywhere, the sound had been immortalised in my mind for ever along with the rest of the experience, which at that time had still been so new to me.

A look of recognition passed across his face at the same moment that I felt it pass over mine and we exchanged glances, holding our gaze for a moment too long, alerting his companion to the fact that we were not strangers.

'Hang on a minute. Do you two know each other?'

He had really raised his voice now, and the other diners had quietened in response to the scene unfolding in front of them, though thcy were politely trying not to stare.

The colour of Birthday Boy's face turned a deep, vivid red and the other man flinched, perhaps having just been kicked under the table.

'Rob, shut it.'

Rob did exactly the opposite, angered now by my apparent defiance.

'Oh, I got it!' he cried, slapping his meaty palm down onto the table so hard that his fork bounced into the air. 'You're the girl from that weirdo club we went to! Nice arse you got there, baby.'

He flailed his hand out to cop a feel and I ducked away

before he made contact, knocking his arm aside in the process. His heavy cufflink caught on the cloth covering the next table and he jerked back, pulling the cloth with him, so that the bottle of wine that had been resting precariously on top tipped over, tumbling directly into the lap of the woman sitting adjacent.

It was red wine and, judging by the elegant outfit of the diner now covered in it, pricey. She leaped out of her chair in shock, and I took this new distraction as an opportunity to disappear, escorting her into the bathroom so that she could dab at her clothes.

I hid in the bathroom for as long as I could, and the woman was very nice about it.

'Wasn't your fault,' she said, glumly soaping up her shirt. 'I know that guy through work. He's a total cunt.'

Not so refined after all, then, I thought, giving the woman another look over.

My boss had been headed for the table just as I rushed for the bathroom, and I knew that he would have the situation under control, but likely in line with the ethos that 'The customer is always right'. At the very least, he'd surely have credited the wine from the bill of the woman with her clothes ruined, and probably the meals too, easily in the region of a couple of hundred pounds.

I wasn't sure I'd be able to talk my way out of this one.

I headed out to face the music just as the men were leaving, Rob looking very pleased with himself, and my manager gritting his teeth in an expression of politeness masking a mood like thunder.

'Summer,' said my boss, after they'd gone, 'come here.' He gestured to the office staffroom.

'Look,' he continued, once we were inside, 'what you do

in your private life is your business, and I know that guy was an arsehole . . .' I opened my mouth to speak but he held up his hand to stop me '. . . but when your private life becomes public, in my restaurant, then that is my business. I just can't have you working here any more, Summer.'

'But it wasn't my fault! He tried to grab me. What did you expect me to do?'

'Well, maybe if you were a little more . . . discreet . . . this wouldn't have happened.'

'What do you mean, discreet?'

'Like I said, Summer, what you get up to outside of work is your affair, not mine, but be careful, won't you? You're going to get yourself into trouble.'

'Losing my job isn't trouble?'

'I'm sorry, really.'

I picked up my bag and walked straight out through the door.

Dammit! That fucking bastard and his fat, clumsy hands. Now I was screwed. I'd already had one extension on the rent, and I knew that I was getting the bedsit at a knock-down price anyway. I didn't want to give the landlord any more reason to replace me. Another late payment might be the final straw.

Shit.

I couldn't call Chris, as then I'd have to tell him what had happened, and I didn't want to give him any more reason to disapprove of my lifestyle. I could call my parents in New Zealand, but I didn't want them to worry; besides, I'd already told them how well I was doing here, so they wouldn't nag me to come home again. Charlotte might help, I supposed, but I was too proud to ask her for money, and I had a sense that she might somehow use the fact of my troubled finances against me. There was the job in New York, with a guaranteed salary, but I'd have to ace the audition first, and I knew the competition would be fierce.

That only left Dominik.

I wasn't going to ask him for a loan – never – but I desperately wanted to see him. His voice would soothe my worries, help me think my way out of this. My every sinew was taut, my muscles tensed to breaking point, my mind racing with anxiety. Nothing could relieve me of this pressure better than Dominik taking over my mind and my body, fucking me with that absurd combination of fury and gentleness that made me feel so relaxed and alive.

I didn't know if I could face him, though, with the episode with Lauralynn so fresh in my mind.

I'd have to come clean, talk to him. There was nothing else for it. The thought made me sick to my stomach, but it was either that or stew over it for ever, and I couldn't have guilt stand in the way of my violin and me. If the music stopped flowing, I would simply cease to exist.

I made the short journey home from my now former workplace, had a quick shower and grabbed some clothes, something suitable for campus and something that would make Dominik feel like I was his. I put on the same outfit that I had worn for him last time, jeans and a T-shirt, a pair of ballet pumps and my lighter daytime lipstick. I hoped it would remind him of our last time together, when I had given myself to him entirely.

I fired up my laptop to Google universities in North London and found a literature course at one, with Dominik listed as the professor. I figured there'd be a list of classes somewhere on the noticeboard in the arts faculty, as there had been at the College of Music. I would find him.

It took me a while to locate the right place, but eventually I did, just as his lecture was beginning.

It was a popular course, full of women, many of them very attractive, their eyes fairly glazing over with lust as Dominik cleared his throat and began to speak. I felt a keen pang of jealousy stab me and took a seat at the front, directly in his line of vision. I wanted to stand and shout, 'He's mine!' but I didn't, and I knew that he didn't belong to me any more than I belonged to him, or any more than anyone ever truly owns another person.

It took a few moments for him to notice me, sidetracked as he was by the task at hand, giving the lecture. When he saw me, his eyes flashed for a moment – was it anger? Lust? – and then his features relaxed and he carried on as if I didn't exist. I hadn't read the book that he was discussing, but nonetheless I followed the rhythm of his words, the musicality of his language. He was like a conductor, starting softly, working up to a crescendo, then falling gently down again. No wonder his classes were popular. He glanced back at me every now and again, and when he did, I made no movement in response, sitting mute, but hoping that he would remember the last time I had dressed this way, worn this lipstick, and he'd chosen a darker colour and painted it onto my nipples and cunt lips, marked me, made me his.

The class finished and the students began to file out. I held my breath. I couldn't hang around all day if he simply chose to ignore me.

'Summer,' he said to me softly, over the clatter of bags and books.

I stood up and took the stairs down to the front of the theatre, where he was packing up his notes behind the lectern.

He straightened his back and looked at me balefully. 'Why did you come here?'

'I needed to see you.'

His expression softened a little, perhaps observing my distress. 'Why?' he asked.

I sat down on the last step, so he was standing above me, and told him everything, Lauralynn, the slave and the way I had worn an artificial cock and thrust it savagely into his mouth and enjoyed it, but how, despite all these things, I wanted Dominik to own me. I wanted to be his.

I told him everything, except the job prospect in New York, and my current status of unemployment. Even sat there in the heart of his world, at his feet, I was too proud for that.

'You shouldn't have come here, Summer,' he said.

He picked up his bag and walked out through the door.

His message came later, after I had arrived home again. I was lying on my bed hugging the violin case, hoping beyond hope that whatever happened between Dominik and me, he would let me keep the Bailly. I felt sweeping shame, again, that I could take anything from this man.

Then my phone beeped. An apology.

'I'm sorry. I was caught off guard. Forgive me.'

'OK,' I replied.

'Will you perform for me again?'

'Yes.'

The specifics of time, date and address came in another

message. Tomorrow, at another, new location, not his home.

This time, he asked me to provide an audience. Select it. A test of my resilience?

I would be playing for him again, I figured, and as a way to repeat the format of our last, successful dates, if you could call our meetings that. He was trying to rewind time, putting us back on the track that we had been headed down.

I thought about who I could invite. Not Lauralynn. That would be adding insult to injury.

There was really only Charlotte, as hesitant as I was to include her in this more sensitive occasion. She had a way of taking over and wasn't empathetic enough to notice if relations were strained between Dominik and me, but she was my only option. I had met other people on the scene, but in the normal way of these sorts of parties, we'd not really drifted beyond the short space of pleasure to anything more meaningful that might be called a friendship.

'Ooh, fabulous,' said Charlotte. 'Can I bring a friend?'

'I guess so,' I replied. He had said to bring an audience, and it would be awkward if I just turned up with Charlotte. On her own, she would definitely get in the way.

All I really wanted to do was fuck Dominik, but I wanted to prove to him that we could make this strange partnership of ours work, and he had asked for an audience, so an audience he would have.

I wore my long velvet dress again, the one I had worn that day on the bandstand, and I took the Bailly along. He hadn't specifically told me to, I thought with a frown, but he had asked me to perform for him, so I must be playing. Besides, my arms felt empty without the violin.

The address was in North London, another anonymous location, but this time, a large living room-type area with a kitchen and shower, fairly swanky, though blandly decorated with a couple of leather couches at either side, some rugs on the floors and a glass table in the middle. There was a king-size bed in the far corner.

Nearly every available space was filled, as Charlotte had turned up with about fifteen people, including the gorgeous escort, Jasper. Did he charge by the hour?

And Chris.

Oh, God, what had she done?

Dominik looked happy enough, though, I noticed, with relief. He came straight over and kissed me warmly on the lips, giving my shoulders an affectionate squeeze.

'Summer,' he said softly, looking as relieved as I was. Maybe he had thought I might not show up.

Chris and Charlotte were deep in conversation across the room, with Jasper. They were chatting in a tight conclave and none of them had seen me. Good. That would give me a chance to talk to Dominik.

Just before I had a chance to open my mouth, to suggest that we find somewhere quiet, just the two of us, even for a short time, Charlotte bounced over and threw her arms around me.

'Summer!' she cried. 'Now we can get the party started.'

Chris threw his arms around my other side and gave me an affectionate kiss on the cheek.

I was surrounded. A look of frustration crossed Dominik's face, but was quickly replaced by his usual composure. He disappeared into the kitchen, Charlotte trailing after him, her expression more mischievous than usual. What was she up to? I looked around the room, at all the couples in attendance, most of them scantily clad but no one actually having sex yet, despite the lusty vibe that filled the room. This didn't seem like Dominik's style at all. I wondered how much of this was his doing and how much was Charlotte's. Mainly the latter, I suspected.

No matter – soon I would begin to play and then forget them all.

Chris seemed pleased to see me and was trying to engage me in conversation, but all I could think about was Charlotte and Dominik in the kitchen. They were having some kind of strange conversation, and what did they have to talk about, other than me? Dominik's face was impossible to read at the best of times, but I could tell by the hard set of his mouth that he wasn't happy about something, and Charlotte was going on and on about whatever it was.

'Earth to Summer . . . Shall we warm up?' Chris was shaking me by the shoulder.

'Oh, sure,' I replied, picking up my case and moving over to a space at the far end of the room, where he had laid his viola, and which I guessed would be our makeshift stage.

Then Dominik called my name.

'Summer, come here.'

I set my case down next to Chris's and walked over to Dominik.

'You won't be playing tonight. Not like that, at least.'

He leaned down and kissed me full on the lips. I caught Charlotte's gaze out of the corner of my eye, just as Dominik pulled away. She looked smug. Whatever argument they'd been having, she'd won. Dominik was hot, and flustered. I could feel the heat rising from his body. I wouldn't have been surprised to see him fill the air with steam.

Somewhere in the room, the snap of a cigarette lighter.

I flinched.

Charlotte had produced a bag with some sort of rope and various attachments inside. She'd told me that she'd been reading up about it, I recalled. I hoped she'd actually enrolled in some proper courses and wasn't just stringing up anyone who would let her.

She pushed the glass table over a foot or two and then climbed up on top of it, giving the entire room a vision of her long, tanned legs and arse, clad in a full-length white dress, which I realised was completely see-through in the light. She wasn't wearing any underwear, but then again, neither was I, and I had to give it to Charlotte, she had great legs.

Dominik squeezed my hand reassuringly. I was not reassured. Charlotte was down on the floor again, pushing the table out of the way. She had attached a long length of rope to a metal ring in the ceiling.

'Will you do this for me?' said Dominik.

Well, I still didn't know what he wanted me to do, but whatever it was, I would do it. I didn't trust Charlotte when she was like this, but I trusted Dominik, even if he was acting weird.

Charlotte took me by the shoulders and pulled me along until I was standing under the ropes.

'Put your hands up, and don't worry – you're going to love it.'

She was going to suspend me, I supposed.

'Take her dress off first,' called a voice, playfully, from one of the sofas.

Charlotte complied, slipping off the thin shoulder straps and sliding down the zip at the back before I had the chance to put my arms into the air. It fell straight to the floor. I was naked for an audience again, though fairly well used to the feeling now.

Chris was thankfully nowhere to be seen. Perhaps he'd got fed up of waiting or had been freaked out by the crowd, who were getting lustier by the minute, and left.

I lifted up my arms and felt the rope brush across my wrists, wrapping both between and round them, creating an intricate pair of handcuffs. She slipped a finger between my wrist and the rope, checking the pressure wasn't too great. Perhaps she had a heart after all.

'That's OK?' she asked. 'Not too tight?'

'Feels fine,' I replied. My feet were still firmly on the ground, and though I couldn't wiggle free, she'd left my arms a little slack so the position shouldn't get uncomfortable too quickly.

'She's all yours,' Charlotte said to Dominik, conspiratorially.

I heard water running in another room, then the sound of a door open and close.

Chris.

He'd just been in the bathroom.

Fuck.

'Hey,' he said to Dominik, 'what the *fuck* are you doing?' His voice was filled with anger.

He didn't ask me what I was doing, just what Dominik was doing. Couldn't he see that I wasn't struggling, that I had made a choice to do this, that I was acting out of my own free will, not just according to the whim of whatever man I happened to be with?

I was angry with him suddenly for not understanding me, for wanting me to fit in with his expectations.

'Oh, just fuck off, would you, Chris! I'm fine! We're all fine. You just don't understand.'

'Summer, would you look at yourself! You've turned into a fucking *freak*! You're lucky I'm just going to let the lot of you get on with your sick little games and not call the police.'

He picked up his viola and his jacket, and stormed out through the door, slamming it shut behind him.

'Wow,' said the voice from the sofa that had spoken earlier, 'and that's why you shouldn't invite vanillas to perv parties.'

A few people laughed, settling the tension.

Fuck him. It was my body and I'd do whatever I damn well pleased with it, and that included whatever Dominik wanted to do with it.

Dominik stroked my hair, kissed me again, softly, and fondled my breast.

'You sure you're OK?' he said.

'Yes, I'm good, better than OK.'

I just wanted him to get on with it now, to fuck me and set me free, to stop my arms from aching and let me play my Bailly.

Then Dominik produced a razor.

10

A Man and His Darkness

The heat was rising.

In the smoke-filled room. In their minds.

Chris had departed, but his words still rang in Summer's ears. Part of her felt the sting of his accusations, while another, more impish and irresponsible part of her was angry at him for having the cheek even to attempt to criticise her and believe he understood the contradictory nature of her impulses.

Summer sighed, shifting her feet to redistribute her weight. She looked up and watched Dominik on the other side of the room as, standing in a corner in deep conversation with Charlotte, his hands wandered freely over her friend's now mostly unclad body. Next to them was Jasper, fully nude and sporting a spectacular erection, lazily stroking himself with one hand while his other actively busied itself in the darkness of Charlotte's crotch. The combined caresses of the two men she was almost sandwiched between did not appear to faze Charlotte and she appeared in full control of the bizarre situation. Dominik, still clothed from top to bottom in black, had shed his jacket, his sole concession to the situation, the smooth wool of his cashmere crew-neck top no doubt rubbing smoothly against Charlotte's breasts as she squeezed against him.

In the dim light Summer could see, and hear, the palette

of other couples scattered across the floor, on the other angled sofa on the far side of the room and even on the large rectangular table, now cleared of food and glasses. They were involved in some form of sexual activity – moans, whispers, embraces. The fingers of someone tiptoeing past her brushed her hair, but she did not turn round, and whoever it might have been did not linger and moved on to another tangle of limbs. Her eyes were fixed on the trio made up of Dominik, Charlotte and Jasper. What could they be talking about? Her?

Summer's mind was racing.

What had begun as yet another stage in the game she had willingly been playing with Dominik was now in freefall.

At brief intervals, all three of the constituent members of the conspiratorial trip would turn and take a look at her, and it appeared to Summer they were laughing, as if she had now become the abandoned rear part of the pantomime horse.

Recollections came flooding back: playing for Dominik alone on the bandstand on the heath, then naked with the blindfolded string quartet, then naked for him, solo, in the crypt, which had ended with them finally fucking, and the episode, still burning in her mind, when he had blindfolded her and she had performed for an unseen spectator (she now believed there had not been more than one other person present and her instinct told her it must have been a man) and was then summarily taken by Dominik in full view of the still unknown stranger. Which had led to tonight.

What had she been hoping for, expecting? Some form

of cruel progression in the ritual of their uncommon relationship? There was no doubt she had missed him while he was away at his Italian conference. His quiet assurance, his soft but peremptory orders. Her body had told her so, and she had compensated for it with her own adventures on the fetish scene.

She had wanted tonight to be special, not just some new variation, some twisted theatrical event.

Summer shivered, still feeling the earlier sharp path of the razor blade across her cunt, looked down and again saw the bare smoothness of her genitals. She shuddered; there was something so shocking about the sight of such extreme nudity. Would she ever get used to it, not be self-conscious about the fact that she had been shaved in front of others, unveiled in the most humiliating of ways? She had vaguely hoped that after being displayed in this way, Dominik would then free her hands and at least allow her to play her precious new Bailly for his invited audience, but somehow Charlotte had taken over the reins of the evening and Summer was left here, not quite hanging, but naked and useless, merely a spectator as the tides of lust she had involuntarily given birth to flowed effortlessly among the small crowd and desires were unleashed. Inside Summer's head was a small voice screaming, 'Dominik, fuck me, take me, in front of everyone, now, right now,' but the words just couldn't get past the ramparts of her closed, parched lips. Because, despite everything she'd done with him, she felt it would be to demeaning to say so. Deep within was a feeling that she must not be the one to ask, beg, that the command must come from Dominik. Not her.

She saw Charlotte lower her head to Dominik's lips and kiss him. Jasper crowded in closer, began nibbling on

Charlotte's ear lobe. The sound of an unseen couple making love on the carpet right behind her reverberated across the room.

Alerted by the soft sounds, Dominik broke from Charlotte's embrace and walked across to Summer and, without a word, untied her hands. She lowered her arms, grateful he had finally remembered her before cramp could set in. He kissed her forehead with all the delicacy in the world and then Charlotte was with them.

'You were beautiful, my dear,' her friend said, stroking her cheek. 'Just wonderful.'

Summer hoped Dominik would now devote himself to her, but Charlotte, trailed by the ever-erect Jasper in all his splendour, took Dominik by the hand as if to lead him away.

Standing there naked, normal circulation returning to her arms, Summer felt a pang of jealousy at the way her friend wouldn't let go of Dominik, wouldn't leave him alone. Didn't she know that in a curious way she couldn't quite explain that Dominik was hers? Summer's? Why couldn't she leave them alone? It was none of Charlotte's business after all.

Finally, Dominik said, 'I think I need another drink. Anyone else need a refill? Summer, some water maybe?' Summer nodded and Dominik left them to make his way to the kitchen, stepping across bodies in motion, slaloming between the various carnal activities in process.

As he disappeared, Charlotte whispered in Summer's ears, 'I do like your guy, sweet Summer. May I borrow him?'

Shocked by the request, Summer fell silent, anger bubbling beneath the surface. Had the circumstances been different, in a bar, at a normal party, anything but in this room full of couples fucking and fondling and rutting wildly as a result of her enforced exhibition and ceremonial shaving, she would have objected loudly, but the twisted nature of this environment of excess somehow forbade it. The curious etiquette of orgies, perhaps?

Inside, however, she was boiling. With anger. How could Charlotte? Wasn't she supposed to be her friend?

Summer was still seething when Dominik returned and gingerly made his way towards them holding a set of glasses.

He handed Summer her water, which she gulped down, past her dry lips. Charlotte, still shadowed by Jasper, put her hands in a proprietorial fashion round Dominik's waist.

'Isn't this fun, guys?' Charlotte said.

Which triggered Summer's moment of madness.

Or spite.

Handing the empty glass to Dominik, she swivelled round to face Jasper and deliberately lowered her left hand and brazenly took hold of his cock.

'Yes, it is,' she said, 'and all among friends, no?'

'So cosy,' Charlotte remarked, noting Summer's gesture, an amused smile painted on her face. Somewhere in the room, someone came with a soft sigh of abandon.

In Summer's hand Jasper's warm cock was incredibly hard. Firmer than any penis she'd ever had the opportunity to handle before, she thought. As she gripped it, she saw the shadow of a grin spread across his features and felt a rush of warmth and desire. Summer refused to look at Dominik to observe his reaction.

She slipped down onto her knees, took Jasper's long, thick and velvety cock into her mouth and felt its girth increase even further.

'Go, girl,' she heard Charlotte say, and felt Dominik's eyes drilling into her from above.

For a brief moment, Summer wondered how Dominik's cock might taste. She had not gone down on him yet and wondered why this hadn't come about. She focused her attentions back on the job at hand, her tongue and lips playing with the escort's cock, sucking, licking, nibbling delicately, according the rhythm of her attentions to the remote pulse driving down from his heart to the very edge of his stem, like a muted drum in some exotic jungle. Out of the corner of her eye she noticed Charlotte moving her hands to Dominik's belt, no doubt with a view to emulate her.

Summer felt a sharp pang of jealousy. She was determined to bring Jasper to climax. But the best of plans are so easily thwarted and just as Summer felt a faint tremor begin to course through Jasper's athletic body in a journey that was likely to end inside her mouth, the escort gently detached himself from her, leaving her mouth open in an O of interrogation and disappointment, pulled her up by the hand and delicately set her down on the nearby now-abandoned sofa. Unlike Dominik and Charlotte, who stood nearby in a semi-state of disarray, she in her corset and stockings, he with his trousers down but his undershorts still on, both Jasper and Summer were naked, their bodies mirror images of desire and pallor. Summer kneeled down, displaying herself to everyone. Summer heard the sound of a wrapper rustling and being expertly peeled over Jasper's jutting member, and then he spread her legs open and positioned himself behind her, his cock dancing teasingly at the gates of her barer-than-bare entrance.

Summer took a deep breath, looked behind Jasper and

saw the deep darkness of Dominik's eyes as he stared at the spectacle she and Jasper were providing, and then felt Jasper's thick cock breach her in a single forward thrust, stretching her unexpectedly wide and investing her with his manhood. Fuck, he was big. Summer exhaled, as if all the air had been forced out of her lungs by the sheer power and determination of Jasper's initial push. As he began his movements in and out of her, Summer switched off, allowing her body to float again in a sea of nothingness, surrendering herself to the moment, shedding all shreds of defence, mindless, open to whatever might now happen, purposefully defenceless, a willing toy on the waves of desire unbound.

She closed her eyes. Flesh as a super-conductor, thoughts like evanescent clouds, her grey cells relocating below for the duration, abdicating all willpower to the mighty fire of desire.

In a hidden compartment of her mind (or was it her soul?) Summer imagined she was now in Dominik's body, not to observe the way Charlotte was possibly giving him an expert blowjob but to witness how his eyes were hypnotically fixed on her being fucked by Jasper. Oh, how he must be watching as the escort's cock plumbed her depths, splashed against her, causing sweat to rise to the surface above her lips and her breath to become halting. Watch, Dominik, watch – this is how another man fucks me, and fucks me well, and wouldn't you want to be him, wouldn't you? Oh, how hard he is. Oh, how he owns me. Oh, how he makes me tremble, shiver, shudder. Oh, how he fucks me hard. And harder. On and on. Never stopping. Like a machine. Like a warrior.

She let out a hoarse cry of pleasure, and realised that it wasn't just the rigorous clockwork movements of Jasper inside her that she found so arousing, but the knowledge that Dominik was watching.

And then she came.

Screamed.

In a moment she finally felt Jasper come in turn, flooding her insides, the warmth of his hot seed inside the thin latex sheath he had slipped into, and a sudden mad thought tortured her mind, appearing out of nowhere – Am I mad? Am I sick? – as she wondered what Dominik's come would taste of had she sucked him to completion, or whether she ever would. Absurd thoughts have a habit of peering over the horizon of one's mind at the most inopportune moments, Summer realised.

She breathed heavily as Jasper withdrew from her, rising above her, his penis now limp but still imposing in both girth and length. She closed her eyes, felt a wave of regret mingle with her pleasure. She no longer wanted to know or see what Dominik and Charlotte were up to.

She was tired, very tired.

She swivelled her spent body, dug her face into the odorous leather of the sofa and began sobbing quietly.

In the room, all around her as Summer lay there as its centre of gravity, the orgy was coming to an end.

'I'm disappointed,' Dominik said.

'Isn't it what you wanted?' Summer asked. It was the following day and they were sitting in the cafe where they had first met, in St Katharine Docks. It was evening and straggling commuters fought the rush hour and cars roared across the nearby bridge. 'Didn't you want to see me fucked by another man and—'

'No.' Dominik interrupted the angry flow of her words. 'Absolutely not.'

'So what *did* you want?' she almost screamed at him, pain and confusion written on her face. Before he could reply, she continued, the devil inside her spurring her on a tide of wrath and hurt, 'I'm sure it turned you on, though, didn't it?'

He looked away briefly. 'Yes,' he admitted in a low voice, as if pleading guilty to a minor charge.

'See,' Summer said, with just a hint of triumphalism, her point made.

'I no longer know what I want,' Dominik said.

'I don't believe that,' Summer responded, her mind still journeying through a storm of anger.

'I thought we had an understanding.'

'Did you really?'

'For my sins, yes.'

'And a multitude of sins they must no doubt be. A veritable herd of them.'

'Why are you so aggressive?' he asked Summer, sensing their conversation was taking a wrong turn, a very bad one.

'So I'm the one who is guilty of taking a step too far, am I?'

'That's not what I was saying.'

'And who was it who was allowing himself to be groped by Charlotte as if I didn't even exist and happened to be standing there like a fool, as naked as the day I was born, shaved like a common slave?' she continued.

'I have never thought of you as a slave, whether past, present or future,' he remarked.

'But you have no problem treating me like one.' She

almost choked on the words. 'I am *not* a slave and I never will be.'

Dominik, in a forlorn attempt at regaining the initiative, interrupted Summer. 'I just thought that by demeaning yourself with that . . . gigolo, you were letting both of us down, that's all.'

Summer fell silent, tears of shame and anger pricking her eyes. She briefly felt like throwing the glass of water she was gripping over his face, then thought better of it.

'I never made you any promises,' she finally said to Dominik.

'I never asked for any.'

'It was an . . . urge. I just couldn't control myself,' she said by way of apology, but then turned against him again. 'You placed me in that situation and abandoned me. It was as if you'd triggered my demons and moved miles away, leaving me alone with . . . God knows what. I just don't know how to explain it, Dominik.'

'I know. It was partly my fault too. I can only apologise.'

'Apology accepted.'

She drank from the glass. The ice had long melted and the water was tepid. Silence fell again between them.

'So . . .' Dominik finally said.

'So.'

'Do you wish to continue?'

'Continue what?' Summer asked.

'Seeing me.'

'As what?'

'A lover, a friend, an accomplice in pleasure. You choose.'

Summer hesitated. 'I don't know,' she said. 'I just don't know.'

'I understand.' Dominik nodded with resignation. 'I really do.'

'It's so complicated,' Summer remarked.

'It is. On the one hand, I want you. Badly, Summer. Not just as a lover, or a plaything, as something more. On the other, I find it difficult to explain that attraction and the way it's become twisted so quickly.'

'Hmm,' Summer said. 'So not a marriage proposal, eh?' She grinned from ear to ear.

'No,' he confirmed. 'Maybe some form of arrangement?'

'I thought that's what we already had.'

'Maybe,' he said.

'And it visibly doesn't work, does it? So many unknown factors at play.'

They both sighed in unison, which made them smile. At least they could see the humour in the situation.

'Maybe we should stay apart for a while?'

It didn't matter which one of them actually said the words; it was on the tip of the other's tongue anyway.

'Do you want the violin back?' Summer asked.

'Of course not. It was always yours. Unconditionally.'

'Thank you. Truly. It is the most magnificent gift I have ever been given.'

'You deserve it a hundred times over. The music you created for me was unforgettable.'

'Both clothed and unclothed?'

'Yes, clothed and unclothed.'

'So?'

'So we wait; we think; we see what comes next and when, if ever.'

'No promises?'

'No promises.'

Dominik left a five-pound note on the table and with a heavy heart watched Summer walk out of the cafe and her silhouette gradually melt into the night.

He looked at his watch, the silver Tag Heuer he had bought himself years ago to celebrate getting his tenure.

He looked not at the time, which was at the imprecise, blurry junction between evening and night, but at the day. It had been forty days since he had seen Summer for the very first time, as she performed in Tottenham Court Road station with her old violin, a date to remember.

The appointment with the headhunter who was filling the vacancies for the orchestra in America went particularly well, and barely a week later, Summer landed at JFK airport, having unceremoniously given up her room in the Whitechapel bedsit and deliberately foregone her deposit. She had not said goodbye to Charlotte or her other acquaintances. Only Chris, whom she had briefly explained herself to as best she could, as she wanted his blessing.

She hadn't called Dominik, though the temptation to have the last word had been strong, among other reasons.

The agency had arranged for temporary accommodation in a shared apartment with other foreign members of the orchestra just off the Bowery. She had been warned they were all from the brass section, as if their instruments somehow determined their personality. The remark – or was it a warning? – had amused her.

It was Summer's first time in New York, and as the yellow cab approached the Midtown Tunnel, she caught her first glimpse of the Manhattan skyline, as impressive as in virtually every movie she had ever seen. It quite literally took her breath away.

This was certainly the way to begin a new life, Summer thought. Her slow early passage through the traffic jams of Queens and Jamaica following the departure from the airport had only offered suburban ordinariness, but now, through the dirty cab windows, her eyes fixed on the distant skyline of tall buildings and recognisable landmarks and she felt filled with joy and hope.

Her first week in the city provided her with little leisure time as she scrambled to fit in the necessary urgent rehearsals, set up the obligatory paperwork for her residence, acclimatise herself with the arcana of the Lower East Side's peculiar geography and catch her bearings in this strange and wonderful new city.

Her flatmates kept to themselves, which presented her with no problem. She had scarcely even been on first-name terms with those she had accumulated back in London.

The day quickly came around for her first public performance with the new orchestra, the Gramercy Symphonia, and its initial programme of fall concerts in a local hall that had recently been restored to its former glory. They played a Mahler symphony, which somehow didn't connect with her, and she found it difficult to impart much feeling into the music. Fortunately, she was just one of over half a dozen violin players in the string section and was technically adept enough to be able to hide among their ranked masses without drawing attention to her lack of empathy.

In a fortnight's time, they would be playing mostly from a more traditional classical repertory: Beethoven, some Brahms and a series of pieces by Russian romantics. Summer was looking forward to this, although not to the final concert of the season, which she saw had pencilled in some Penderecki, which was a bit of a nightmare for string players and in no way to her personal taste: strident, impersonal and, she felt, awfully pretentious. This was still some time ahead, though, and those rehearsals were not planned until later in the fall. She would try and enjoy herself before then.

The weather in New York was unusually balmy, although Summer seemed to make a habit of getting herself caught in seasonal showers on the rare occasions she strayed far beyond her Greenwich Village or SoHo patches. The way her thin cotton dresses, once drenched, would stick to her skin as she rushed towards some form of shelter or made her way home in the rain reminded her of late spring back in New Zealand. It was an odd feeling, definitely not one of nostalgia, as if that had been another life altogether.

She felt no need to go out and socialise, meet men, have sex. A holiday, that's what this was. Back in the solitude of her sparsely furnished room at night, she would listen to the sounds of the street outside, sirens blaring all through the night in between the blankets of silence, every sound the breath of this new city. Sometimes, through the thin wall that separated her room from one of the apartment's other bedrooms, which was occupied by a couple whom she thought were actually married, brass players hailing from Croatia, she would hear them making love. A mini recital of voices in a foreign tongue, of repressed whispers and the inevitable sound of straining bed springs and heavy breathing. Then the inevitable clarion cry of the flute player as she came in a loud deluge of Croatian swear words, or at least that's what it sounded like to Summer as she attentively listened to their scrambling movements and tried to imagine the spectacle of cock and cunt in love and war between the bedcovers and the ferocious hammerhead of the trumpet player's member as he fucked his wife. Summer had often seen him wandering around the apartment in his underwear, impervious to her presence. He was short and hairy, and his penis seemed to stretch his jockey shorts to the limits of the material. Somehow, she sort of guessed he was not circumcised and imagined the way the head would emerge from the untamed folds of his flesh when he unrolled to full length in arousal. All the time banishing from her mind the memories of other cocks she had known, cut or uncut.

Then she would masturbate, her delicate fingers splaying her cunt lips open and playing her usual clever tune there. Oh, yes, there were distinct advantages to being a musician . . . The music from her body swirled through the otherwise empty room of the shared apartment like a torrent and brought both pleasure and forgetfulness, driving away the lingering ache she felt when her mind turned to thoughts of Dominik.

Time was running short as the orchestra neared its first performance of the season, and Summer and her colleagues had had to spend most of the weekend in the bowels of a damp rehearsal space near Battery Park, going over their parts until she felt she would be sick if she had to pull another arpeggio out of her Bailly.

She'd cleaned her face under cold water in the ground-floor washroom of the rehearsal space and was one of the last to leave the building. The day's last echoes of the sun were fading over the Hudson river. All she desired right now was a bite to eat, maybe a takeaway sashimi plate from Toto on Thompson Street, and a good night's sleep.

Emerging onto the pavement, she was about to head north when a voice called out to her. 'Summer? Summer Zahova?'

She turned to see an attractive middle-aged man of medium height with salt-and-pepper hair and a short, carefully sculpted beard in the same shades of grey. He wore a seersucker jacket with thin blue stripes, black trousers and heavy dark shoes polished to within an inch of mirror shades.

No one she knew.

'Yes?'

'I'm sorry to bother you, but I was allowed by some acquaintances in the orchestra's management to watch and listen to your rehearsal. I was highly impressed.' His voice was rich and deep, with an unusual lilt to it. He was not American, but she couldn't place the accent.

'It's still early days,' Summer said. 'The conductor is putting us through our paces, aiming for more cohesion.'

'I know,' the older man said. 'It takes time. I have experience watching orchestras, but I thought you integrated well, even at this early stage.'

'How did you know I was a newcomer?'

'I was told.'

'By whom?'

'Let's just say we have friends in common,' he grinned.

'Oh,' Summer remarked, ready to continue on her way by now.

'It's such a beautiful violin,' the man said, his eyes fixed on the case she held in her right hand. She was wearing a short leather skirt that finished high above her knees, a tightly cinched belt with an oversize buckle, no hosiery and brown boots that stopped at mid-calf level. 'A Bailly, I would say.'

'It is,' Summer confirmed, a smile playing on her lips at last as she recognised a fellow aficionado.

'Anyway,' he said, 'I knew you were new in town and was wondering whether you might be willing to join me and some friends tomorrow night. I'm having a little party. Mostly musical friends, so you should feel at home. I know how big a city it is, and it's still early for you to have made many friends, no? Nothing fancy, just drinks in a bar and then maybe some of us will repair to the place I'm renting for some further conversation. You can bail out at any stage.'

'Where are you renting?' Summer enquired.

'A loft in Tribeca,' the man said. 'I only live in New York a few months a year, but I hold on to it. Normally I'm in London.'

'Can I think about it?' Summer said. 'I doubt tomorrow's rehearsals will end before at least seven. Where are you all meeting up?'

The man handed her his card. 'Victor Rittenberg, PhD,' it said. He must be Eastern European, she decided.

'Where from?' she asked.

'Ah, it's a complicated story. Maybe one day . . .'

'But originally?'

'The Ukraine,' he admitted.

Somehow this snippet of news was comforting.

'A set of my grandparents came from there,' Summer pointed out. 'They travelled to Australia and then to New Zealand. That's where my name comes from. I never knew them.'

'So that's one more thing we have in common,' Victor

said, a broadly enigmatic smile spreading across his bearded features.

'I suppose so,' Summer said.

'Do you know the Raccoon Lodge in Warren Street in Tribeca?'

'No.'

'That's where we are all meeting up. Tomorrow from seven-thirty. Will you remember it?'

'I'm sure I will,' Summer said.

'Great.' He turned on his heels with a small wave at her and walked down the street in a different direction to her way home.

Why not? Summer thought. She couldn't stay a hermit indefinitely, and she speculated as to who their common friend might be.

Victor's seduction of Summer was a gradual process in which his cunning was deployed to great purpose. Knowing what he already did of her from London, from what Dominik had said and described to him under casual interrogation, he had soon realised that Summer, whether she was aware of it or not, had the characteristic traits of a submissive woman. What a wonderful coincidence it had been that, at her lowest ebb, the job in New York that Lauralynn, his old accomplice in mischief, had pointed out to her had coincided with his own move to the Big Apple, something that had been arranged long before, when he had accepted the post at Hunter College, where he now lectured on post-Hegelian philosophy.

A libertine of old standing, Victor was also a fine connoisseur of submissives and knew the many ways to manipulate them and bring them round to him in the most devious fashion, exploiting their weaknesses and playing to their needs.

From the way Summer had fallen willingly into the arms of Dominik and what he had observed on the one occasion he had been allowed to see her in action and play, he now knew the right triggers to push, the nerves to reach for, the invisible strings that could be pulled. Exploiting her loneliness as a newcomer to New York, Victor took care to tease her natural submission into the open, one careful step at a time, giving her exhibitionistic streak a subtle nudge here, or indulging the foolhardy form of pride that led her into awkward situations of a sexual nature on a whim there.

Compared to him, she was an amateur, never realising she was being played.

Victor knew Summer's desires had been stirred and her sexual needs heightened by her experiences with Dominik. New York was a big city and could be a lonely one. Dominik was the other side of the ocean and Summer was here, unprotected, alone.

During their first evening together, at the party he held in his loft in Tribeca, Victor carefully revealed his interest in BDSM, guiding the conversation onto the subject of certain private clubs in Manhattan and the more distant wilderness of New Jersey. He saw Summer's reaction, the burning desire in her eyes, the inability to deny her sexual mores. The flame was lit, and she quickly gravitated towards it like a moth unable to control its dance towards the light.

Try as she might, she could not resist the call of her body, the complex web that Victor wound. Summer missed Dominik, his strange, sexy games and the way that she enjoyed playing along. Victor's voice was different, his tone firm and unyielding, without the softness of Dominik's lilt, but still, if she closed her eyes she could almost imagine that it was Dominik instructing her, bending her to his will.

It quickly became apparent to Summer that Victor knew more than he should about her, and she began to suspect Lauralynn had been his informer. She was no dupe, but she was willing to see where all this might lead. The call of twisted thoughts and the siren song of her body in a state of want could not be ignored much longer.

By their third meeting, in a dark bar on Lafayette Street, she found herself at ease with Victor's subtle grooming and was far from surprised when halfway through a normal, civilised conversation about the ugliness of more modern forms of classical music (although she personally had an indulgent appreciation of the works of Philip Glass, whom Victor couldn't stand), he suddenly turned to her and, out of the blue, asked, 'You've served before, I believe?'

She nodded in response. 'You're a dom, aren't you?'

Victor smiled.

The time for psychological games had come to an end.

'I think we understand each other, then, Summer, don't we?' Victor said, laying the palm of his hand over hers.

They did; the real world, that secret world she had been orbiting somewhat like a headless chicken, was summoning her again, beckoning in dulcet tones.

You know you're embarking on a path that is a dead end, but you do it anyway, because not doing so would leave you incomplete.

Summer's next meeting with Victor followed a long rehearsal session with the Symphonia, just two days prior to their first official performance of the new concert season.

She was feeling high on the way the music flowed and how the sound of her exquisite Bailly now embedded itself into the corpus of the orchestra. Her hard work was bearing fruit. With the adrenaline going, she felt ready to tackle any damn perversion Victor might conjure. She was actually looking forward to it.

It was at an improvised dungeon in the basement of an imposing redbrick building uptown, just a block off Lexington. She had been asked to report at 8 p.m. and had decided to wear the corset she had worn for the maiding experiment back in London what now seemed like an eternity ago. Wearing the outfit that Dominik had bought for her, she could imagine that it was a party she was attending at his request, it was his will she was following.

As she fitted herself into it in preparation, Summer marvelled again at the softness of the material. She drew her fingers across it and couldn't help briefly thinking of him. Why was she finding it so difficult to banish his memory?

However, the insistent thought was not given the opportunity to linger as her mobile phone vibrated. The limo Victor had sent for her was waiting outside. She slipped on her long, red leather trench coat. It was in no way appropriate for the warm weather, but it covered her up all the way to the ankles, concealing the shocking spectacle of her laced-up corset, her exposed breasts and the black stockings she had been asked to wear, which reached to mid-thigh and bared territories of pale milk skin all the way to her almost invisible thong. She'd noted with some irritation that her pubic hair was beginning to grow again in thin patches and she was a bit messy down there, but she didn't have the time to rectify the situation.

Victor was wearing an elegant dinner jacket, as did all his

male guests, while the accompanying women proved a visual cocktail of couture dresses in all shades of the pastel rainbow. Her trench coat was taken from her shoulders and Summer felt self-conscious at being the only bare-breasted presence in the large dining room, where the crowd was sipping drinks and smoking. A thick haze of cigarette and cigar smoke lingered in the air.

'Our final arrival,' Victor proclaimed. Pointing to her, he said, 'This is Summer. As of today, she will be joining our intimate little group. She comes highly recommended.'

Recommended by whom? Summer wondered.

She felt the gaze of the twenty or so strangers landing on her, exploring her, interrogating her. Her nipples hardened.

'Shall we?' Victor said with a flourish, indicating the door to the basement.

Summer followed the movement of his hand and walked unsteadily on her high heels towards the opening. She felt a little dizzy now, as the moment approached. This was her first scene since the London orgy that had ended so badly and torn Dominik and her apart.

A dozen steps brought her down into a large, well-lit basement or cellar, the walls of which were lined with exotic-looking carpets of Arabian provenance. She'd once known what they were called, but the word eluded her as she noted the presence of six other women standing in a circle at the centre of the improvised dungeon. Summer actually counted them.

Every single one of them was naked from the waist down. No underwear, or even stockings or shoes. Above, they wore an assortment of blouses or shirts or flimsy silk tops with varying degrees of transparency. They all had their hair pinned upwards in the form of a chignon, and their hair colour varied from almost platinum to jet black. She was the only redhead present. Two of the women wore thin velvet chokers round their necks, while the others were adorned by collars, some metallic, another more like a dog collar with a line of metal studs, and yet another a thin leather belt closed by a heavy metal lock.

Slaves?

The guests trooped into the dungeon and circled the walls.

'As you see, my dear –' Victor had silently moved to her side and was whispering in her ear – 'you are not alone.'

Summer was about to respond, but he quickly brought a finger to her lips in a demand for silence. It was no longer her role to speak.

His hand brushed against her flank, affectionately tugging at the tight elastic of her minuscule thong.

'Expose yourself,' he ordered.

Summer raised a leg and pulled the thin undergarment down and stepped out of it.

'The rest?' he continued.

She caught sight of the other women and how they were bottomless and understood his command. Aware that all eyes in the basement were on her, and attempting to keep her balance and not fall to the ground, Summer rolled down her stockings and kicked off her shoes, Victor offering her no support. The ground was cold under her feet. Stones.

Now she was as bottomless as the others, just her corset contricting her waist and her breasts uplifted by its delicate but firm engineering, on full display, at attention.

Looking at the other silent women standing in a circle on similar display, Summer realised how abominably obscene they all were. Nudity was natural, even in public, but this was something more, a travesty of sexual reality, a form of clever humiliation.

There was a nudge on her shoulder and she was guided towards the exposed women, who parted to fit her into their circumference. She noticed they were all shaven too. Terribly smooth, she reckoned, as if the depilation were permanent. Something they had committed to at some stage, determining their status as slaves, the loss of power. She felt conscious of her own untidiness there.

Just as this thought crossed her mind, Victor said, 'You should have been cleaner, Summer. Your cunt is messy. In future you must be totally bare. I will punish you later.'

Could he read her thoughts?

Summer's face reddened and she felt the heat run under the skin of her cheeks.

Someone struck a match and her heart seized, fearing for a moment that this was the beginning of some rite of pain, but it was just to light a cigarette.

'So, Summer, you join us,' Victor said, now circling her and threading fingers through the tangle of her hair, allowing his other hand to lie against her buttocks.

'Yes,' Summer whispered.

'Yes, sir!' he roared, and his hand landed with fierce strength on her right bum cheek.

Summer flinched. There was an intake of breath from the audience. One woman's smile as she observed the scene had all the ugliness of a fairy-tale evil queen. Summer spied another licking her lips. In anticipation?

'Yes, sir,' she said meekly, repressing her reluctance to fall into the role this easily.

'Good,' he said. 'You know the rules: you will serve us;

you will not ask questions; you will afford us respect. Is that understood?'

'Yes, sir.' She knew the routine by now.

His hand moved to her nipple and squeezed it hard. Summer held her breath to control the pain.

Victor was now standing behind her, his words drilling into her ear. 'You are a little slut.' When she did not respond, she felt the hard slap of his hand against her arse again.

'I am a little slut.'

'I am a little slut *what*?' Again the sting of his palm drew a lightning spasm of pain.

'I am a little slut, sir,' she said.

'Better.'

There was a moment's silence, and out of the corner of her eye Summer noticed one of the other slaves smirking. Were they laughing at her?

Victor continued, 'You like it that everyone can see your body, slut, don't you? You like to be seen, to be exposed?'

'Yes, sir, I do,' she answered.

'You'll do well, then.'

'Thank you, sir.'

'From this moment on, I own you,' Victor proclaimed.

Summer felt like protesting. On one hand, there was something terribly exciting about the idea, but on the other, a core of her personality rebelled.

For now, though, standing in this dungeon, with her tits and unevenly shaved cunt on full display, the wetness oozing from her centre unwittingly confirming how excited she was, it was only words.

Summer felt emboldened to face whatever the future held in store.

II

A Girl and Her Master

The first smack was so fierce I knew that the mark of his hand would remain on my rump for hours to come, delineated in pink like a child's version of an abstract painting.

I swallowed hard.

All eyes were on me, awaiting my reaction, hoping to see me flinch. I just gritted my teeth. I didn't want them to have the pleasure. Or not yet, at least.

There was a harshness in Victor's voice I had not perceived previously, as if his true nature was now rising to the surface. Then, making me shed what little garments I had on but retaining the corset, I finally reached a state of exposure that satisfied him. 'Sir' this, 'Sir' that, authoritarian, insistent. I obeyed his instruction, though it irked me to do so. The way I should address him. Dominik had never asked me to call him 'sir'. I had always found the term silly, felt it reduced a situation from risqué to ridiculous. I tried to retain my dignity despite the sheer tawdriness of the situation.

I stood there, motionless, one of a parade of slaves, all in line like ducks on a shooting range. The slim blonde with small breasts, the olive-skinned brunette with the low-slung centre of gravity, the mousy-haired woman with voluptuous curves and a prominent birthmark on her right thigh, the tall one, the small one, the round one. And me, the redhead with her constrictive corset, the one whose clothing drew even greater attention to her sexuality, nipples hard, cunt moist and expectant.

'Kneel,' a voice said. This time it wasn't Victor, who had retreated into the crowd of guests, where he blended seamlessly into the dark-costumed throng of men and women.

We all kneeled.

'Heads down.'

The women on either side of me did so, their chins almost scraping the stone floor. If this was total subservience, it didn't sit well with me. I lowered my head but still kept it at a minimal distance from the ground. I felt a foot against the small of my back, forcing me down and increasing the curve of my spine to bring my arse further upwards in offering.

'That ass looks succulent,' a woman said. 'She has such a small waist that it just dominates her landscape.'

The foot retreated. Dark polished shoes and five-inch heels began circulating round me and the other slaves as the guests navigated between us, judging us, evaluating our wares. From the corner of my eye I saw a suited knee touch the ground next to me; a hand appeared beneath me, weighing my hanging breasts. Another invisible participant slid a finger across my arse crack, dipped into my cunt and tested my wetness, then withdrew and probed the tightness of my anal opening. I clenched, trying to keep him out, but he inched his way in for a moment. I was surprised he had managed to breach me there, albeit briefly, with no form of artificial lubrication. Mind you, the position I was in, with my intimacy on full display, made it easier.

'Not been extensively used here,' he commented, then

slapped my arse playfully before moving on to another exposed body.

Suddenly, Victor's breath was in my ear. 'You like to be shown off, don't you, Summer?' he remarked with a note of amusement. 'It gives you a kick. I can see it from how wet you are already. You can't hide it. Have you no shame?'

It was clammy down there and a warm blush no doubt coloured my cheeks as he kept on examining me up close.

'Can she be used?' someone, a man, asked.

'Not totally,' Victor remarked. 'Her mouth only today. I have more interesting things for her in store.'

'That's good enough for me,' the other answered.

'She enjoys being displayed, used publically, this one,' Victor continued. There it was again, the soft shuffle as he dragged his foot along the floor, just a few inches from my nose. He had a very slight limp, which made his gait recognisable. I felt furious, but had no leisure to indulge in my anger. Victor's hand was under my chin, forcing me to raise my head. He placed me at eye level with the other guest's trousers, zip open, as the stranger pulled out his cock and presented it to my mouth. A faint smell of urine wafted in my direction and I almost gagged, but Victor's hand now gripped my shoulders, conveying his will. I parted my lips.

The stranger's cock was short and thick. He began his frantic thrusts, holding me by my hair so I had no alternative but to take him whole, in a parody of greed.

He came quickly, the jet of his come hitting the back of my throat. The man maintained his grip on my head and refused to withdraw until I had, reluctantly, swallowed and cleaned my mouth of his emission. Then he let go. His bitter flavour lingered and I longed to run to a bathroom to scrub his semen from my tongue. At that moment I would have gargled acid to get the taste out of my mouth.

I quickly glanced around me and noted that all the other hapless slaves were in use, alternately being face-fucked by the male guests or ridden doggy style like pieces of meat, aside from the one who reminded me of a suburban housewife. She was busy going down on one of the female guests whose scarlet silk dress had ridden up all the way to her waist and who emitted little birdlike cries every time the slave's tongue connected with her clit or wherever her pleasure points were.

I had no time to consider the situation further, as I was approached by Victor and ordered onto my back after he had laid a thick blanket over the stone floor. With my legs wide open, he advanced towards me, trousers down to his ankles, his respectably sized cock already sheathed. I noted that, unlike Dominik, he had chosen to wear a condom. Was it that he didn't trust me, my health, or just that Dominik had happened to be irresponsible?

He pushed himself into me with force and began to fuck me. I realised, suddenly, that though I had chosen to surrender my body to Victor's will, my mind was still my own, to do with what I wanted. I searched for that place in my head, the door that would take me away from all this mentally, if not physically. Soon, my surroundings faded, the men and women and the slaves shifting into some absent dimension, bodies and grunting sounds and all, and I abandoned my grip on reality and allowed the tides of arousal to sweep over me as I closed my eyes. He quickly satisfied his lust and took a couple of steps back.

I barely had time to blink before another man's penis was being presented to my still-recovering mouth. A different shade of pink and brown, a large head, another faint scent, this time of herbal-scented soap. I didn't look up to see the face it belonged to. Did it matter? I bridged the gap between it and my lips, and tongued its warmth in a semblance of appetite.

The rest of the evening went by in a blur.

Men as anonymous as they come. Women with a touch of cruelty in their commands and a sweet sickness rising from their assorted fragrances. I'd quickly disconnected from my thinking self; my mind and body were on automatic pilot.

The next time I opened my eyes properly and looked around, the earlier crowd had mostly dispersed, the late stragglers flushed or adjusting their clothes. Just us circle of slaves still at the centre of the room, soiled, tired, resigned.

Someone patted my head as one would a pet.

'Well done, Summer. You certainly show promise.'

It was Victor.

His comment surprised me. I knew I had been detached, faraway, mechanical, totally disengaged, just an actress on a set. A porno set at that.

'Come,' he said, his arm extended in my direction, his hand outstretched towards me to help me up from my unbecoming crouch. He had retrieved my trench coat from the hall where I'd had to leave it on arrival and helped me into it.

Outside the brownstone, the limo was waiting for us.

He dropped me off first. The drive downtown took place in silence.

*

You become a zombie out of sheer tiredness, mental and physical. Days completing the rehearsals, two performances on average a week, and whenever I was free, Victor would call on me.

Of course, I could have said no, I should have said no, informed him he was going too far and I was no longer a willing participant in the games he was orchestrating with such deliberate cunning, but I realised that part of me sought further episodes with a morbid sort of curiosity. As if I was testing my own limits. Every encounter was a bridge further down the river, a challenge that my body was drawn to.

I was losing control.

Without Dominik to anchor me, I was a sailboat with no engine now, drifting in the high, unexplored seas, at the mercy of wind and storms. On the prayer of a song, and not one I could play on my violin.

We had a guest conductor from Venezuela in town for a season of post-romantic works by Russian composers and he was driving us hard. Our initial sound was not to his liking. He wanted more verve and colour in our playing. The string section was affected the most. The predominantly male brass section appeared to be adept at switching their emphasis, but us string creatures found it more awkward, accustomed as we were to a more discreet angle of attack on the music. Many of us also had Eastern European roots and old habits die hard when it comes to adding a touch of added bravura to pieces we already knew so well.

That afternoon's rehearsal had been a ragged affair and Simón, the conductor, had been quite critical of our efforts. By the end of the double session, our nerves had been frayed.

As I walked up West Broadway on my way home, my phone buzzed. It was Chris. He was passing through Manhattan. The band had been booked on a short East Coast tour of minor rock clubs and he was on his way to Boston. It seemed he had attempted to ring me the day before to invite me to join the guest list for a gig on Bleecker Street, but I remembered that I had left my mobile phone uncharged or switched off for several days, absorbed as I was by the Venezuelan's rehearsals and Victor's demands.

'We missed you,' Chris said after we had exchanged warm greetings.

'I'm sure you didn't,' I replied. I'd never even played on all the songs when the band performed. A fiddle adds a particular sound to a rock band and if overused, provides too much of a country touch.

'We did,' Chris replied. 'You as both a person and a musician.'

'Ah, flattery will get you everywhere.'

He was only in the city for an evening. We agreed to meet as soon as I'd had the opportunity to shower and change following today's nervous exertions.

We both had a taste for Japanese food. Raw. Sometimes I judge people on their taste in food, and I seldom approve of those who profess to dislike raw fish or tartare-style dishes, or oysters. Culinary cowards, I felt.

The sushi bar was a small place on Thompson Street where you seldom found more than a handful of customers, as most of their business was takeaway. Consequently, the underemployed sushi chef was generous with the size of his portions.

'So how's the classical world?' Chris asked as we sipped our first sake of the night.

'Keeping me on my toes, that's for sure. The conductor we're working with right now is a bit of a tyrant. Very demanding and temperamental.'

'Haven't I always told you that us rock 'n' rollers are a much more civilised bunch than your classical old fogeys?'

'You have, you have, Chris.' Every time we spoke almost. The shared joke had long become something of a cliché, but I tried to raise a smile.

'You look tired, Summer.'

'I am.'

'Is everything all right?' he asked, with a look of concern.

'Just tiredness. Busy with the music. Not sleeping too well,' I confessed.

'Is that all?'

'Should there be? Do I have black bags under my eyes?'

Chris smiled. My old sparring partner, one I was unable to lie to.

'You know what I mean. So . . . have you been up to . . . mischief? I know you, Summer.'

I speared a slice of yellowtail tuna with my chopsticks.

Chris knew most of what had happened in London, with Dominik. Well, maybe not all the specific details: a girl has her pride. He was certainly aware that coming to New York at such short notice had been a way of escaping.

'Don't tell me he's followed you here? Surely not.' He dipped his California roll into the wasabi-infused cup of soya sauce.

'No,' I said, 'not him.' Then, overcoming my reluctance to reveal my true feelings, 'If only it was him.'

'What do you mean, Summer?'

'There is another man I've come across. Similar . . . but I think worse. It's not easy to explain.'

'What is about you that attracts the bastards, Summer? I never thought you were a sucker for punishment.'

I remained silent.

'Look, I know Darren was a bit of prick, but the guys you now appear to be strangely attracted to are a dangerous lot.'

'They are,' I confirmed.

'So why do you do it?' Once again he was on the way to losing his temper with me. Why did this happen every time we met up now?

'You know I'm not into drugs. Well, the common ones. Maybe this is a bit like a drug. I get a kick out of it. As if I'm putting my hand into the flames and seeing how far I can go, juggling the line between pain and pleasure. But you know, it's not all bad, Chris . . . though I know it must seem that way to you. Different strokes for different folks. Don't knock it until you've tried it.'

'Hmm . . . I'm not sure it's really for me. You're crazy, girl.'

'I sure am, Chris, but you know me, you have to take the good with the bad, no?'

'But are you happy?' he finally asked, as the Oriental waitress began to clear our plates and bowls, and set down the complimentary pineapple squares.

Again I declined to answer, but I fear the look in my eyes betrayed me.

We moved on to a nearby bar and shared a round of beers before we both parted on an uncertain note.

'Keep in touch,' Chris said. 'You know the number. Whenever you feel like it. Or if there is a problem. We return to England at the end of next week, but I'll always be there for you, Summer, believe it.'

It was night-time. Greenwich Village was alive with electricity, and music flooded the narrow streets with melodies unknown and a touch of cacophony. The sounds of the big city.

I needed to sleep badly.

The Prokofiev performance at one of Manhattan's more classy venues was a triumph. Everything had come together with perfection, justifying all the agony of the rehearsals and the frayed tempers on both sides of the rostrum. My own few solo measures in the second movement flowed like a dream come true, and I was even gifted by a wink of approval by Simón, the young maestro, as we all took our final bow.

My mood deflated soon after when I found Victor waiting for me at the stage door.

'What took you so long? The concert ended over an hour ago,' he remarked.

'We had a little celebration,' I said. 'It went surprisingly well. Not at all what we'd expected,' I pointed out.

Victor frowned.

He gestured for me to walk with him as we took Third Avenue, heading north. Maybe because I was wearing heels, Victor suddenly appeared to be smaller in height than I'd previously thought.

'Where are we going?' I asked him. I was still feeling a little giddy, a combination of the celebratory glasses of vermouth and the natural high the semi-perfect performance had triggered in me.

'Don't you worry,' Victor said brusquely.

What had he in mind? I was still wearing my black velvet performance dress and normal day-to-day underwear. Not even stockings, just tights, or hose, as they called it here. And a thin cardigan top I'd picked up the day before at Anna Taylor Loft. Dominik's corset, which Victor often insisted I wear for our scenes, was safely tucked away in a drawer by my bed.

Maybe it would just be a social occasion.

Knowing Victor, though, I doubted it.

'You have lipstick in your handbag?' Victor asked as we continued moving up Third.

'Yes.' I always did. Girls will be girls.

Then the fleeting memory of a more recent episode involving lipstick flashed through my mind. And I knew. It must have been Victor who had been my secret audience that evening in Dominik's loft, who had seen me adorned like the Whore of Babylon, as Dominik had described me.

The venue was a large chain hotel in the Gramercy Park area. Its top floor reached to the sky, with neon lights blazing above its canopy and a forest of small, square doll's house windows piercing the night. It looked to me like a daunting fortress. A fortress, or a dungeon? Oh dear, what a one-track mind I was developing.

The night porter doffed his hat at us as we made our way into the lobby and advanced towards the bank of elevators. We took the one on the left, which rose all the way to the penthouse. This was not accessible to the general public and required a key, which Victor pulled out of his pocket and slipped into the lock by the penthouse-floor button.

We rode up in strained silence.

The elevator doors opened directly onto a large, empty foyer with nothing more than a sizeable leather bench, where earlier arrivals had draped their coats and bags. I slipped off my knitted top and, reluctantly, set down my violin case. We stepped out of the foyer into an immense room bordered with bay windows through which you could see half of Manhattan and its dazzling horizon of night lights. Guests were milling around, glasses in hand. In a far corner of the circular room was a small elevated area, like a stage, and to its left a set of doors connecting, no doubt, with the rest of the suite.

I was about to step over to the small bar where a variety of bottles, glasses and ice decanters stood, but Victor warned me off.

'You mustn't drink tonight, Summer. I want you at your best,' he said.

I was about to protest – since when did he think I was some sort of lush? – but just then a stranger in a dinner suit that made him look more like a waiter than a man of the world approached us and heartily shook Victor's hand.

The guy brazenly looked me up and down, and, royally ignoring my presence, turned to Victor and commented, 'Very nice, my dear Victor. Very nice indeed. A particularly striking slave.'

My first instinct was to kick him in the shins, but I held back. Is this how Victor had presented me?

I was not and would never be a slave. I was me, Summer Zahova, and I was an individual with a mind of my own, a submissive, not a slave. I had no issue with the concept. I knew that other men and women desired to give themselves away completely like that, but it just wasn't me.

Victor smiled at the other man, evidently self-satisfied. The bastard. He patted my rear with awful condescension. 'Isn't she? Isn't she just?'

Both ignored me as if I wasn't there any longer, just a part of the furniture.

'She will fetch a good price,' one of them said, but my head was already on fire and I was unable to make out who had said this.

I felt Victor's hand grip my wrist. The mist cleared in my mind and I faced him.

'You will do as you are told, Summer. Do you understand? I know that inside you are conflicted about all of this, and I quite understand. However, I also know that you are at war with your own nature, and a moment will arise when you come to terms with it. The craving you have to be exposed, to be publically whored, it's part of you. It's the real you. It brings you to life, allows you to experience sensations you have never experienced before. The resistance you feel is just old-fashioned social mores, education. You were born to serve. And that's when you are at your most beautiful. All I want is to bring out that beauty, see you flower, see you assume your condition.'

What Victor said was profoundly disturbing, but there were kernels of truth I recognised. In moments of excess my body betrayed me. The drug of submission beckoned and it was as if the real Summer appeared, wanton, brazen, unashamed, a side of me that I enjoyed but feared, scared that it would one day lead me too far, that the pull of danger would be stronger than my need for safety. The animalistic side of me sought out this sexual oblivion, while the rational half questioned my motives. They often say that most men are guided by their cocks; in my case I was guided by the hunger in my cunt, but paradoxically that hunger also resided in my mind. It's not that I needed a man, or particular men, to own me, use me; it was this yearning for something else, for the zone of nirvana that I reached in those moments of senseless sex and even degradation or humiliation, and which made me feel more alive than at any other time. Perhaps I should have taken up rock-climbing.

I was aware of my contradictions, accepted them, but acceptance didn't make finding the right path any easier.

As my mind unfogged, there was a hush in the room, unspoken words indicating that the time had come.

Victor on one side and the tuxedoed stranger on the other, I was led to the small elevated stage at the other end of the room, where I was swiftly stripped naked. I remember thinking how inelegant I must look while they rolled down my unappealing tights, but it all happened so fast, too fast for me to protest.

The stranger, who was the master of ceremonies for this curious evening, waved his arms with a flourish and announced, 'This is Slave Summer, the property of Master Victor. I'm sure you will agree she is a splendid specimen. Pale skin –' he pointed at me – 'and a most exquisitely rounded ass.' He indicated for me to turn and display my rear to the onlookers. Deep breaths were drawn. I already had new admirers.

A tap on my shoulder indicated I should turn round again to face the small crowd. They were mostly men, I realised, but there were also women in fancy evening wear dotted here and there. All appeared normal; there were clearly no other slaves serving tonight.

The circus master's hand passed across my left breast and raised it a little, showing it off, displaying its shape. 'Petite, but in her own way voluptuous,' he indicated, his fingers moving further down and demonstrating how my thin waistline accentuated the curves of my breasts and arse.

'A wonderfully old-fashioned – or should I say classical? – body.'

I gulped.

He saved my blushes by not moving on to my once again impeccably shaved pussy and describing it to the audience. They could see it anyway, and complimentary words would have made no difference in the present circumstances.

'A wonderful specimen, and our compliments to Master Victor, who once again provides us with a perfect and highly individual body. I am informed that she has not yet been properly broken, which should add to the appeal.'

Broken? Fuck, what was he on about?

Behind me, a hand darted between my legs and forced me to part them. It was Victor's. I could recognise his touch.

I was now on display and could feel the gaze of at least two dozen eyes running across my skin, exploring me, assessing me, enjoying the spectacle of my total vulnerability.

Oh, Dominik, what did you give birth to?

I realised, though, it had been there already, before him, and he had sensed it and brought it to life, brought me to life.

The jumble of thoughts swirled around inside my head.

In a daze, I followed the 'auction' as if I were merely a spectator.

Images raced through my mind, of bad films seen an eternity ago, of events in exploitative BDSM novels that had once tickled my fancy, picturing myself in some Arabian or African marketplace, sand swirling all around, while the burly, dark-skinned slave masters advertised my wares, fingers testing my tautness, others roughly holding me open for the eyes of the crowd to demonstrate the nacreous shade of pinkness of my insides and the contrast with my pale skin. Maybe in those wakening dreams I was wearing a veil, maybe I wasn't, but in every loop that flew across the horizon of my imagination, I was nuder than nude, so terribly exposed, my intimacy on display for all to see. Or I was dragged from a bamboo cage on the bridge of a pirate ship, the consequence of kidnapping on the high seas and soon about to be acquired by some Oriental prince for his amusement and a place in his crowded harem. Was this what becoming a slave was all about?

The bidding began at $500. A woman began the process. I wasn't sure that I could serve a woman. I had fancied Lauralynn, true, but from what I had seen so far, I preferred the male brand of domination.

Soon a gaggle of male voices joined the fray and the bids came in at a rapid pace. Each time someone raised the odds, my eyes darted across the audience to try and distinguish the face of whoever was putting a value on me, but the action was too fast, and it soon became a jungle of voices and unfamiliar features.

Finally, the struggle between the two most regular bidders dragged to an end, when all the other voices dropped out. The winner actually appeared to be Arabic in appearance, at any rate Oriental. He wore an old-fashioned if elegantly tailored tweed suit and glasses. He was balding, swarthy, and the curl of his lips betrayed a world of cruelty.

My new owner?

Why would Victor wish to pass me on? Surely not for the money. I had reached just over $2,500. A flattering enough amount, but surely not what a woman was actually worth these days.

Victor handed the lucky winner a dog collar with a leash attached, which he then fastened round my neck. 'She is yours for the next hour,' I heard him say.

So this was only a temporary, one-off transaction. I would be going back with Victor after all. Another side to the game we were playing as we explored our darkness.

The man who had bid highest for me, ignoring the leash now dangling by my side, took my hand in his, his prize, and led me to the door. It opened onto a large bedroom. He pushed me onto the bed, closed the door behind him and began undressing.

He fucked me.

He used me.

And when he was done, without a word, he left the room, left me open, numbed by the relentless hammering he had just completed, ignoring me totally.

I caught my breath.

Abandoned like a rag doll in a toy house.

From the other side of the door, I could hear the muted sounds of the private party, the clinking of glasses, the drone of low-flying conversations. Could they be talking about me, discussing my performance, how I rated?

Was that it? Would another stranger walk into the room and take the relay baton in the fuck-the-new-slave sweepstakes?

But nothing happened.

I felt a wave of relief mixed with an inexplicable sense of disappointment. Another stage in my exploration of perversity had been completed. I was still here, still unfulfilled, relatively unruffled, all things considered. How far would I go before it was enough?

Victor came through the door. He didn't compliment me or make any comment on what had happened.

'Stand up,' he said, and I meekly obeyed. I couldn't be bothered to argue with him.

He was holding the lipstick tube he had retrieved from my bag. He came towards me, brandishing it like some inoffensive weapon.

'Keep straight,' he ordered, as he approached, and I felt his warm breath on my naked skin.

He began writing on me.

I tried to look down, but he tut-tutted as if it were none of my business.

The lipstick danced across my front; then he swivelled me round with a movement of his other hand and continued tracing whatever hieroglyphics he was creating across the curve of my bum.

Job completed, Victor took a step back to admire his handiwork, took out a small digital camera from his jacket pocket and snapped away to his heart's delight. The result seemed to please him.

He pointed me to the door, indicating I should rejoin the milling crowd on the other side. I felt weak, drained by the battering I had just taken, in no mood to argue any longer.

As I walked into the main circular room with its endless glass frontage overlooking the lights of Manhattan, I saw heads turn towards me, smiling, appreciative, lecherous. I didn't know what to do. Walk further? To where? Stand still?

Victor's hand on my shoulder stopped me in my stride.

Finally, once everyone present had a full view of me and my inscriptions, he said, 'You may dress. It's over for tonight.'

In something of a daze, I slipped back into the jettisoned black velvet dress and, of all things, almost forgot my violin case!

Outside, he hailed a yellow cab, bundled me into it and gave the driver my address. He didn't join me, just called out, 'I'll be in touch. Be ready.'

The first thing I did on reaching my place was undress and look at myself in the full-length bathroom mirror. Fortunately, none of my Croatian flatmates were around.

The thick red letters criss-crossed my skin like waves of infamy. Across my stomach he had written, 'SLUT', above my genitalia, 'SLAVE', and on my rear, which I had great trouble deciphering as I had to both twist my body round to catch a sight of the inscription and read from back to front, he had in bold red letters spelled out, 'MASTER'S PROPERTY'.

I felt sick.

It would take me three days of showers, baths and determined rubbing to feel clean again.

Victor called me the next morning.

'You enjoyed it, didn't you?'

I denied it.

'You say that, but I could read the contrary on your face, Summer. And the way your body always reacts.'

'I'm—' I gathered a weak protest.

'You were made for this,' Victor declared, 'and we're going to have a wonderful time. I will train you. You will be perfect.'

The bile was rising from my stomach to my throat, that terrible feeling of being on a runaway train, helpless to change its course, tethered to its thunderous wheels as it rushed down the track.

'And next time –' I could hear at the other end of the line how he was savouring every single word – 'we will make it official. We will register you.'

'Register me?' I queried.

'There is a slave register on the Internet. Don't fret – only people in the know will be aware of your true identity. You will be assigned a number and a slave name. It will be our secret. I was thinking of Slave Elena. It has a nice sound.'

'What does it entail?' My indignation was battling my curiosity.

'It will mean you will fully accept my ownership, my permanent collar.'

'I'm not sure I'm ready,' I said.

'Oh yes you are,' he continued. 'You will be given a choice of a ring or a tattoo in the most private of places, with your number or barcode, indicating your status and ownership. Of course, only those of us in the know will ever set eyes on it.'

Listening to his words, I felt a sense of both shame and excitement rise inside me. Surely in the twenty-first century, these things didn't happen any more?

Nevertheless, the temptation was strong; a siren call was already tickling my senses and imagination, tempered by the hard reality of knowing I would also be losing the treasured independence I had fought for years to retain.

'When?' I asked.

Victor purred. He could read me like an open book. 'I will let you know.'

He hung up, leaving my life in limbo.

I collapsed back onto my narrow bed. There were no rehearsals for another week. So much time to kill, too much time to think. I tried to read, but the words of every single book I picked up just became a blur and I was unable to concentrate on plot or subject matter.

Neither would sleep come and soothe the storm raging within.

I waited for Victor's call for two days. I spent my hours roaming through Greenwich Village looking for distractions of the shopaholic variety and dropping in to see mindless action movies in the hope they might help me take my mind off things, but the call never came. It was evident he was torturing me on purpose, ensuring my mind was ablaze with yearning by the time he made contact with me. Every time I entered an auditorium, I adjusted my mobile phone to vibrate in the hope of news during the screening, but to no avail.

I was becoming scared of my own thoughts, of the inevitability of the path I was moving towards.

Then, at three in the morning, one balmy night with the windows open wide to the New York heat and the regular sound of sirens from ambulances and police cars rushing down the canyons of the avenues, it came to me.

A final gamble.

Maybe putting the decision out of my hands.

London was five hours behind, not an unreasonable time to call.

I dialled Chris, hoping his phone wasn't switched off and he was in the middle of a gig in Camden Town or Hoxton.

It kept on ringing for ages and I was about to switch the phone off when he finally picked up.

'Hi, Chris!'

'Hi, hon. You back in town?'

'No, still in the Big Apple.'

'How are you?'

'A bit of a nervous wreck,' I confessed.

'Things not getting any better?'

'No. Maybe even getting worse. You know me – I'm sometimes my own worst enemy.'

'Don't I know it.' There was a moment of considered silence. 'Summer? Come back to London. Just drop everything and do it. I'll help if you need something, you know that.'

'I can't.'

'So?'

I hesitated, rehearsing every word around my dry tongue, and then said it. 'Can I ask you a huge favour?'

'Of course. Anything.'

'Can you contact Dominik? Tell him where I am?'

'Is that all?'

'Just that.'

A throw of the dice. Would Dominik respond?

12

A Man and His Blues

Their sex was regular, perfunctory.

Dominik had a strong libido, though when the occasion warranted it, he could easily forego carnal pleasures in order to concentrate on other pursuits, research projects or the various literary endeavours he was regularly involved with.

With Summer gone, Dominik had precious else to occupy his time. He had long since fine-tuned his lectures, though he was careful to vary his material, keep things fresh. He had enough notes ready and was quick enough on his feet that he needed very little time to prepare these days. He much preferred to improvise on any given subject.

His current intake of students was dull in the extracurricular sense; no one interested him in that way. Not that he would actively pursue a relationship with a student: it was too risky. He left that to the less moral professors, such as Victor, who had quickly vanished off campus to take up a new post in New York that had arisen at short notice. He was still a man, though, and he couldn't help but notice those girls who caught his eye, who smiled invitingly when he looked their way, even if he didn't act on it, at least until the term was finished.

Dominik had imagined he was in for a sexual hiatus, a proverbial dry spell, to compensate for Summer's sudden departure, and in some respects he had relished that, wallowed in it, looked forward to evenings alone catching up on his neglected pile of reading material, a new series of books that had so promised to captivate his attention when they arrived in the post from a dealer a few weeks ago but which had been left gathering dust while he concentrated his energies on plotting new scenes for Summer.

Then Charlotte had appeared, turned up at one of his evening talks at the City Lit. Dominik hadn't believed for a second that she had happened upon his class by accident, having almost overnight developed an overwhelming interest in mid twentieth-century literature. He knew that she had tracked him down, her pride hurt no doubt as a result of his unenthusiastic response to her fumblings at the party where he had shaved Summer. He was surprised that Charlotte had gone to the extent of finding and reading one of his books, but not flattered. Dominik merely saw that she had wanted something and had set out to get it.

They had fallen into a relationship easily enough, simply by continuing to indulge their appetites in the sexual sense. Neither Dominik nor Charlotte had ever formalised their arrangement in words. Sometimes he wondered what she wanted from him. Not money: she had enough of her own. Not sex: he knew that she still saw Jasper on occasion, and, he suspected, other men too, with regularity. He didn't care. It almost seemed to Dominik that Charlotte simply wanted to spite him, to taunt him, to ensure that Summer never left his mind.

He noticed that she had begun waxing her cunt bare, so that every time he saw her nude, he was automatically reminded of Summer's once newly shaved genitals, of the ritual that had seemed so perfect in his mind, the ultimate crescendo in their orchestra of lust, an act of depravity that had somehow been snatched out of his control, his fantasy used against him, an act that had pushed them apart instead of bringing them together.

He fucked Charlotte more roughly because of it, took her whenever the mood struck him, though she was always willing of course, and seemed to enjoy it. He rarely indulged in cunnilingus, a task he normally revelled in. He could have licked Summer's pussy for days, until she begged him to stop, but he never touched Charlotte with his tongue, and he didn't plan to. She never mentioned it, and continued to perform fellatio with surprising regularity. Sometimes, just to spite her, he held back his orgasm, let her continue to suck and suck until her jaw ached, too proud to give up, to admit that she had failed to make a man come with her mouth.

She was attractive enough, he supposed, in the typical sense of the word, but though his cock responded readily to the presence of her flesh, his mind was unmoved. In a physical sense, he found her dull, a doll of a woman, nothing original, unique or surprising about her. It was as if her personality had deserted her. Maybe he was just attracted to more complicated women. And her scent of cinnamon gave him a headache.

Dominik sighed. He shouldn't be so cruel. It was not Charlotte's fault that she was not Summer, that their sexual tastes were not fully aligned. She might have set out to light the spark that fanned their relationship, but he was as much a party to it as she was.

Charlotte turned, sighed softly in her sleep, snuggled her rump against his crotch. Dominik felt a momentary spark of affection for her. The only time that Charlotte ever seemed completely genuine, without guile, was in her sleep. He slung an arm around her and drifted into a fitful slumber.

He was haunted by the most perverse dreams. All of them involved Summer, most, Jasper too, or some other faceless man, plumbing her depths, her genitals on awful display, the shaft of a stranger's cock pumping against the inner walls of her vagina, her face a picture of ecstasy, her body writhing in orgasm, while he watched, powerless, uninvolved, obsolete, consumed by jealousy. Sometimes he imagined her being filled by a legion of different men, one after the other, each filling her with his seed while Dominik stood back, helpless, forgotten.

He spent the mornings after these dreams wondering where she was and to what extent she was pursuing her desires without him. Dominik knew that he had started it; he had taken the lid off that simmering pool of submission, that deep well of darkness within her.

He missed her emails and text messages informing him of her adventures. True, it had been a way of taming his jealousy – he didn't own her, though he wanted to – but it had also been a way to keep an eye on her while she was still growing into her new skin. To check that she was in control of giving away her control, that she had not been pushed too far.

How far would she go? he wondered. Would she ever draw a line in the sand? Where would Summer's line be?

It was after one of these dreams, when he was particularly cranky, that Charlotte started on him.

'You never come up with scenes for me,' she said. 'No

naked concerts, no fucking for an audience, no rope, no showing me off in public. We never do anything.'

She was right. He never did any of those things for her, but she didn't inspire him to do so, like Kathryn had, or Summer had.

He shrugged. 'What is it that you want me to do?'

She raged. 'Anything! Anything other than just fuck me. What kind of dom are you, anyway?'

Flecks of spittle flew across her lips as she spoke. He watched her mouth move with a curious disengagement, remembering a nature programme he had recently seen that featured an animal with an abnormally large oral cavity. It had reminded him of Charlotte.

She yelled at him often, her ready temper pushed to the surface by his apparent disinterest. Each time she lost her prized sense of composure Dominik felt a small thrill of victory, a battle won.

He had agreed, in the end, to attend a swingers club with her, partly because he had always wondered what these establishments were like. He had never had the right person to go with, except for once, years back in New York, when the etiquette of swinging was still in its infancy. Either the girl was straight-laced and would have been horrified at the idea, or his romantic feelings for her were too strong and he could not bear the thought of giving her up to another man. Perhaps Charlotte was just the right person for him to attend such an evening with.

Besides, the thought of sex in public had distracted Charlotte from her desire to have him dominate her. Dominik didn't feel that way about Charlotte, had no desire to spank her or have her give herself to him. Charlotte was a hedonist, a player; she liked to dip a toe into whatever water she stumbled upon, just to try it out. Charlotte was indulging a whim, not submitting to him, and that didn't inspire him. She didn't move Dominik in the way that Summer had.

The club was in an industrial centre in South London, tucked between a series of minor factories and dated office buildings. It was discreetly signposted, the only light on the outside of the building from the headlamps of infrequent taxis, pulling in and out to deliver new patrons or take them away.

They were met at the door by the club manager, a simpering man dressed in a full suit with jacket, despite the closed heat in the small reception area. He seemed pleased with Charlotte, looking her up and down in the manner that someone might admire a racehorse, and gave Dominik a cursory glance, tolerating his presence at least.

Dominik paid the rather exorbitant entry fee and declined the offer of yearly membership, which also entitled them to early-bird tickets for a couples-only cruise around the Mediterranean the following year. He always got seasick, anyway.

He could not think of a prospect more awful than spending a week in a similar situation on board a boat, with no escape route available, other than diving overboard. An option he might actually consider, he thought, as another man, similarly suited, took their jackets and mobile phones away. Dominik was about to protest that he needed it to call a cab later when the man waved to a sign on the wall that advised that the use of any device that contained a camera was prohibited.

They were ushered through into the club proper and

introduced to Suzanne, a hostess, who promised to show them round and help them settle in.

'Hiya!' she said, with a cheerfulness that did not seem to be forced.

Charlotte responded with an enthusiastic greeting in return. Dominik nodded an acknowledgement, once.

She was young, in her early twenties, Dominik guessed. On the short side, and a little bulky. It was unfortunate that the uniform for the hostesses was so unflattering, as the short pink crop-top and tutu-style miniskirt that Suzanne was wearing did not add to her appeal.

'Is this your first time, guys?' she continued, seeming uncertain now whether to direct her questions toward Dominik or Charlotte. In most situations like this, he supposed, it would be reasonably obvious which member of the couple was the driving force. Perhaps not so in their case.

'Yes,' replied Charlotte smoothly, saving the hostess from embarrassment. 'We can't wait.'

Suzanne waved a plump hand towards the bar, indicating where they could buy drinks on the lower level. They followed her as she led them upstairs, to another smaller bar, and a 'play area', a labyrinth of dark corridors with a series of adjoining rooms of varying sizes. Some were obviously designed for orgy-like encounters, easily holding twenty people at a time. Others were more like small booths, for two or perhaps three sets of couples, at a push. Most were entirely open, so that anyone would be able to watch, or join in, but one or two of the smaller rooms had bolts on the inside, so that a couple looking for a quiet moment could shut themselves in.

Their hostess pointed out the features of all the rooms,

without a moment's blush. She did not seem at all discomfited by her attire, or her role at the club.

Dominik's gaze travelled around the room, noticing the poles in the bar area, inviting patrons to cavort in the manner of amateur strippers once enough alcohol had been consumed. Females, at any rate, he hoped. A series of couches lined a lounge area, alongside the bar, and in one corner a piece of equipment a bit like a swing hung from the ceiling, made from a wide mesh, allowing free roam around the body of whoever lay within, with arm and leg restraints so that an individual could be strapped inside, unable to free herself.

Each empty surface was filled with a large clear bowl of condoms with multi-coloured wrappers – enough condoms, Dominik guessed, to sustain a club full of copulating couples for a month. They gave the place a strangely cheerful look, like bowls of sweets in a doctor's surgery.

Adjacent to the rooms was a thin, black curtain fixed to the ceiling and falling full length to the floor, with a slit in one side to form a makeshift tent. The tent was full of holes, some the size of an eye, others the size of a fist, so that spectators could peer inside at any figure or figures within, or reach an anonymous hand and grapple at whatever happened to be within reach. Dominik peered inside. It was empty.

'It's always quiet like this until midnight,' Suzanne said apologetically, 'but then it really picks up. In an hour or so, all this will be heaving.'

Dominik held back a grimace.

He had never quite understood the appeal of watching people rutting in public, and the thought of such mindless fucking reminded him of Summer and Jasper, a picture that he could not get out of his head.

Dominik's personal brand of voyeurism required some kind of connection with the subject, an unwritten contract, an agreement of sorts that allowed or invited his stare. Without any kind of connection to the participants, he was no more moved by the spectacle they provided than he was by watching animals mating on a nature show.

Charlotte, however, held an entirely different view. She enjoyed the physical sensation of sex for its own sake, enjoyed demonstrating her daring and allure by indulging in public displays, and she liked to show off. Swinging was a favourite pastime of hers.

She had already begun to saunter over to the bar area, making eyes at the few people who gathered around the countertop: a young man and woman who were studiously avoiding eye contact with anyone besides each other, a beefy older man in a polo shirt and cheap mock-leather belt, who seemed to be alone and was leering at the hostesses in their pink tutus, and an older Indian couple, the type who looked as though they came every week.

Charlotte ordered drinks for them both, an elaborate cocktail for her and a Pepsi for him.

He sat alongside her and sipped it as she struck up an easy conversation with anyone who approached the bar.

Suzanne, the hostess, was right: the club was beginning to fill up.

So far he hadn't noticed anyone he was attracted to. Some pretty enough girls, but most of them were decked out in ridiculously slutty clothing, cheap PVC mini-dresses and too much make-up and fake tan. No one who interested him. The other guests in attendance either bored or repulsed him.

'Are you just going to sit there?' Charlotte hissed in his ear.

Dominik couldn't be bothered to listen to her. 'Go and enjoy yourself,' he replied. 'I may join you later.'

She didn't need to be told twice. Charlotte disappeared into the crowd, flashing Dominik a vision of her arse cheeks as she slipped off the high bar stool, her long, tanned legs in stark contrast to her short white dress. She had barely left his side before men began to flock to her, like flies to a honeypot.

Dominik remained silent as she glanced at him, a malevolent expression on her face, and took first one and then another man by the hand. Neither of the men was terribly attractive. One was the single man with the polo shirt and cheap belt who had been at the bar earlier. The other was younger, but turning to fat already, his face surrounded by more than one chin too many and his gut barely constrained by his shirt.

Charlotte led them both over to the swing in the corner and then proceeded to clamber onto it, lying on her back with her legs spread in the air. It became patently clear that she was not wearing any underwear, her intimacy on display to the entire occupants of the room.

Dominik moved closer, out of curiosity more than anything else.

The two men strapped Charlotte's legs into the restraints. She wrapped her hands round the ropes that fell from the ceiling over her head. She was more than a willing participant in this.

The man in the polo shirt had unbuckled his belt now

and had begun to stroke his still flaccid cock. The fat one had his out too, his trousers pooled round his ankles and his shirt tails framing his bare arse untidily. He snatched up one of the coloured wrappers and applied a condom to his shaft, then stepped forward, between Charlotte's long legs, and pulled the swing towards him so that he could enter her.

Dominik moved nearer, observed the man's penis enter Charlotte's cunt. She looked up at him, her malicious expression now replaced by lust, by need, a need greater than her need to prove a point, to hurt him.

Was she hurting him? He supposed that was her intention, but he felt entirely detached from the situation, completely unmoved.

He watched as both men filled her, first one, then the next, their shafts pumping in and out, coated with Charlotte's juices, listened to her loud moans as she made no effort at all to hide her enjoyment out of any deference to his feelings.

A crowd had gathered; several men had unbuckled their trousers and stood near her, fondling their genitals. Some moved forward to touch her, hands darting in and out wherever the owner saw an opportunity, a clear space to be groped.

Dominik made no attempt to stop them. Charlotte still had her hands free to bat away any unwanted attention, and she had a voice, could cry out if she wanted to. Besides, she appeared to be revelling in the attention, her mouth now an open O, her face a picture of lust and desire.

He conjured up an image in his head, tried to imagine Summer lying there, ignoring his desires, giving herself up to the touch of strangers, her legs spread for other men to fuck. He recalled the way that she had opened herself up to Jasper, had taken him in her mouth, how she'd kneeled on the couch with her legs spread in readiness, like an animal waiting to be mounted.

At least his thoughts of Summer made him feel something, not this dull absence of consciousness, the uncaring emptiness that filled him without her.

Dominik did not care to watch Charlotte any longer. He pushed past the eager onlookers who had gathered to catch a glimpse of the depravity and stumbled down the stairs to the lower bar, waited there for her to finish, ignoring the efforts of the hostesses to engage him in conversation and the attentions of the occasional woman looking for an easy fuck.

Eventually, Charlotte sat down next to him. As she pulled herself onto the stool, her skirt rode up and she made no effort to hide her pussy, obscenely naked, swollen, still slick with juices. Charlotte lazily spread her legs, giving him a better look.

'There's no need for that,' said Dominik, glancing away.

'Jesus Christ, what the fuck is wrong with you? What did you think it would be like?'

'Charlotte, I don't care who you fuck. You're free to do what you like. I thought you knew that.'

'You cared who your precious Summer fucked.'

'You're not Summer.'

'And I don't want to be! That weak little slut. She doesn't care about anything other than her precious violin. She was using you for it, playing you. Don't you see that? Do you think she cared who she fucked? Gave a shit about you?'

Dominik felt a sudden desire to slap her, to watch her face flinch in pain, but he had never, and never would, hit a woman, not like that.

He got up and stalked out.

Her apology came the next day, by text message.

'Come over?'

At least, it was likely the closest that Charlotte would ever come to an apology.

He owed her no more or less in return.

The terms of their relationship were obvious: they fucked, hurt each other. Summer was always at the centre, gone from both of their lives yet present in it every day, her absence like the open wound that neither of them was able to stop picking at.

He went over.

Fucked her again, more cruelly than ever. Again he closed his eyes and imagined that Charlotte's hair was red instead of brown, her waist smaller and her legs shorter, her skin creamy white instead of tan, her arse curved, that she shivered under his touch. He felt his cock expand, harden within her as he thought of Summer, and was filled with anger, anger that Charlotte was not the woman he wanted her to be. He raised his hand, brought it down hard against her arse, listened to her yelp, first with surprise and then pleasure. He raised his other hand, brought it down on the other side, watched the skin redden, hit her again and again. She pressed herself back against him in delight, raised her arse in the air to be used.

He watched her thrusting towards him and again remembered how Summer's anus had looked so inviting, how she had orgasmed for the first time for him when he had told her that he intended to make her fuck her own arse.

Dominik regretted not having broken that virgin territory of Summer's before she had disappeared. He had been saving it, planning to keep that entrance for a ritual, just as he had been saving the shaving of her cunt for him alone.

He bent forward, spat on Charlotte's anus to lubricate her hole, pressed his thumb gently against the circle of her sphincter and began to breach it further, surprised by her tightness. She jumped forward, pulled away from his touch, and then, when he removed his hand, she moved back again, finding his cock, directing it once more into her still wet cunt.

Dominik was surprised. Despite her open sexuality, it seemed that Charlotte was not a fan of anal sex.

He thrust his cock into Charlotte again, as hard as he could, feeling the base of his head hitting her cervix. He drifted away into his thoughts as she pumped back against him, listened to her screech out an orgasm.

He pulled out of her carefully, peeled off the condom and disposed of it discreetly, before she could notice that it was empty. He had not reached his own climax.

Charlotte draped herself over the bed lazily, and Dominik lay down beside her, running his hand up and down the smooth skin of her torso.

'You haven't done that before,' she said, her voice silky, soft, full of the pleasure of a recent orgasm.

'No,' he replied, unable to think of anything more to say on the subject.

'Don't take this the wrong way . . .'

'I won't. What is it?'

'What kind of dom are you? You don't normally seem to want to . . . dominate me.'

Dominik considered. 'I've never been one for the "scene",' he replied, 'the trappings of it, the stereotypes. Nor do I have any interest in causing pain.' He noted her still red backside and added, 'Usually.'

'Would you try it?' she asked. 'Humour me.'

'What is it that you want?' he asked, a little impatiently now.

'Rope. A beating. Surprise me.'

'Has it not occurred to you that instructing your dominant to dominate you is not very submissive?'

Charlotte shrugged. 'You're not really a dominant, though, are you?' She was goading him now.

'All right, then.'

'All right?'

'I will give you your scene.'

Dominik considered. He had no wish to hurt Charlotte. He was using her as much as she was using him. Neither did he have any wish to put on some foolish act of dominance that he didn't feel. To begin play-acting. Their relationship had become ridiculous, sordid, a parody of itself, a mockery of what he had shared with Summer.

Even so, she pushed him, and if she pushed him, then Dominik would push back.

He waited until she was in the shower, then dipped into her oversized designer handbag for her mobile phone. As he suspected, she did not have a password. Charlotte was open in every way. He skipped by all the messages from other men, uninterested. 'Hey, baby,' or, 'Hey, sexy,' they read, one after the other.

He found Jasper's number, jotted it down, then, once he was back home, he called.

'Hello?'

'Jasper?' Dominik replied.

'Uh. Yes?'

Jasper's tone was uncertain. Dominik smiled to himself. This was evidently Jasper's work phone; perhaps he was wondering whether he had a male client.

'It's Dominik. We met at a party recently. Charlotte was in attendance. And Summer.'

'Oh, yes.'

Dominik felt a moment's irritation as Jasper's voice audibly perked up at the mention of Summer's name.

'How can I help?'

'I'm planning something special for Charlotte. I think she would like it if you were in attendance. I would compensate you, of course.'

'Then I would be delighted. When were you thinking?'

'Tomorrow?'

Pages rustled as Jasper checked his diary.

'I'm free, and looking forward to it.'

Dominik finalised the arrangement.

Then he texted Charlotte.

'Tomorrow night, at yours. Be ready.'

'Ooh, goodie,' she replied. 'What shall I wear?'

Dominik fought the urge to reply, 'I don't care.'

Then, in a rush of hurt and anger, he decided to opt for maximum humiliation: 'A school uniform,' he replied.

He met Jasper outside Charlotte's flat, went over the ground rules. Dominik was in charge, at Charlotte's request.

'Hey, you're paying,' said Jasper. 'Whatever you kinky cats want is cool with me.'

They stood on the porch together, complicit in Charlotte's future subjugation, and rang the bell. Dominik still hadn't invited Charlotte to his house. It didn't feel right having her there. He wanted to keep himself private from her.

She answered the door, dressed in a tartan miniskirt, white blouse, knee-high socks and black closed-toe shoes with a low heel. Charlotte had met his request to the detail, Dominik realised, as he took in her slicked-back, high ponytail and thick-rimmed black spectacles. He had not expected that, and he was surprised by his own response. He was getting hard, achingly so. Perhaps this wouldn't be such a chore after all.

She grinned from ear to ear when her eyes landed on Jasper, and Jasper grinned back at her, two easy conspirators in crime. Like Summer and me, Dominik thought with a pang.

'Hello, sirs,' Charlotte said demurely, with a slight curtsy.

'We've come to punish you,' Dominik said, 'for being such a naughty girl.'

Dominik grimaced at the sound of his own voice, the foreign nature of those words. Charlotte's eyes flashed with delight.

He stepped past her, into the flat, spun her round and put his hand on her lower spine. 'Bend over,' he said. 'Show me your arse.'

Charlotte giggled, but was quick to follow his instruction.

Dominik circled her. Remembered, before he could push the thought away, how Summer had stood for him, bent over in the crypt, almost unwilling, perhaps afraid, but she had done as he asked anyway, because he had asked her. Why she felt bound to do so, he couldn't say. Perhaps the motivation driving her was not so very different from the one driving him, the powerful streak of dominance within him that was so drawn to her opposite.

Charlotte began to wiggle her knees. Unlike Summer, who was locked into place as if she had been set in concrete, unable to move once she had been bidden, Charlotte was role-playing, and she was uncomfortable, impatiently awaiting his next play in this absurd game. He had half a mind to just sit down and watch Jasper fuck her. That was all she seemed to want, anyway.

But no. She had asked for domination, and domination she would have.

He hooked a finger through her panties, pulled them sharply down to her feet. Charlotte didn't usually wear underwear. Today she was wearing a plain white cotton pair. All part of the act.

'Spread your legs.'

She shifted her weight, tried to straighten, to stretch her back out, but Dominik refused to allow it. Each time she tried to rise, to reduce her discomfort, he pressed his hand against the small of her back and guided her down again.

He gestured to Jasper. 'Fuck her. Right now. No prelims. No wasting time. Just do it.'

He watched as the young man produced his enormous erection and sheathed himself.

Charlotte sighed with pleasure, her discomfort forgotten, as soon as she felt Jasper's hulking penis breach her entrance.

Dominik left them momentarily, exploring Charlotte's

bedroom until he found a bottle of lube. Cinnamon-flavoured. Typical.

He returned to the living room to find that Jasper had moved Charlotte towards the couch, so that she could support her body weight on the cushions. He guided them both back into the centre of the room. Charlotte whimpered. In pain? Dominik found that his own cock had hardened at the thought.

He squirted some lubricant onto his fingers, then laid his hand gently on her arse, separated her cheeks with his palm and inserted his index finger into her hole. Charlotte jumped and he felt her sphincter muscles tighten, gripping his digit with clamp-like strength, but she did not protest. His erection grew, expanding in response to the shrinking circle of her hole, his cock now rock hard and straining to burst out of his trousers.

Through the thin wall separating the walls of Charlotte's anus and her vagina, Dominik could feel Jasper's thick shaft driving in and out of her hole in the manner of a battering ram assaulting a rampart. He inserted a second finger, began to match the escort's rhythm, fucking her arse now with increasing ferocity.

Charlotte began to wriggle, her hands unable to find purchase on the floor beneath the steady onslaught of their joint attack on her body.

He removed his fingers, very slowly, from the grip of her arsehole, feeling her muscles pulse and release as he made his exit. He gestured to Jasper to pull out.

Dominik pulled Charlotte up to standing. Her eyes were filled with tears.

'Good girl,' he said. 'Now that we have loosened those nice, tight holes of yours, the real work can begin.'

Charlotte lowered her head, nodded once.

He picked her up and carried her into the bedroom, remembering as he did so the occasion when he had taken Summer home, carried her into his study and she had masturbated for him on his desk.

'On all fours,' he said to Charlotte imperiously. She complied, her head down, not looking back at him. 'Wait here,' he added.

Dominik turned to Jasper, who was in the process of unrolling the barrier from his cock and applying a new one. 'Don't touch her.'

Dominik returned to the living room, collected the lubricant and stopped by the bathroom to wash his hands. He glanced into the mirror as he did so, stared for a moment at his own reflection.

What had he become?

He pushed the feeling from his mind and returned to the bedroom, where Charlotte and Jasper were waiting, Charlotte still dressed in her school uniform outfit, her panties bunched round her ankles, the short tartan skirt cutting a line into her arse cheeks. Jasper stood to one side, completely naked now, his jeans and T-shirt folded in a tidy domestic pile on Charlotte's dresser.

Dominik approached, took a handful of her hair in his hand and pulled her head back. 'I'm going to fuck your arse,' he said softly into her ear.

She did not respond. Although the displeasure painted across her face made it clear she felt she had been duped, she should not have revealed to Dominik that anal sex was particularly low on her sexual menu and that she normally actively disliked it.

He flipped up her skirt and spread her legs apart.

Charlotte had such long legs that fucking her from behind was like riding a pony. He ran his finger through the folds of her labia, dipping a finger into her hole. She was wet, still slippery from her fuck with Jasper, who was now standing stock still by Charlotte, silent, his member standing to full attention.

Dominik squeezed a liberal dose of lubricant onto Charlotte's arsehole, watched her shiver in response to the cold sensation, felt himself get hard again in response.

He unbuckled his belt. Dominik was still fully clothed.

He pulled out his cock, brought it to the base of her opening so that he could feel the heat radiating from her hole to him. Then he considered, rolled a condom onto his shaft and pushed the head of his cock gently against her sphincter, struggling to find purchase.

'Relax, sweet Charlotte,' he said.

Jasper leaned forward and stroked her hair. 'It's OK, babe,' he said.

Dominik looked across at Charlotte and Jasper. She had laid her head against him, her face now relaxed, resting gently against his torso. He was lightly stroking her hair.

Romantic, Dominik thought, realizing that he had been completely forgotten, he was adding nothing more to the scene than any other cock would. He could have just as easily been a dildo, any other person wearing a strap-on.

He couldn't bring himself to blame her. He didn't care for her either.

Dominik pulled the condom off and buckled up his trousers, glancing back at Jasper on his way out the door, ready to reassure the escort that he could carry on with Charlotte if he wished, his contract to Dominik had been fulfilled. But Jasper was on the bed, embracing Charlotte before Dominik had even managed to leave the bedroom, and within a few minutes he could hear them, breathlessly at it.

As he passed through her living room, he glanced around. He was acutely aware that Summer had never invited him into her home, the final redoubt of her privacy. Charlotte had no such qualms; she was an entertainer and had guests of all descriptions over to visit regularly. Her apartment was virtually bare, quite a large room but just the one couch, swing seat and a Mac and office space in the corner. She had a large kitchen bench, which boasted one of the more expensive models of coffee machine. Antipodeans were so fussy about their espressos and flat whites, fussier even than the Italians, who practically invented the stuff.

Dominik noticed a light winking on top of the coffee machine. Could it be? No. Surely not. He approached for a closer look.

It was Charlotte's phone, lying on its side and set to video mode. It was recording.

Dominik picked it up, stopped the recording, rewound. She had filmed the scene, or at least the part of it that occurred in the living room. The impudent bitch.

It was a strange sensation, watching himself on film. If he had ever happened to be copulating in a room with a mirror, and had caught a glimpse of his own expression in the act, Dominik had always looked away. He had no wish to observe himself fucking.

Charlotte had managed to catch most of the action. She had aimed the camera into the middle of the living-room floor, not over onto the sofa, or in the bedroom. She had guessed where the action would be likely to take place.

Perhaps he had not been so mysterious, or surprising, after all.

Dominik erased the film and placed the camera carefully back into position, leaving the record button off. She might notice, of course, that it had been tampered with, but these sorts of devices often cut out of their own accord. It was a better alternative than filming himself walking away from the camera. He collected his jacket from where it lay across the arm of the sofa. He had paid the escort already, so that part was organised. Any additional cost that he might think to charge, for whatever activity took place after Dominik left, was Charlotte's problem.

Then it hit him. What else had she filmed?

He walked back to the coffee machine, picked up Charlotte's phone and scrolled through the saved videos. They were sorted in date order. One of them was the date of the last evening he had spent with Summer, before their fight in the coffee shop. The night that he had shaved her, that Jasper had fucked her, in his presence.

Dominik pressed 'play' with a heavy heart. The picture was small but clear. Charlotte had indeed filmed Jasper and Summer having sex. Had she known what would happen? Paid him to do it? Organised the whole thing? The camera must have been fixed between the cushions of the couch, or balanced on the window ledge above, perhaps. The angle had captured Summer's face, her expression caught between pleasure and pain. Perhaps the escort's cock had been too big for her. Once or twice she glanced behind her. Was she looking for him, for Dominik?

He played the tape over and over, unable to wrench himself away from the spectacle that Charlotte had recorded, without Summer's consent, he was sure. He pressed a few buttons, sent the recording to his email address, then deleted it from Charlotte's phone and placed the device carefully back again. Not that he would care if she realised she had been discovered. He didn't ever wish to see Charlotte again.

Dominik walked out of the door without a glance behind him.

It was late evening now. He slid behind the wheel of his BMW and took a breath before expertly backing out of his parking space. The road had been nearly empty when he arrived, but was now jammed with cars, all the residents of Charlotte's peaceful street having returned to their homes for the evening. He had been locked in, another BMW ahead of him and one behind. Three in a row. The last thing he needed was to take out one of their head- or tail-lights.

Dominik stared into the windows of the houses as he drove slowly towards the main thoroughfare, where he would find the A41 and head up Finchley Road towards Hampstead. He watched the lights glowing in bedrooms and living rooms, saw a slim silhouetted shape, a woman he guessed, glance out onto the street and then pull a pair of curtains together.

Thoughts of Summer still flooded his mind, the image of her looking back at him over her shoulder, as Jasper filled her, ran through his mind on repeat as he negotiated the odd car coming the other way on the narrow avenue and barely avoided a cat, racing to safety on the other side.

He wondered, idly, if Charlotte's house was the only home entertaining the less-usual pleasures tonight, or if suburban men and women throughout the neighbourhood were busy indulging in, hiding from or covering up secrets of their own.

Back home, he quickly slipped out of his clothes and collapsed on his bed, not even bothering to shower.

He had a review deadline in the morning.

13

A Man and a Girl

Victor's call came the following day.

'Summer?'

'Yes?'

'Be ready in an hour. A car will be coming to collect you at midday.'

He hung up the phone without waiting for me to reply.

I responded to his call in much the same way as I had responded to his other calls, like a wind-up toy soldier that had been set on a path from which I now seemed incapable of moving away.

A slave register? The idea was absurd; it couldn't be true. Soon, I thought, I would wake up and find this had all been a dream.

Still, I showered and shaved carefully, as Victor had ordered. I didn't want to give him any motivation to step in and do it for me. With a razor in hand, I did not think he would be as gentle as Dominik had been.

Dominik. Would he call me? My heart ached at the thought of him. He would understand all of this. They shared a similar core, Victor and Dominik, but Victor was so very different. Dominik didn't want to break me, or be served mindlessly. He wanted something more. He wanted me to choose him.

The car arrived, another enormous, sleek machine with

tinted windows, the sort that you would see in mafia movies. I didn't bother to look out of the windows, follow our journey to see in which direction Victor was taking me this time. Another anonymous address, another improvised dungeon. What did it matter? I'd chosen to go. I wouldn't need to call the police to report my own kidnapping.

My phone vibrated in my purse, its buzz barely audible over the purr of the engine. I had a constant and terrible fear that Victor would call during a rehearsal, so I always had it set to vibrate or silent mode. The conductors or orchestra managers would be furious if the screech of a mobile phone interrupted one of our performances, even more so if Victor asked me to report immediately and I felt obliged to set down my violin and follow his summons.

I began to fish through my purse for my phone, to check who had rung. Was it Dominik? My fingers froze in fear. Did Victor have cameras installed in here? A microphone so that he might hear any call that I made? I leaned forward, trying to catch a glimpse of my chauffeur, but my view was obscured by the pane of glass separating the back and front seats of the vehicle. The driver might even be Victor; that was exactly the kind of trick he would get a kick out of playing.

The car began to slow, and through the dark-glass window I could see Victor's squat form appear on the pavement. So he wasn't the driver. Any moment now my door would swing open: there was no time to call, to send a text message, to even check if it was Dominik who had rung. All I could do was hold my thumb over the off button so that it wouldn't vibrate again and alert Victor to the fact that we were in touch.

I could only hope that Dominik, if it was him, would

keep trying, and that at some point during whatever bizarre scenario it was that Victor had planned this time, I would find a way to reach him.

Victor pulled the passenger door open and offered his hand to me. I took it, allowed him to assist me out of the car. Was this what I had fallen to? Ironically, the idea of Victor helping me out of the back seat, like some ridiculous creature unable to stand up on its own, offended me more than the sexual acts that he had subjected me to, that I had submitted to. I wanted to rise up, tower over him and push him down onto the pavement, but I didn't, I couldn't. I just took his hand and followed him meekly.

We had arrived at his loft in Tribeca. It had been transformed, for this event, into a harem of sorts. The whole thing was like a parody, ornate cushions everywhere, bits of colourful, flimsy chiffon draped all over the ceilings. Men and women, the mistresses and masters, decked out in outfits that they seemed to think signalled their 'rank', but which I found patently ridiculous.

'Lower your head, slave,' Victor hissed into my ear. I complied, but with a thrill of satisfaction. So I seemed too confident, with my head up and shoulders back. Good.

Victor removed my purse from my shoulder.

'Strip!' he commanded.

My small rebellion had evidently angered him. I removed my dress and handed it to him. I was not wearing anything underneath. What was the point? I could almost elegantly slip out of a dress, but I felt so foolish wriggling out of a pair of knickers that I just left them off these days.

'You will have no need of possessions here,' he said, taking the dress away and setting it to one side, along with my purse.

Thank God I had left my violin at home. My arms felt empty without the case to hold on to, but at least my Bailly was safe. I was terrified that Victor would see how attached I was to the violin and try to destroy it. I didn't think he could break me in any other way, but taking my violin away would probably do it.

With my head down, I could see only the floor and catch glimpses of the other characters in the room. I listened carefully to as many snippets of conversation as I could pick up.

'She's Victor's latest catch,' said a small, dark-haired woman, stretched out lazily among the cushions nearest to me. I could just catch a vision of her out of the corner of my eye. She was made up like a 1940s movie star, sporting vivid red lipstick and a chic bob.

'Sure looks feisty,' her companion replied, a tall, lean man with a thin moustache that just grazed his lip, like something he had forgotten to wash off in the shower.

'Victor will find a way to break her. He always does.'

I watched carefully as Victor placed my purse, with my phone in it, and my dress, away in his drinks cabinet. He locked the door with a tiny key, which he placed in his pocket.

Then he turned back to me, a triumphant smile spreading across his face from ear to ear.

'Tonight, the preparations begin. The ceremony will be held tomorrow.'

Oh, Dominik, I thought, casting a sideways glance towards the cabinet where my phone was locked away. Where are you?

*

Dominik was aware that Chris had always been a close friend of Summer's. They had known each other since she had arrived in London from New Zealand. Both were musicians, and she had also on occasion helped out on fiddle with his small rock group. Nevertheless, it had never occurred to him to contact Chris after Summer had so suddenly vanished. Of course he had made attempts to contact her, but her phone number was dead, and when he visited the flat in Whitechapel where she lived, the landlord had angrily responded that she had left without legal notice and grumbled offensively about it.

Maybe something inside him, his pride, his pain, had prevented him from investigating further.

Never before had he felt so mixed up about a woman.

It wasn't that she hadn't made herself available to him and willingly consented to his games and the often left-of-field sexual activities they both were visibly into, but the fact he had always sensed that she was holding back. Controlling her core of darkness, topping him from below in ways he couldn't quite understand.

So when Chris called him out of the blue, he was taken aback. Couldn't she call him herself?

'In New York?' he queried.

'Yes, that's what I said.'

'And what did she want?'

'How the fuck should I know? To tell you where she is, I suppose. As her mate, I ain't at all happy about this, you know,' Chris said, his irritation growing with every word. 'All her problems seemed to begin when she met you, so I can assure you you're not my flavour of the month, Dominik. And if I had something to say in the matter, I'd rather she kept well clear of you.'

Dominik processed all the information, phone to his ear, eyes darting across the study where he had taken the call as he had been drafting a book review for an academic journal. The nearby bed was strewn with books and papers.

'Is she OK?' he asked Chris.

'No, she isn't, to be bluntly honest about it. She's having bad problems. That's all I know. She wouldn't tell me more. Just said to get in touch with you and let you know where she was.'

New York, a city he had always loved and which had become a Sargasso Sea of memories of women and affairs past. Images flooded back in a rush: the Algonquin Hotel and its tiny rooms with antique furniture in which you couldn't swing a cat, let alone spank a willing arse; the Oyster Bar below Grand Central Station; the Iroquois Hotel, where the rooms were larger but more shady chic in spirit and it was not an uncommon occurrence to see the odd cockroach sprint across the wall. He recalled a Taste of Sushi on 13th Street, where the Japanese food had been a revelation but the toilets stank of the Middle Ages and would never pass a British Health and Safety inspection; Le Trapeze Club in the Flatiron District, where he had taken Pamela, the banker from Boston, and watched her indulge in her deepest fantasies; the Gershwin Hotel right next door, where his room had a Picasso image daubed across the wall behind the bed that he couldn't escape seeing on every occasion he'd fucked a companion there in the missionary position and inevitably raised his head. New York, New York.

And now Summer was there, of her own accord. Not even taken there by him as a reward or a distraction.

Dominik returned to his senses and heard Chris's laboured breathing at the other end of the line.

'Do you have a phone number for here there? Can you let me have it?'

Conquering his obvious reluctance, Chris read the number out and Dominik jotted it down on a corner of his reading notes.

An uncomfortable silence followed between the two men, and both felt a profound relief when the other finally hung up.

Dominik sat himself down in his black leather office chair, facing the computer screen on which he was working, and watched with remote fascination the blinking signal of the cursor, which he had abandoned halfway through a word when the phone had rung.

Finally, he took a deep breath and dialled the number he had obtained from Chris. Even though New York was miles and five hours away, the ringtone felt as if it was in the next room.

But it rang and rang and no one picked up.

Dominik consulted his watch to check on the time difference. It was still daylight there. Maybe she was working and unable to take calls right now. Might she have found work in music there? The Bailly would have helped.

He put the phone down. A wave of conflicted feelings washed over him.

He tried to concentrate on the job at hand, but the subtle shifts in the relationships between English and American writers living on the Parisian Rive Gauche during the years of existentialism failed to regain his full attention and he gave up and paced up and down his study.

Having allowed, he thought, enough minutes to elapse,

he dialled Summer's New York number again. It began to ring and the space between each successive sound seemed to get longer and longer, stretching to relative eternity. As he was about to put the phone down, a message clicked into action, a standard AT&T 'customer unavailable' loop.

Dominik left a message, enunciating calmly into the mouthpiece, controlling his inner panic. 'Summer . . . it's me . . . Dominik . . . Call me back. Please. No more games. I just want to hear you.' Then, as a second thought, 'If you can't get through for one reason or another, just leave a message, text, anything. I miss you terribly.'

He reluctantly hung up the phone.

Still pacing up and down the room an hour later, he went online and checked the next flights to New York and the availability of seats. There were several from Heathrow early in the morning, all arriving in New York around midday local time. He impulsively booked himself on to the first flight out in business class.

Hopefully she would be in touch before he left, as he had no clue what he could do on arrival with no indication of her location.

A case of hope against hope.

I stood stock still and waited for Victor to make his next move.

Perhaps sensing my impatience to find out what he had planned next, Victor took his sweet time before producing the next item in his arsenal of tricks, a bell, not unlike the one that Dominik had provided for my evening of maiding, but larger. Its clear sound reverberated through the room like a death knell, a sound with an automatic echo. It had an empty quality to it that set my teeth on edge.

At the sound of the bell, a door opened from down the hall and a woman emerged. She was dressed, if you could call it that, in a completely see-through white gown, cut a little like a toga. Her hair was piled on top of her head in a loose bun, the escaping tendrils framing her face and giving her the appearance of a modern-day medusa.

She ignored me completely and inclined her head to Victor as she approached. She was very tall, probably over six feet, I guessed, and barefoot. He seemed to prefer his women that way. I guessed having us lower made him feel less concerned about being short.

'Cynthia will be orchestrating your preparations tonight, slave. Kneel to her.'

I kneeled, my face pressed almost against the floor. As I did so, I noticed that a thin silver anklet was draped elegantly round Cynthia's ankle, a little like a charm bracelet, but with only one charm, a tiny padlock. It was really quite pretty. If this was an option, instead of a piercing or a tattoo, maybe it wouldn't be so bad.

Then again, I didn't think that Victor would allow me to have any say in thc matter, and in the mood that he seemed to be in now, he would probably opt for the most humiliating and permanent mark that he could think of: a tattoo.

'Victor,' called the glamorous dark-haired woman reclining on the cushions on the floor.

'Yes, Clarissa?' he asked. He did not call his fellows 'lady', 'mistress' or 'master' unless speaking of them to a slave.

'Where are all your service slaves tonight? I've been sitting here with an empty glass for an age. Can't seem to get a champagne top-up for love nor money.'

I had seen her drain the dregs from her glass about three seconds earlier.

'Oh dear,' he replied. 'I will identify the culprit and give them a thrashing later.'

'Good,' said Clarissa. 'I hope you will allow me to watch. In the meantime, might I have a drop to soothe my aching throat? And would you ask your new girl to bring it for me? I do like the look of her.' Clarissa eyed my naked, kneeling figure and smirked.

The moustachioed man lying alongside her perked up and cast a glance over me also.

'Actually,' he said, in a slow drawl, 'I could use a top-up too. Do you have any harder stuff perchance? The ladies seem to love this champagne, but I prefer something . . . a little stronger.' He stared at me as he said these last words, and I hunkered down further into my crouch.

Victor's tastes, physically at least, had so far been fairly ordinary – nothing I couldn't handle, or even enjoy if I pretended that it wasn't Victor in the driving seat – but I knew perfectly well that he might have doms of a more violent persuasion in attendance, or perhaps sadists, who might be into things that weren't my cup of tea, that might really hurt, or leave me with injuries. I had so far been fortunate that all of the marks Victor and his friends had left had been relatively mild, scrapes and bruises that I could cover with long sleeves or explain away. I might not always be so lucky.

'Certainly,' said Victor, maintaining his composure outwardly, though I sensed that his guests' request for my service had interrupted his plans and left him irritated. He pulled me to my feet. 'Pour Mistress Clarissa a glass of champagne, and find some whisky for Master Edward.'

They always chose such ridiculous pseudonyms. Victor

had an excuse, I supposed, for something more classical; he was of Ukrainian descent after all.

He rifled in his pocket for the key to the drinks cabinet and handed it to me.

'If you touch anything besides the whisky,' he whispered softly into my ear, 'then you will not be given the option to choose where I place your marking.'

I poured the champagne first and took it to Clarissa.

'Forgive me, mistress, master,' I said, 'for not bringing the two drinks together, but mistress looks thirsty, and I did not wish to risk the champagne warming.'

'Oh, she is good,' Clarissa said Victor. 'When will she be available for use?'

'This evening,' he replied abruptly.

'Oh,' she said. 'I thought you were going to mark her tomorrow, with the others?'

'I had planned to,' he replied, 'but this one is special.' He stopped and looked at his watch. 'Two hours from now. Six. That gives us enough time. Keep an eye on her for a moment, would you, Clarissa? I need to make the arrangements.'

Victor pulled his phone out of his pocket and disappeared down the hallway.

'Excuse me,' I said. 'I will return with the whisky.'

As I expected, Clarissa paid me no attention as I reached into the drinks cabinet and slyly flicked my phone on again. I checked the 'missed calls' list. Dominik had called twice and left a message. There was no possibility that I could listen to it, and neither could I type out a lengthy reply: Victor might be back in the room at any moment. I tapped out a brief text: 'Got ur message. I'm in NYC. Call me again. S.'

I just had to hope that he would keep trying.

I put my phone back into the cabinet and shut the door carefully, but didn't lock it.

Victor returned to the room, and I handed him back the key.

'Good girl,' he said. 'You will make an excellent servant, Slave Elena.'

'I look forward to it, master.'

'Your time will come very soon. Now you will bathe.'

He snapped his fingers and Cynthia appeared again by his side and held out her hand to me. I followed her down the hall, into a bedroom, where a large, ornate bathtub sat, filled with steaming water. It looked as though it ought to be scented, but wasn't. No soap or bath products lined the rim. I guess he wanted me just how I was, only cleaner.

I sank into the hot water, and Cynthia sat in a corner of the room in silence. My guard? Did I even need a guard? Was I a prisoner?

I didn't think so, no. I'd come here of my own accord. Victor had my clothes and my phone, but there was nothing stopping me walking straight out of the door and calling the police. I could scream my head off and neighbours would probably come to investigate. None of the other 'slaves' in attendance was physically restrained; they were all here of their own accord, playing roles in a sexual theatre piece, all indulging their not-so-private fantasies as much as the mistresses and masters were indulging theirs.

I remembered what Victor had said, that this was my proper place, where I was my most beautiful. His words had hurt, but I couldn't deny there was some truth to them. His behaviour sickened me but aroused me at the same time. That way he had of pushing my mind into the space where nothing mattered, where I was physically restrained but mentally free.

The door opened. Victor. He had changed into a formal suit, a tuxedo. For a moment, he reminded me of Danny DeVito playing the Penguin in *Batman Returns*. I stifled a laugh.

'Slave Elena,' he said, 'your time has come.'

Dominik's flight landed at JFK International under clear skies. Because of the time difference, it was only just past midday in New York. The queues at immigration and passport control were awful and slow. Maybe because it was the wrong time of the week, he wasn't sure, but the couple of handfuls of international flights from Europe had all arrived within minutes of each other and disgorged their human cargo into a veritable bottleneck inside the terminal. Ninety per cent of the arriving passengers were foreign nationals and had to make do with only three uniformed immigration officers, who seemed totally indifferent to the general air of impatience.

Dominik only had walk-on baggage with him, but it made no difference as the luggage carousels were beyond border controls anyway.

Asked whether he was visiting for business or pleasure, he hesitated briefly before opting for the latter.

This caused the official to ask, 'What sort of business are you in?'

Should have pretexted a holiday, he reckoned.

'I'm a university professor,' Dominik finally said. 'I'm here to give some conferences at Columbia,' he lied.

He was let through.

Finally settled in the back seat of a yellow cab some time

later, he watched as the car joined the stream of vehicles racing onto the Van Wyck Expressway in the direction of Jamaica and Queens. The driver at the front, behind a flimsy security grille, wore a turban. His ID badge and photo had almost faded away to invisibility. His name was Mohammad Iqbal, it seemed. Or maybe that was his cousin or whoever he shared his licence with.

The cab's air-conditioning wasn't working, so both driver and passenger had to rely on the open windows. The change in temperature since leaving London at an early hour was significant and Dominik was already sweating uncomfortably. He slipped off his grey linen jacket.

Past Jamaica Hospital, the slow traffic began to clear and the cab raced forward towards the city. The driver made a turn onto the road that led to the Midtown Tunnel.

All of a sudden, Dominik remembered he had switched off his mobile phone while in the immigration queue, as demanded. He turned it on and watched it power up, more in hope than in expectation.

There was a text.

Summer.

'Got ur message. I'm in NYC. Call me again. S.'

Damn! He already knew she was in New York. This was no help at all.

He rang her number and once again ended up with the messaging service.

Damn again. With no further clues, it would be like looking for a needle in a haystack.

He was about to send her a text when the car dived into the Midtown Tunnel. He had made a booking at a hotel on Washington Square, which is where he had asked his driver to drop him off. Once out of the tunnel, he decided to wait until he was in his room before attempting to reach Summer again.

Even though check-in time was not until 3 p.m., he was allowed to check in early as a room was available. He badly needed to shower and change clothes.

From his window the balmy sight of the Washington Square Arch blinked at him in the sun. The sound of musicians playing jazz by the central fountain reached his ears.

A while later, still wet under the fluffy white bathrobe, he tried Summer's number once more, but again was unable to reach her. What was this all about? he wondered. Why get in touch with him and then instantly become incommunicado?

He was picking a clean short-sleeved shirt from his overnight bag when his phone finally rang.

He hurried to the desk and picked it up.

'Summer?'

'No, it's not Summer. It's Lauralynn.'

'Lauralynn?' Dominik at first didn't recall who she was and was about to hang up on her, for fear of missing Summer's expected call.

'Yes, Lauralynn. Remember? I played in that . . . special string quartet. Blonde. Cello. Ring a bell?'

Dominik now remembered her. What did she want from him? He was growing impatient. 'Yes, I do.'

'Good,' Lauralynn said. 'I'd hate to be the sort of gal men don't remember,' she laughed gently.

'I'm in New York,' he informed her.

'Is that so?'

'Just arrived here.' Then he came to his senses. 'What was it you wanted?'

'A bit difficult at such a distance,' Lauralynn remarked. 'I was going to say how much I'd enjoyed our little event. I was just wondering whether you might be interested in organising something else one coming day, but seeing you're not even in the country, that might be a trifle complicated.' Her tone dripped with mischief. 'You're right. Maybe we can speak another time, when I'm back in London.' Dominik was being polite and had no intention of setting up such a scene again.

'I understand,' Lauralynn said. 'Pity. It's just that with Victor also in New York, I'm a bit short of gaming opportunities.'

'You know Victor?' Dominik queried.

'Of course. He's an old – how shall I put it? – friend,' she said.

'I thought he'd come across you and the other musicians who played that day through a card on the college's noticeboard.'

'No,' Lauralynn revealed. 'Victor actually briefed me about the likely unusual nature of the concert and selected the location. Didn't you know?'

Dominik swore under his breath. A dark cloud began forming in his mind and his chest tightened.

Victor, that devious libertine of a man, and Summer, both in New York? It couldn't be a coincidence, could it?

He strengthened his resolve.

'Lauralynn? Would you know how I could get in touch with him while I'm in the city by any chance?'

'No problem.'

'Wonderful.' He wrote down the address she gave him.

'You mentioned Summer? Is your trip to New York related to her? Just curious,' Lauralynn remarked.

'It is,' Dominik said, and hung up on her.

He put his jacket on and decided to walk in the nearby park to clear his mind and gather his thoughts before he attempted to reach Victor. Past the small children's playground, then the dog enclosure, catching sight of the army of squirrels galloping through grass and trees. He found a bench and sat himself down.

Cynthia stood and helped me out of the bath, then wrapped me in a large towel. The water had gone cold. I hadn't even noticed.

Victor took my hand and led me into yet another room. How big was this place, anyway? A makeshift tattoo parlour. I'd once considered getting a tattoo, before I left New Zealand. Something to remind me of home. I'd decided against it in the end, simply because I couldn't come up with an image that I wanted to have emblazoned on my skin for ever. Perhaps this would solve that problem: I would get a tattoo, but leave it to someone else to choose the image for me.

I lay down upon the bench that Victor gestured to, still completely naked. He squeezed my hand, the only sign of tenderness that he had ever shown me.

I closed my eyes. I was right. It seemed that he wasn't going to give me the option to choose a piercing after all.

My mind fell into a blissful nirvana almost without my bidding, preparing for the ache of the needle, which I expected to begin at any moment. The gentle sound of traffic flowing past outside faded to a soft hum. The people in the room, whom I am sure had gathered to watch, became inconsequential, barely even shadowy figures in the background. I thought of my violin, of the sweet journeys that took me on. Sex, and submitting to the power of others, gave me a sense of peace, of calm, but it wasn't quite like the visions that unfolded as I played the Bailly.

I remembered playing for Dominik, Vivaldi, the first time, though I had been unaware of his presence, and the second time, on the heath. Both times he had witnessed my reverie, seemed to take pleasure in watching the effect that the music had on me.

Dominik. I had almost forgotten my text message. Was my phone buzzing away silently in the cabinet? Had he tried to reach me again?

A hand passed over my navel, then my shaved mound, hovered above me for a moment, perhaps surveying my landscape, choosing the best place to mark me. Would Victor apply the tattoo himself? I wondered.

'Slave Elena,' he said, in a deep, formal tone, 'the moment of your marking has arrived.'

He took a breath and paused for a moment as if about to launch into a speech. Had he prepared vows, like at a wedding? How odd.

'Now you must forsake your former life and promise to serve me, Victor, in all that I would ask of you, until I choose to release you from service. Do you agree to submit to me, slave, to make your will mine to hold for ever?'

I was on the brink of a precipice, at the edge of one of those moments when the course of your life turns on a knife's edge, a fleeting choice made in no more time than it takes to draw a breath, but one that might alter your path for ever.

I replied, 'No.'

'No?' Victor whispered, incredulously.

'No,' I answered him again. 'I don't choose to submit to you.'

I opened my eyes and sat up, suddenly conscious of my nakedness. I tried to summon all the authority that I was able to, in my undressed state. At least Dominik had given me plenty of practice at that.

Victor looked aghast, but small with it. How had I ever felt under the thumb of this man? He was just putting an act on, like they all were.

I pushed through the throng, their faces a mix of shock, embarrassment and concern, some murmuring to each other that this must be part of Victor's display.

I took my dress from the cabinet, pulled it over my head, picked up my purse and phone, and headed for the door. It was unlocked.

Victor put his foot in the doorway as I swung it shut behind me. 'You will regret this, Slave Elena.'

'I don't think I will. My name is Summer. And I am not your slave.'

'You'll never be anything but a slave, girl. It's in your nature. You will surrender to it eventually. You can't help it. And look at you – have you not seen yourself? You were wet from the moment you took your clothes off, dripping. Your mind might fight it, but your body will always betray you, slave.'

'Do not contact me again. I will call the police if you do.'

'And what will you tell them?' he sneered. 'Do you think they will believe a slut like you?'

I turned on my heels and stalked from the room, head held high, though his words still rang in my ears. All I wanted to do was go home. Go home and play my violin.

I walked up Gansevoort Street and hailed a cab, fiddling

with my phone from the moment that I got inside so that the driver would not try to engage me in conversation or query my upset state. New York cab drivers are a funny bunch, some as silent as the night and others so friendly it's hard to make them shut up. I dialled my voicemail and sank into the seat as Dominik's voice washed over me.

He had missed me. He'd never said anything like that before. I had missed him too, dreadfully.

I stared out of the window at the hubbub of traffic, the sights of the city that had seemed so exciting to me when I first arrived, and now just seemed foreign, other, reminding me that I wasn't at home, that I didn't have a home any more.

Dusk was beginning to fall as we passed Washington Square Park, the trees casting dim shadows across the grass like long arms and hands, a choir of greenery. It wouldn't be really dark for a while yet. There was still time to play.

I had promised Dominik that I wouldn't take the Bailly out in public, busk with it, that it was too dangerous with an instrument so valuable, but I thought he'd understand, just this once.

The cab dropped me at the door to my apartment and I gave the driver a good tip to thank him for keeping quiet for the whole journey.

I ran up the stairs two at a time, dropping the black dress on the floor as soon as I got inside. I wasn't sure I wanted to wear it ever again. Perhaps I'd get a new outfit for concerts, one that didn't hold so many memories. I put on some ordinary clothes, so I wouldn't draw any more attention to myself than was necessary, picked up the Bailly and headed for the park.

The Washington Square Arch was my chosen spot to

play. It reminded me of the Arc de Triomphe in Paris, and of places that I wanted to go, of the pictures that Dominik had shown me from his visit to Rome.

I stood by the main fountain, overlooking the arch, and placed the Bailly to my chin, gripped her neck firmly and drew my bow along the strings. As to the question of what to play, my body made that decision before my mind even had time to think.

I closed my eyes and concentrated on the first movement, the 'Spring' *allegro*, of Vivaldi's *Four Seasons*.

Time passed, the minutes of my performance going unnoticed until I drew the last section to a close, opened my eyes and realised that it was nearly dark.

Then I heard clapping. Not the raucous clap of an entire audience, just the firm, clear clap of one individual.

I turned, the Bailly held protectively to my side, in case a psychopath was about to launch himself on me and run away with my instrument.

It was Dominik. He had come for me.

Dominik opened his eyes.

It was the witching hour of the night, and just the light of the Washington Square Arch peered through the window of his hotel room. The air-conditioning's peaceful hiss breezed through the bedroom like a kind, cool wind.

Next to him Summer slept. The quiet sounds of her breath rising and falling in unison with her heart, her shoulder uncovered, just a glimpse of the underside of her breast in the window of vision created by her folded arm, which she held between her chin and the pillow.

He held his own breath.

He remembered the feel of her lips around him as she

had taken him for the first time into her mouth, her velvet caress and the delicate way her tongue had curled round the stem of his penis, almost playfully toying with it, tasting it, exploring his texture, inch by minute inch, grazing over the skin and its valley of veins and minuscule promontories.

He had not asked, nor ordered her to do it. It had just happened naturally, like the right thing to do at that moment, as they had both lowered their defences, exposed themselves fully to each other, banishing the past, the mistakes, the roads taken in error and now regretted.

The echoes of the lust he felt for Summer still rushed across his whole being, and Dominik mourned for all the days that he had wasted. Before her, after her. Those days he could never recapture.

He watched her sleep.

Sighed.

In happiness and in sorrow.

Outside the window, joyous voices passed by, trekking back from the bars on Bleecker and MacDougal on their way uptown, and for a brief instant, Dominik felt truly happy that he had found Summer again.

The moments they had shared tonight had been normal, not part of any game.

He fell asleep, lullabied by her presence at his side, the warmth radiating from her naked body next to him as she spooned herself against him like a balm.

He awoke again with dawn still a fillet of light on the Manhattan horizon. Now Summer was awake too, her eyes fixed on him, her gaze curious and affectionate.

'Good morning,' she said.

'Good morning, Summer.'

And then silence again, as if they had all too quickly run out of things to say to each other.

'You'll find out I'm also a man of silences,' Dominik said, apologising for his being lost for words.

'I can live with that,' Summer replied. 'Words aren't that important. Wildly overrated, I believe.'

Dominik smiled.

Maybe this would work out after all, go beyond the bed and the sex and the darkness he well knew they both harboured deep inside their souls. Maybe.

She extended her hand towards him, rose slightly, one breast cheekily emerging from the covers. Her fingers settled on his chin.

'Your beard is hard. You need a shave,' she remarked, stroking him.

'Yes,' Dominik confirmed. 'It's been at least two days,' he added.

'I'm not partial to all marks,' Summer grinned.

'Marks won't always be necessary,' Dominik pointed out.

'No, that's OK,' she said. 'I'm sure we'll find a balance.'

Dominik smiled, touched her uncovered breast with all the delicacy he could muster. 'Does that mean we can still be—'

'Friends,' Summer interrupted him. 'Maybe not.'

'More than friends,' he added.

'I think so,' she said.

'It won't be easy.'

'I know.'

Dominik delicately pulled the covers away from her body, exposing her all the way to her pale thighs.

'I see you're still shaved,' he remarked.

'Yes,' Summer said. 'It felt too messy and awkward

growing back, and I came to like it that way.' She didn't tell Dominik that Victor had ordered her to remain smooth, although it was true that she had learned to enjoy the vulnerability the smoothness of her condition evoked in her heart and mind, and the sheer sensuality of being able to feel herself so naked down there when she touched herself.

'And if I asked, would you agree to either leave it that way or grow your hair back again?' Dominik asked. 'At my whim, or maybe command?'

'I'll have to think about it,' Summer said.

'And if I ordered you to play the violin for me, would you again?'

Her eyes were shining in the faint morning light.

'I would,' she replied. 'Anytime, anyplace, with clothes or without, any tune, any melody . . .' She smiled.

'A gift from you to me?'

'A submission. In my own style,' Summer said.

Dominik's hand moved to her pussy, lingered over her lips, parted them open and slipped a finger inside her with slow deliberation.

Summer moaned softly.

She'd always enjoyed making love in the morning, straight from the drowsy embraces of sleep.

He withdrew his finger, shifted his whole body, slid down the bed and brought his lips to her. Summer gently threaded her fingers through the tousled curls of his hair to hold him in place and control her pleasure.

I opened the door to my apartment, set my violin case gently down on the floor and headed over to my wardrobe. I'd popped back home to pick up a change of clothes.

Dominik had just one more night in New York, and he had asked me out for dinner, and a Broadway musical, to celebrate.

It would be an odd celebration. Bittersweet. Our last night together until some unknown point in the future, with the time in between to be spent in the embrace of separate continents.

Could it work? I mused, pulling my short black dress out of the wardrobe, the one that I had worn for him, briefly at least, for one of our early recitals.

I thought so. We were two halves of the same whole, Dominik and me. Even an ocean couldn't keep us apart indefinitely.

I packed a small overnight bag with my outfit for that evening, gave the Bailly one last glance and headed out through the door.

Dominik still hadn't visited me at home.

Perhaps next time I would invite him in.

Acknowledgements

We would like to thank all the people who made the writing of the Eighty Days series not just a possibility but a pleasure – Sarah Such at Sarah Such Literary Agency, Jemima Forrester and Jon Wood at Orion for believing, and Matt Christie for photography – www.mattchristie.com.

Special thanks to all the unnamed individuals who assisted along the way with research, support and violin lessons; the Groucho Club and Chinatown restaurants for hosting our perverse speculations; and to our respective partners for standing by at all hours of night and day as we typed away in overdrive and neglected them.

One half of Vina Jackson would like to thank her employer for her extraordinary support, understanding and very open mind.

And a final thanks to First Great Western trains for facilitating the wings of fate through the lottery of online booking which brought us together.

If **Eighty Days Yellow**
left you breathless for more,
get ready for the next two books
in Vina Jackson's compulsive
new trilogy

Eighty Days Blue

and

Eighty Days Red

Coming soon in 2012